DOUBLE ACROSTIC

On a liner homeward bound from India a young man falls in love with a beautiful girl. Once home, there is no further contact. Soon after, a passenger from the boat is killed; then the girl is found dead in equally suspicious circumstances. Inspector McLean is assigned to the case and believes his main clue is a sketched cryptogram, torn from a diary, that was found with the girl's body. Unravelling the ambiguous meaning of the acrostic will surely provide the sole means to identifying the killer . . .

DOUBLE ACROSTIC

An Inspector McLean Mystery

·BLACK·
DAGGER
·CRIME·

First Published 1954
by
Rich and Cowan
This edition 1998 by Chivers Press
published by arrangement with
Mrs. B. A. Roberts

ISBN 0 7450 8528 7

British Library Cataloguing in Publication Data available

**Printed and bound in Great Britain by
Redwood Books, Trowbridge, Wiltshire**

I

IT WAS not without a pang of regret that Harry Montague stood at the rails of the *Rantala* and watched the lights of Bombay fade until they were no brighter than the myriad stars overhead. Inwardly he said his farewell to India, where for ten years he had followed his profession of electrical engineer, and which he had a strong feeling he would never see again. His regrets were not so much concerned with the country itself as with the many friends he was leaving behind. The new Indian Government had taken over the Company for which he had worked, and he had had the option of signing a fresh contract with the new management or throwing in his hand and accepting the comparatively small compensation offered him. Weighing up all the pros and cons he had decided on the latter course, and now he was wondering if he had been wise.

There was a certain thrill in the prospect of this return to the land of his birth—the reunion with old friends and numerous relations—the thought of excursions to almost forgotten beauty spots, but he was conscious of the fact that great changes had taken place in England since last he had seen it, and that many of the friends he had once possessed were now scattered over the surface of the globe. Ten years was a long time in the life of a man still in the early thirties. In those ten years both his parents had died, his brother had been killed in the Normandy Landing, and his sister married. She at least would be glad to see him, for between them there had always been ties of the deepest affection. But the husband he had doubts about, for Helen had drawn a vivid pen picture of him, and Harry had got the feeling that Mortimer Arkwright was a little god in his own particular kingdom. "But," she concluded, "he's quite a darling."

The *Rantala* was quite a small ship, and Harry had chosen her in preference to the palatial liner which was due to sail a week later, because he disliked floating palaces, and the sort of people who invariably favoured them. Also the future was not so bright as to justify him in spending large portions of his limited capital.

But when he came to look over the ship he liked its lay-out and its simple but comfortable appointments. It was a one-class boat and its passengers numbered some three hundred. Going down to his cabin he met for the first time the man who was to share it with him. He was a jovial Irishman named Joe Murphy, but he spoke English without a trace of national brogue. He was about Harry's own age, and built like a bull.

"Toss you for bunks," he said.

"Oh no. You take your choice. I'm quite indifferent."

"Saves a lot of mental effort to let the coin decide. Heads you have the porthole—tails you don't."

Harry laughed as Murphy spun a coin with the dexterity of the born gambler.

"Heads it is!" said Murphy. "There it is. No argument. Home for a spot of leave?"

"Home for good."

"Quitting?"

"You can call it that. What about you?"

"I'm an insurance man—here today, gone tomorrow. Usually I travel by air to save time. My Company likes it that way, but this time I'm having a cruise, and I'm going to like it. Play Bridge?"

"Yes."

"Fine! We ought to be able to fix up a nice little Bridge four. You don't happen to snore, do you?"

"No one has ever accused me of that."

"Better and better. The last time I shared a cabin my sleeping companion snored all the way from Hong Kong to Naples, and I had to do my sleeping in the daytime. We'd better hunt up some food. Dinner's been on a long time."

They shared a table in the dining-saloon, which was packed with an interesting assemblage of people. A few of them wore dinner-jackets from long habit, but the majority suffered from no such qualms of social conscience. Murphy was the born talker, and kept Harry amused throughout the meal with narratives of his roving life. There seemed to be scarcely a place on earth which he had not visited in his quest for business.

6

"We insure everything," he said. "Buildings, ships, jewels. I've even insured a woman's legs, and a violonist's hands. All's grist that comes to my mill. I've got my wife insured against every illness under the sun, except hay-fever."

"Why omit hay-fever?"

"Because she has it every year. I've tried everything, but it's quite useless. I once took her to Scotland to a place where there was nothing but rocks and waterfalls. There wasn't a hayseed for miles and I reckoned I had the old jinx beaten, but I hadn't. I'm certain that if I landed her in the middle of the Sahara in the right season the old hay-bug would soon find her out. Are you married?"

"No."

"Leaving it a bit late, aren't you? I was spliced before I was twenty-one. Shall I tell you something? Married life's a hell of a success in spite of what the cynics say. I wouldn't be unmarried for all the tea in China."

"I don't think you're a fair sample," laughed Harry. "Three parts of your life seem to be occupied in chasing ladies with legs to insure. Your family must be wondering who the strange man is who very occasionally spends a night under the domestic roof. But no doubt you mean well."

After the excellent meal Harry went up on deck while Murphy hunted round for the other half of the Bridge party. It was the most perfect night imaginable, with the sky full of stars, and enough breeze to temper what would have been stifling heat. From the ballroom came the sound of dance music, and from close at hand low conversation and laughter, mingled with the hiss of the vessel's movement through the ocean.

Lying back in a long chair Harry found the situation pleasant enough after the heat and dust of a long railway journey to the port, and he rather hoped that Murphy's quest would be vain. How much better it was to lounge and ruminate than perspire and suffocate in the smoke-laden air of the card-room.

A wondrous star, lying well down in the southern sky, fascinated him. It did not seem part of any system, and was all the brighter by reason of its loneliness. Some half-forgotten lines ran through his mind:

Bright star, would I were stedfast as thou art . . .
Not in lone splendour hung aloft the night . . .

How did the thing go?

And watching with eternal lids apart,
Like nature's patient, sleepless Eremite,
The moving waters at their priestlike task
Of pure ablution round earth's human shores. . . .

The rest eluded him, and he was still seeking them when
Murphy burst upon him, smoking a huge cigar and oozing
enthusiasm.

"I've nailed 'em," he said. "They're in the card-room
waiting. Hey! Wake up! We've work to do."

"Who are *they*?" asked Harry.

"Tea planter from Assam named Winters, and a fellow
whose name I didn't get, but Winters knows him. Let's hurry,
or they may get snapped up."

"All right. But no wild gambling. I've had to work too
hard for money to fling it away on the turn of a card. Lead on,
Macduff!"

Harry was not greatly impressed by the other two Bridge
players. Winters had all the appearance of an incorrigible soak,
and the fourth man, who gave his name as Peyton, looked in
little better shape. Obviously Murphy must have recruited
them from the bar. But at least they were first-class players
at the game, especially Peyton, whose occasional psychic bids
were almost uncanny.

Murphy, who partnered Harry in the first rubber, proved
quite unreliable. He bid on very little, and when he did hold
a fair hand no amount of opposition would stop him. The wily
Peyton was not to be put off by the Irishman's kite-flying, and
Harry found himself pencilling large penalties above the line
in his opponent's favour.

Rubber followed rubber, and drinks followed drinks. When,
in the early hours of the morning, the session was brought to
an end Murphy was well down, but Harry had held his
own. Wisely he had signed off drinking at the second round,
for it was clear to him that he could not stand the pace
set by his companions. Murphy was humorously drunk,

but neither Winters nor Peyton showed the slightest ill-effects.

"Och, the luck was against me," hiccoughed Murphy. "I'll have my revenge tomorrow."

Harry helped him to their cabin where Murphy wanted to indulge in post-mortems on the game.

"No," said Harry. "I've had enough cards for one night. I'm going to stretch my legs before turning in."

Harry imagined that Murphy on the following morning would be a little sorry for himself, but to his surprise Murphy was out of bed and humming a lilting Irish air when Harry opened his eyes and blinked at the well-lathered face which he saw in the mirror over the wash-basin.

"Oh, it's you," he said. "I wondered where that gurgling was coming from."

"Sure it's me," said Murphy, turning his head. "Who did you hope it was?"

Harry sat up and stared through the porthole at the vast expanse of sunlit sea and opalescent sky. Only now was he fully conscious of the changed circumstances, and the regrets of yestereve had vanished. The new day had brought a new world, and the clean fresh air which entered the cabin was a joy to breathe.

"Homeward bound," he muttered. "I never dreamed it would be so pleasant. What's the time?"

"Breakfast time. You'd better get a move on if you want a bath. I've had mine."

"You think of nothing but eating and drinking. I should have thought that after last night you'd be willing to give breakfast a miss."

Murphy turned his half-shaven face. In his blue eyes was an expression of surprise.

"What happened last night?" he asked.

"I got the impression you were a little—just a little—sozzled."

"Me—sozzled, on a couple of whiskies!"

"Your arithmetic is faulty. You've omitted the first cipher. But we'll let it pass."

"Man, your standard of intoxication is deplorably low. It was one of the most sober evenings of my life. That fellow Peyton's a dark horse. I thought perhaps he might loosen up

9

after a few drinks, but not a bit of it. You might as well try to get blood out of a stone. Here, you can have the wash-basin. Better forgo that bath."

"I'm damned if I do. I'll catch up with you. If not, I'll see you in the dining-saloon."

Murphy was half-way through his breakfast when Harry found him, but he had reserved a place for his cabin companion, and Harry, whose breakfast needs were few, soon caught up with him as promised.

"You don't eat enough to keep a cat alive," commented Murphy.

"That depends upon the type of cat. Anyway, I appear to thrive on about two thousand calories. Now would you mind passing the toast and marmalade?"

Later Harry was enabled to get a closer view of his travelling companions as they engaged in various forms of exercise and relaxation. He himself was satisfied with a book from the excellent library, and a comfortable chair; but the restless Murphy liked life at a quicker tempo and was soon roped in to a deck-tennis tournament.

Looking up from his book from time to time Harry was interested in the stream of people that passed him and re-passed at regular intervals. They ranged from fuzzy-headed negroes to sleek Hindus, the women in the main beautifully dressed, but doll-like by comparison with their European sisters. There was a large smattering of very obvious Anglo-Indians, mostly, like himself, burned to a deep tan by the merciless Indian sun. There were numerous children, some in charge of amahs, and others roving free and happy in their games.

A young woman, alone, drew Harry's attention every time she passed. She was one of the most beautiful women he had ever seen, and her nationality was doubtful. He judged her to be about twenty-five, and she walked like a goddess. It was on her nth perambulation that she loitered and then took a vacant chair next to Harry's. Their glances met and she smiled.

"My daily dozen," she said in excellent English.

"Quite a noble resolution," he replied. "I'm afraid I'm rather a slacker where exercise is concerned."

"So am I," she confessed. "I have to make myself do it.

The trouble with ships is that they are too well provided with most delicious food."

"That's true. Are you travelling alone?"

"Yes. I have a married sister at Karachi. Her husband has a job at the airport. I had the offer of an air passage, but I much prefer the sea."

"So do I—when the sea is like this."

He nodded towards the colourful quiet ocean, and then reflected that her eyes were of the same hue, forming a wonderful contrast with her mass of flame-like hair.

"Are you going all the way to England?" he asked.

"No. I get off at Naples. I have some friends in Rome, and shall stay with them for a few days. I think I shall resume my journey in short stages—Florence, Venice, and the Italian lakes. I've never seen that part of Europe."

"You have a treat in store. I went to all those places long ago, when I was rather too young to appreciate them. But I can still remember Botticelli's pictures in the Ufizzi, and the gondolas on the Grand Canal, and over all the wonderful Italian skies. Rome I have never seen, and Naples only from the sea."

"Shall you go back to India?"

"No. I am now a man without a job. This ship is full of men without jobs—and most of them are wondering 'where do we go from here'."

"Was it an interesting job?"

"Very. Chiefly electric generating plant. I've always been mad on electricity, and India is virtually having its teething troubles in that respect. It's still living in the dark ages."

"And yet they don't want you any more?"

"They did, but on their own terms. I had to make up my mind quickly—and here I am."

"With regrets?"

"Not now. I find myself wondering what the passage of time has done to the old country. One hears awful stories of shortages, crippling taxation, ever-increasing loss of liberty. I want to find out for myself."

"You'll find out quick enough," she said, with a laugh. "But the outlook isn't as gloomy as some would have you believe. There's a lot to be said for the Welfare State, and you English are still wonderful people."

This remark caused him to look at her sharply.

"So you are not English?" he asked.

"No. But my mother was. She married a Frenchman in the Colonial service, and I was born in Algiers. My name is Denise Rostan."

"But you speak English perfectly."

"My mother saw to that. She insisted upon my being bi-lingual."

"My name is Montague—Harry Montague, and I'm not even bi-lingual. Languages have always been my weak point, but I do know a little Hindustani—mostly swear words."

Their pleasant conversation was interrupted by Murphy, who descended on Harry like a hurricane. He was dripping wet with perspiration, but on top of the world.

"Toughest game I ever played," he gasped. "Come out of that chair, you lizard. They've got the swimming bath going. Don't you want to swim?"

"I hadn't given it a thought. But meet Mademoiselle Denise Rostan. Mademoiselle—my friend Joe Murphy, who burns the candle not only at both ends, but in the middle as well."

2

DURING the next few days Harry did his best to resign from the Bridge party. He found it much more pleasant to pro-menade with Denise, and sometimes to dance with her, but he was constantly being sought by Joe or his friends, who always seemed to have difficulty in finding that fourth man, without whom their evenings were ruined.

"If we don't play Bridge we drink too much," pleaded Joe.

"I haven't noticed any difference in the amount you drink, whether you play Bridge or not," replied Harry. "Surely you can find another player in all this crowd?"

"We found one last night," said Joe. "He went to sleep in the middle of the game, and then woke up and trumped my ace. Have a heart, laddie. Give the girl a break."

Harry glared at him. He thought Joe was taking too much for granted.

"I hate to mortgage my future," he said. "Tell you what

I'll do. I'll play Bridge every other evening, and you can rope in your ace-trumping friend when I'm enjoying myself in my own fashion. How's that?"

"You win," said Joe, with a grin. "But watch your step, my boy, or you'll mortgage that future of yours to the end of your life."

He skipped out of the cabin just in time to avoid the pillow which Harry flung at him.

The new arrangement worked very well, and Harry kept his bargain with meticulous regularity. The Bridge game was now rather less burdensome, but there was still far too much drinking for Harry's liking. He managed to hold his own in the matter of stakes, but Peyton's superior play told against the other two.

"Cunning as a fox," said Joe. "You never know what's taking place in that mind of his. Wouldn't surprise me if he was some sort of secret agent."

"For whom?"

"Lord knows!"

"Possibly he finds our conversation boring."

"Everyone else's too. You never see him in the daytime. He comes out at night, like an old owl. There's something very queer about him."

Harry had already arrived at this conclusion. At times, while waiting to start the game, he had endeavoured to lure Peyton into talking about himself, but without any success. Yet there was nothing impolite about the man. He never indulged in post-mortems, and when the game went against him, or his partner made an obvious mistake, he would remain as imperturbable as the Sphinx.

"Why worry about him?" asked Winters. "We got him to play Bridge, and he does that most excellently. Do you expect him to talk about his secret vices?"

"But it's unnatural," protested Joe. "Yesterday I asked him what he did with himself in the daytime. D'you know what he said?"

"No. Do tell us," said Winters.

"He said he spent the day minding his own business."

"You asked for that," laughed Harry. "All the same, I am prepared to admit that Peyton is unusual. He listens to everything, but contributes nothing. Possibly he is wrapped up in some particular study, and thinks that everything outside that subject is beneath contempt."

"If he is he keeps it a dark secret," grumbled Joe.

One evening Harry got a surprise. It was his Bridge night and he was sitting at the table with Peyton, waiting for the others to join them, when he saw Denise enter the room with another woman and go to a table where two men were waiting. She looked as lovely as ever, and he felt a mild stab of jealousy as he saw the younger of the two men rise and kiss her hand in continental fashion. Then she saw him and gave him a smile.

"I haven't seen her here before," said Peyton. "A friend of yours?"

"Only since we sailed. Someone must have worked very hard on her to induce her to play Bridge. I got the impression that she hated it."

All through the play which followed he was thinking more about Denise than he was of his own cards, with the result that he made one or two very bad mistakes, which caused Peyton to arch his eyebrows, but as ever that worthy made no comment.

Harry did not see Denise again until the following evening when a formal dance was held in aid of some charity, with evening dress optional.

"I'm not being caught on the wrong foot," said Joe, as he dug his evening dress out of his cabin-trunk. "They'll all dress. You mark my words."

Joe was not far wrong, for at dinner the large dining-saloon was resplendent with gleaming shirts and powdered backs. But Peyton refused to be bludgeoned into any kind of convention, and growled something at Harry and Joe as he passed their table.

"What did he say?" asked Harry.

"Sounded like 'popinjays'. Oh, there's your girl-friend—looking like a princess, and that horse-faced guy ogling her. You ought to do something about that."

"Would you suggest shooting him?" asked Harry.

"Choose your own method, but do something, or he may ruin my secret hopes—for you."

"In any case I am afraid you are going to be disappointed," said Harry, "for I intend to remain a bachelor. Why is it that married men do their utmost to induce their unmarried acquaintances to follow their own dismal example?"

14

"It's like toothache," grinned Joe. "It doesn't feel so bad if the other fellow has it too."

The dance which followed was quite a successful and jolly affair. It started with a Paul Jones to get people nicely mixed up, and Harry found himself dancing with all kinds of strange females, some of whom could do no more than lisp a few words of broken English. But afterwards he gravitated towards Denise and was soon dancing with her.

"You told me you didn't dance," she said.

"And you told me you didn't play Bridge," he retorted.

"That was almost true. The fact is I am a very bad Bridge player."

"The same goes for my dancing."

"I think you dance very well."

"It's nice of you to say so, but it simply isn't true. Where I have been for the past ten years there were no opportunities for dancing."

"No women?"

"Just a handful."

They were passing the doorway when Harry saw Peyton, his hands thrust deep into his pockets, glowering at the pirouetting couples.

"Isn't that one of your Bridge companions?" asked Denise.

"Yes. He lives for his after-dinner Bridge. He must be hating us all for upsetting his personal programme."

"Who is he?"

"His name is Peyton. He drinks like a fish, and plays Bridge like an expert. That is all I know about him. He never talks about himself, and for the major part of the day he stays in his cabin. Joe Murphy, who likes to know everybody's business, wastes a lot of time trying to discover more about him."

When next they passed the spot where Peyton had been standing he was no longer there.

"Gone to the bar, I expect," said Harry. "He's almost a chain drinker, and yet it never seems to affect him. It must be useful to be constituted that way."

"Useful, but very expensive. Oh, that's the end. Thank you very much."

"What about the next dance?" asked Harry.

"Sorry. I promised that to Captain Loveday."

"The tall man with whom you played Bridge?"

"You are very observant. Yes—he's the man. Just retired from the Indian Army. He's quite charming."

As Harry conducted her back to her seat the captain arrived with his late partner. Harry walked away without waiting to be introduced, for he had the feeling that he and the gallant captain had but one interest in common, and that one which could not be discussed.

He stole out and went to the bar where, as he had surmised, Peyton was sitting in a corner before what appeared to be an immense whisky and soda. He beckoned Harry with a crooked finger and then drained his glass at a gulp.

"Have a drink," he said. "Hey, waiter!"

The drinks were brought and Peyton paid for them from a wallet which was stuffed with notes.

"Well, good health!" he muttered.

"Same to you!"

Peyton's whisky went the way of all drinks in a couple of gulps.

"Tired of it?" he asked.

"Tired of what?"

"Shuffling round that floor."

"Not a bit. I found it rather a pleasant change. I only came out for some fresh air."

"A pity. We might be playing Bridge. Winters is in the writing-room—killing time. If you could get hold of Joe——"

"Nothing doing. Joe is having the time of his life. Besides, I have a reason for going back."

"I understand. How long does that damned thing go on?"

"Midnight, I think."

"Quite early. What do you say to coming along to my cabin after the dance? It's my birthday, and I've got a magnum of champagne there. Winters is coming, and if you'll pass the word to Joe we shall be a nice little party."

"I'll come," said Harry, after a slight pause. "But where is your cabin?"

"B Deck—No. 26."

"I'll be there—with or without Joe."

"Good!"

Harry left a few minutes later, and wandered back to the dance, where he found Joe engaged in a fast waltz with a girl who seemed to be as excited as Joe was himself. When Joe was free Harry told him of the invitation.

"Golly!" said Joe. "So the old iceberg is thawing out. Sure I'll come."

Harry's hope of getting another dance with Denise was vain. She seemed to have attached herself completely to the captain's party, and after attempting a rumba with a partner who was at least as inefficient as he was himself, he gave up dancing and went on deck, to sit and stare at the heavens until finally he heard the strains of the National Anthem.

He found Joe after some trouble, and the pair walked to Peyton's cabin, where Winters had already arrived. It was quite a commodious place, containing but a single bed, numerous comfortable chairs, and a circular mahogany table. Beside the table was an ice bucket, with the neck of the large champagne bottle projecting from it.

"Here we are—all complete!" hiccoughed Peyton. "Joe, bring over those glasses. Winters, don't go to sleep."

"I never go to sleep when there's champagne in the offing," said Winters.

Harry looked at Joe, as he brought the four champagne glasses, and Joe winked significantly. For the first time since they had met Peyton they found him more than slightly intoxicated. He seized the napkin and fumbled with the stiff wires on the head of the bottle.

"Here, let me do that!" said Joe.

Under Joe's muscular fingers the cork came out with a resounding bang, and all four glasses were soon full of bubbling liquid.

"By rights you ought to have a cake with ninety-four candles on top," said Joe.

"Forty-nine—not ninety-four," hiccoughed Peyton. "How did you know?"

"I didn't. Well, chaps—here's wishing Peyton many happy returns of his ninety-fourth birthday. He doesn't look a day older than ninety-three."

"Forty-nine," said Peyton. "And that's as long as any sensible man would want to live."

"Don't be so morbid," said Winters. "I'm ten years older than you and don't find life so bad. What have you got to complain about?"

Peyton stared at them fixedly, and the hand which held the half-full glass of champagne trembled so much that some of the wine spilled over the brim.

"Hey!" ejaculated Joe. "Don't waste that!"

Instantly Peyton's hand grew as steady as a rock, and he raised the glass to his lips and finished the contents.

"I was thinking," he muttered. "Fill 'em up again, Joe. Don't play with it—drink it."

His companions drained their glasses, and Joe filled them all again. It was clear to all of them that Peyton was in a most unusual mood—half-reflective, half-derisive—as he stared into their faces and gave vent to one of his sinister laughs.

"You're all wondering who the hell I am—what I'm doing on the ship—where I'm bound for, aren't you?"

"It's none of our business," said Harry.

"But it is. I know a good deal about all of you, and you've a right to know something about me. Well, you shall. I'm a potential homicide."

"Here, take it easy," said Joe, while Harry and Winters stared at each other.

"You don't believe me, eh?"

"I'm thinking whisky and champagne don't mix," said Joe.

"Mix be damned! You heard what I said. I'm on my way to kill a man. In my mind he's already dead, because I've planned everything to the last iota. What's more, he deserves to die—slowly and painfully. But I shall speed his departure humanely. He'll never know a thing about it. Not a thing until he wakes up in Hell."

There was dead silence on the part of his astonished auditors, for none of them knew just how to react to this remarkable outburst. Joe was clearly about to treat the whole thing as a macabre jest, but he caught Winters' admonishing eye, and held his silence.

"Shocked, eh?" said Peyton. "Of course you would be. I don't look that sort of fellow, do I? And a man who intends to do that sort of thing doesn't talk about it, does he? Well, I'm the exception to the rule. Now let's have another spot of drink before it goes flat."

Thereafter the subject was dropped like a hot brick, and Joe told a few slightly improper jokes, but the life had gone out of the party, and very soon it broke up.

"What do you make of that, Harry?" asked Joe, when they were in their cabin.

"He was drunk."

"Sure he was drunk, but not drunk enough not to know what he was saying."

"I'm not denying that, but a man can say things when he is drunk that are not responsible statements. When he's sober again he probably won't even remember what he said."

"I'd like to take a bet on that. I've hit up against a lot of habitual soaks in my time. When in drink some of them were comic, others were pathetic and maudlin. But Peyton was neither. He meant every word he said, even though it may have slipped out against his better judgment. Did you notice the look in his eyes, and the set of his jaws?"

"Well, we'll probably never know the truth of the matter, for in a few days he'll disembark at Naples, and it's a hundred to one we'll never see or hear of him again."

"Did he say he was getting off at Naples?"

"Winters said so."

"But he told me when I first met him that he was going all the way."

"He may have changed his mind. Or Winters may have misunderstood him. Anyway, what does it matter?"

When next the Bridge party was in session Peyton was his normal phlegmatic self. Joe made one rather indiscreet reference to the birthday celebration, but Peyton pretended not to hear and cut the pack of cards for Winters to deal.

"Cagey!" said Joe afterwards. "He doesn't want that little matter revived."

All this time the ship had encountered nothing but perfect weather and calm seas, but on entering the Red Sea the conditions changed. It was still intensely hot, but the sea was piled up in vast waves under a driving wind which carried with it stinging particles of red sand from the Arabian desert, and made promenading most unpleasant. Rather surprisingly, Joe was a victim of the ship's violent and unpredictable movements, and lay for two days on his bed cursing his luck. But Harry rather enjoyed the sight of the tormented ocean, and found that Denise shared his enjoyment. They spent hours watching the surging waters.

"Where's the gallant captain?" he asked.

19

"In his cabin. He hates the sea when it's rough. But why do you ask?"

"Just common politeness. Is he also getting off at Naples?"

"Oh no. All his party are going to Southampton. Oh, dear —I shall be sorry to leave the ship. This voyage has been so enjoyable."

"But think of that lovely trip through Italy."

"Yes—it's a nice thought. But I shall miss all the friends I have made here."

"Including me?" he asked, with a smile

"Of course. Are you fishing for compliments, Harry Montague?"

"Naturally. It's human and normal to want to be liked by a young and beautiful woman. I wish we were starting the voyage rather than getting near the end of it."

"So do I. But all good things have to come to an end."

"Couldn't we celebrate a bit when we reach Naples? I hear that the ship will stay there the night, and most of the passengers will be going ashore."

"I'm afraid it's impossible. My friends will be at the port waiting for me, and will take me back to Rome in their car. I had a wireless message yesterday."

"Then tell me how I can keep in touch with you. May I write to you at Rome?"

"I shan't be there long enough. When I get to England I shall have to make fresh arrangements, because I gave up my flat when I went to India. You'd better give me your address and I'll drop you a line as soon as I settle somewhere."

Harry took an old envelope from his pocket and scribbled his married sister's address on it.

"It's a promise," he said, as he handed it to her.

"Yes—a promise."

Later he helped her along the heaving deck, in the fierce wind, and it was necessary to hold her closely to prevent her falling. At least so he persuaded himself. In that warm embrace he was reminded of what he had hitherto missed in life.

3

It was a month later that Inspector McLean of Scotland Yard was instructed to proceed to Farley Heath, in one of the most picturesque parts of Surrey, to investigate the discovery of a dead man. The site was given as a hundred yards north of the stones of the old Roman temple, at which point an official from the County Constabulary would meet him.

Sergeant Brook, who loved nothing better than a rural excursion on a beautiful late summer morning, pricked up his ears at receiving this information. He took it for granted that he would accompany McLean, but he was in doubt about the exact location.

"Never heard of a Roman temple up there," he said. "Must be a mistake, sir."

"It's no mistake," replied McLean. "It may not be marked on the Ordnance Survey map, but it's there all right. Ever heard of Martin Tupper?"

"Can't say I have."

"He was quite a character in his day, and mixed a little archaeology with his literary gifts. He has the credit of first discovering the place, but in course of time his excavations got overgrown, until some years ago when a young and enthusiastic archaeologist organized a 'dig' and found Martin Tupper right in some respects, but wrong in others. The old walls of the temple were properly charted, and permanently outlined. Anyway, we're in a hurry, so get the car."

The journey by road was a pleasant experience, for the latter part took in scenery comparable with anything in Southern England. They went by way of Epsom, turning off at Effingham to cross the North Downs. Then through beautiful Shere, and over Albury Heath until at last they passed through the hamlet of Farley, and mounted the gentle rise which opened up a wide stretch of upland country commanding superlative views.

"Where's the temple?" asked Brook.

McLean laughed.

"If you're looking for a second Stonehenge you're mistaken," he said. "It's about a quarter of a mile further on. Ah,

I can see a car parked off the road. That will probably be our colleagues."

As they approached the car two men stepped out of it. One was in plain clothes and the other in police uniform. McLean's car pulled up by the side of the other vehicle, and he and Sergeant Brook got out. The plain-clothes officer introduced himself as Inspector Stephens, and then laughed.

"But we've met before, Inspector," he said.

"Yes—ten years ago. I heard you had been promoted, but understood you had been transferred to the North."

"I was, but I came back here last year. The doctor is still with the body, over there. You can't see him for the tall bracken. Headquarters weren't long in handing you the case. It was only two hours ago that the body was found. Shall we go now?"

"Yes."

Brook was still looking around him for some sign of the Roman temple. His eagerness in this respect was quite pathetic.

"Where is this bloomin' temple, sir?" he asked, as they moved through the bracken.

"Twenty paces and you're in it," replied Stephens.

Brook seemed quite disappointed when, a few moments later, they came upon a rectangular clearing, so small as to appear diminutive in the immensity of the heath.

"Not much to shout about," he said. "Give me Hampton Court every time."

McLean lingered a moment to note that the site had been well cared for.

"You expect too much, Brook," he said. "You lack the true archaeological spirit. No, you won't find any Roman coins lying about."

They entered a narrow track in the bracken, and very soon they came to a depression in the ground which looked as if it might be an old bomb-crater. Here, kneeling beside a bulging waterproof sheet, was a police surgeon whom McLean knew very well.

"Hullo, Nutting!" he said.

Dr. Nutting, a well-built man of about forty, rose to his feet, picking up his bag as he did so.

"McLean! Glad to see you again—even if only on business.

I've been trying to extract a bullet, but it's too far down. You'll have to wait for the post-mortem. He's been here at least a week. Not a very pleasant sight."

"I'm not unused to unpleasant sights. Open up!"

The doctor drew back the covering, and revealed the body of a tall and rather gaunt man. His dark suit hung on him like a sack, and the face was a dreadful sight, so dreadful that McLean winced.

"Rats," said Nutting. "He was shot through the chest. I can find no other injuries."

"He looks as if he were starved."

"He was—until he was finally shot. His body is emaciated. Poor devil."

"Blood on his clothing, but none on the ground."

"No. My impression is that he was dumped here after death. In this thick bracken he might have stayed undiscovered for months. And it's only eighty yards to the road."

"Who discovered him?"

"A man named Tom Jenkins," said Stephens, "who is gardener at a house across the heath called 'Uplands'. He was going to work this morning with his dog, who doesn't often accompany him. The dog found the body and set up a yelping. He wouldn't come when Jenkins whistled for him, so Jenkins, imagining he had caught a rabbit, came and had the fright of his life. You'll find him at the house if you want to question him."

McLean nodded and thrust his hands into the various pockets of the clothing.

"No use," said Stephens. "I have been through them with a view to establishing identity. There wasn't a single article. Everything appears to have been systematically removed. You'll notice that a tailor's tab has been cut away from the coat at the back of the collar, and some small bits of red thread on the shirt suggest that a laundry mark was also removed. Looks like a perfect job to me."

McLean smiled at Stephens' loquacity, but in this case he was justified in his observations, if not in his conclusions.

"What about the ambulance?" he asked.

"On its way," replied Stephens. "I told them to delay sending it for a couple of hours. I thought you would like to see the corpse *in situ.*"

"Thanks," said McLean. "Now I'd like to look over the ground. He's all yours, Nutting. I'll see you later about a detailed physical description. We may find him in our list of missing persons. I think that must be the ambulance coming up the hill."

McLean and Brook were still searching the site long after the ambulance had left with its grim cargo, and also Inspector Stephens, who said he would have to report at headquarters. But he found nothing which promised to throw any light on the matter. He had in fact not expected to find anything, for there was no possibility of footprints on the thick carpet of undergrowth.

"We are in debt to the gardener's dog," mused McLean. "Without his aid we might have found little more than a skeleton. Identification is going to be very difficult."

Later, at County Police Headquarters, the post-mortem was arranged for late afternoon, and McLean decided to wait for the result. It was about seven o'clock when he saw Nutting with the County pathologist, and was handed the bullet which had been removed from the body. It was undamaged and of common calibre. On its base the grooves from the barrel of the weapon which fired it were perfectly clear.

"What about his emaciation?" he asked.

"Just as I expected," replied Nutting. "He hadn't had a meal for a long time before death. It suggests he was being slowly starved until finally it was decided to make an end of him."

"Any body scars?"

"Yes. Here's the description you asked for. Height—five feet ten inches. Age, between forty and fifty. Hair, light brown, grey at temples. Nose large and aquiline. Eyes brown. Large mole on left forearm, about two inches from elbow. Small wart behind right ear. Condition of organs suggests very heavy drinker."

"That ought to help," said McLean, and took the slip of paper from which Nutting had been reading. Following the physical description was a very detailed list of the articles of clothing.

That night at Scotland Yard McLean went through the list of missing persons. The general description fitted two of them roughly, but in one case the man had been missing for over three months, and in the other the probable age was given as thirty. In neither case were the mole and wart mentioned. The first man was missing from a hotel, and the second from his home.

"The first man has been missing far too long, I think," said McLean. "And the wife of the second man is not likely to have overlooked the wart and the mole in her description. But we shall have to act."

On being approached the manager of the hotel who had lost his guest was not very co-operative. He said he doubted very much whether he would be able to identify the missing man, and suggested that the chambermaid might be a better person as she had taken tea to the man's room every morning. The chambermaid didn't like the idea of staring at a disfigured corpse any more than the manager did, but she finally agreed to face up to the situation.

The wife of the other man had no such compunctions. She really did want to know what had become of her absent husband, since she was left penniless and held an insurance policy on her husband's life for the sum of £500. McLean made a mental note of that fact.

Early the next morning the two women were motored down to Guildford, and taken to the mortuary where the body lay. They endured the ordeal most courageously. The wife said at once that it was not her husband. The chambermaid took a little longer to make up her mind, but finally said she was almost certain it was not the man who had vanished from the hotel. He was a much younger man.

McLean had to accept this failure, but instantly he took steps to use the Press and also the B.B.C., giving very precise details of the dead man's physical make-up and his clothing.

"That ought to keep the telephone ringing," said Brook.

This proved to be true, and within ten minutes of the broadcast appeal the calls came in from all parts of the country. It was not astonishing to McLean that the callers took scant notice of the details given. There was always something completely at variance with the facts.

"Same old story," grunted Brook, as he took shorthand notes. "Hundreds of people all hoping to collect insurance money."

But among this flood of useless information there was one

message which aroused McLean's immediate interest. The caller was a woman named Helen Johnson, who stated that she was a charwoman who did cleaning work in a block of self-contained flats in Tottenham Court Road. Among her clients was a Mr. Peyton, who had taken a small furnished flat a month previously. Every day she went to the flat to clean it. But a fortnight ago she found the place locked up, and a note on the door to inform her that the tenant would be away for a few days. She had been there several times since, but had found the flat still locked up. She had seen the suit described by the police, and had once taken it to be cleaned and pressed. The other details all fitted Mr. Peyton, and she had even seen the wart behind his ear, when he had been shaving himself.

Half an hour later this lady was in McLean's office. She was a buxom woman with a ruddy complexion, and answered McLean's questions promptly and intelligently.

"Is there anything you can tell us about this Mr. Peyton?" asked McLean. "Where he came from—what his business was?"

"No, sir. He was rather a curious gentleman. If I passed the time of day to him he would only grunt. But he wasn't bad-tempered. It was as if he was thinking of something else all the time."

"Is there a porter at the flats?"

"Oh no. There are only six flats in all, and a self-operating lift. They are numbered one to six, and Mr. Peyton had number five. The postman delivers letters direct to each flat."

McLean then passed her the full description of the dead man.

"Read that again, and tell me if there is anything you disagree with," he said.

She read the details, and shook her head.

"It sounds exactly like Mr. Peyton," she said. "I never saw the mole on his arm, but then, I never had a chance."

"Would you be willing to come with me and see a dead man, who might be this Mr. Peyton?"

"Oh, dear," she said. "Must I?"

"No. But it would help the police very much if you would. I would take you in a car, and bring you back again. Naturally, I would see that you are recompensed for any loss of time."

"How—how long would it take?"

"Two hours in all."

"You want me to come now?"

"Yes."

"All right. But can I telephone to a neighbour of mine to give a message to my daughter, or she'll wonder what has happened to me?"

By the time Mrs. Johnson had got her message through the fast police car was waiting. Sergeant Brook escorted Mrs. Johnson to the car while McLean got a message through to the County Constabulary. Then Mrs. Johnson was whisked through the countryside at a speed which took her breath away.

Well within an hour she was gazing at the repellent corpse. McLean had warned her that the ordeal would not be pleasant, and was prepared for trouble, but Mrs. Johnson, despite her pallid face, was equal to the occasion.

"It's 'im," she murmured. "I'm certain of it. Yes, yes— it's 'im."

McLean then showed her the brown suit which the dead man had been wearing.

"Is this the suit you took to the cleaners?" he asked.

"Yes. I can prove it too. There was a hole in one of the trouser pockets, and I offered to mend it for him. I think it was the right pocket."

McLean pulled out the pocket and saw the neat piece of mending.

"Thank you, Mrs. Johnson," he said. "I think you have cleared up an important point. Now we'll take you back to your home. But tell me—how did you get the cleaning job?"

"From the agents in Holborn. Their name is Robson and Smith. I've had the job ever since the old house was converted—six years ago."

"I suppose you haven't the note which was left by Mr. Peyton to tell you he had gone away?"

Mrs. Johnson wasn't sure, but promised to look for it when she got home. When McLean finally left her, he gave her a pound note and reminded her about the note. Then he and Brook went to the flat from which Peyton had vanished, the exact address of which had been given him by Mrs. Johnson. He found the door locked against him.

"Looks as if we'll have to wait until the house agents' office is open," said Brook.

"I don't want to waste all that amount of time. Go down to the car and bring some tools. We shall have to make a forced entry."

Brook was soon back, and within a few minutes he had forced the lock with a short crowbar. They entered a narrow hall where McLean switched on the light. It revealed two doors on the left of the hall, and another door beyond them, which was open, and led to the sitting-room. McLean and Brook went along to this and entered a small and simply furnished room. It was equipped with an electric fire, and the two windows looked out on the street below.

In this room there were no personal belongings of any sort, only a couple of newspapers, dated two weeks previously. In one of these a crossword puzzle had been started but not finished. McLean tore out the puzzle and slipped it in his notebook. The small kitchen had no information to give, for the crockery was all neatly stacked in the racks and shelves above the small electric cooker.

McLean then tried the bedroom, and here the state of affairs was much the same—the bed made, and everything tidy. There was no sleeping suit to be seen, and when McLean opened the wardrobe and chest of drawers they were found to be completely empty.

"So he didn't intend to come back," said Brook.

McLean made no comment but passed into the bathroom through a communicating door. Here he found something inconsistent with Brook's conclusion. On a small shelf above the wash-basin was a shaving kit, and a hair-brush and comb.

"My impression is that he had every intention of coming back," he said.

"He might have overlooked those few things. Why should he take all his main belongings if he intended to return?"

"Everything can be explained on the assumption that he was kidnapped, starved for a time, and then shot. The person or persons responsible would have possession of the key of this flat, which would be on Peyton's person. They were careful to remove everything from his pockets before they disposed of the body. I think they came here immediately after his abduction and took away all his belongings, lest anything he possessed should help subsequent enquiries."

28

"And left that written message to allay any suspicions on the part of the charlady?"

"Exactly. That's why I asked Mrs. Johnson to try and find the note."

"Smart work!" said Brook. "I take off my hat to them."

"I hope you'll confine your respects to persons more worthy of them. This is murder. Now we're here we'll see what the neighbours know of the late Mr. Peyton."

One by one four of Peyton's neighbours were seen, the remaining one—a woman—being away from home. The result was disappointing. Not one of them had even caught sight of the new tenant of No. 5. The charlady had mentioned him in her gossip, but beyond that they knew nothing.

On the following morning McLean saw the senior partner of the firm which had charge of the flats. He was an elderly gentleman with a bald head and gold-rimmed spectacles, and he looked aghast when McLean told him the bare details.

"My goodness—how horrible!" he said. "But how can I help you, Inspector?"

"Did you yourself arrange for the letting of the flat to Mr. Peyton?"

"Yes. We advertised it and he came in response to the advertisement."

"Was there a lease?"

"No. I agreed to accept him as a temporary tenant. It was on a monthly basis, rent payable monthly in advance. It was just a simple document, embodying the terms."

"Did he not provide references?"

"No. He explained to me that he was in England on holiday, and was finding the cost of hotels rather prohibitive. To get references I should have had to write to Australia. So I waived the point."

"Did he pay you by cheque?"

"No—in cash, on signing the document. Would you like to see the agreement?"

"Yes."

Mr. Robson pushed a bell-button, and his secretary appeared in the doorway. He told her what was required and in a minute or two the agreement was in McLean's hands.

It gave Peyton's address as Wombara, Alice Springs, Australia, and Peyton's full signature—Robert Edward Peyton—was appended in bold letters.

"I should like to retain this for a day or so, to make a photostatic copy," said McLean.

"Certainly. The whole thing is most distressing. Shall I be wanted at the coroner's inquest?"

"I think not, but I will let you know. Regarding the slight damage to the property, I will have that attended to. One more question. Where was Peyton staying prior to his occupation of the flat?"

"The Argosy Hotel—in Compton Street."

Later, at the Argosy Hotel, McLean found Peyton's name in the register and, as on the agreement, his home address was given as Alice Springs. The writing tallied with the signature on the tenancy agreement. Enquiries showed that Peyton had stayed at the hotel only four days, after which he had paid his bill in cash and moved on. It was the porter, who had taken Peyton's baggage to his room on his arrival, who gave some information which was of prime importance.

"I think he came by way of Naples, sir," he said. "There were five suitcases in all—three fairly large, and two small ones. Two of them had coloured hotel labels on them from a Naples hotel, but I can't remember the name, and on the smaller cases there were labels which said 'S.S. *Rantala*. Not wanted on voyage.'"

"Are you sure about the name *Rantala*?" asked McLean.

"Yes, sir. I once backed a horse of that name, and it stuck in my mind."

"Any other labels on the baggage?"

"Yes, sir. One was a Paris hotel, but I can't remember the name."

McLean felt that some progress was being made, and when he got back to his office this feeling was reinforced by a letter left by Mrs. Johnson. It contained a very grubby piece of paper, on the back of which was a cooking recipe, which Mrs. Johnson explained she had got on the radio. On the other side was the message which Mrs. Johnson had mentioned. McLean gave a grunt and passed it to Brook.

"You were dead right, sir," said Brook. "It's nothing like the signatures we have seen."

"Take care of it," said McLean. "One of these days we may find the person who wrote it."

The *Shipping List* was then consulted, and McLean found that the *Rantala* was owned by a Company which ran a number of ships on the India service. On telephoning the Company's office he was informed that the *Rantala* had never been on the Australian service. She was now in dock undergoing an overhaul, and her last voyage had been from Bombay to Southampton, where she berthed just over a month previously. McLean asked if they would find out if a Mr. Robert Peyton was on the passenger list, and was told he would be rung back.

"The date is right," he said. "Everything is right. For reasons best known to himself he appears to have lied about his home address."

"Unless he broke his voyage at Bombay."

"We shall soon know."

Half an hour later McLean got the information he sought. It was that Peyton had booked a passage in Bombay for Naples, and there also had given his address as Alice Springs, Australia.

"Just as I said," commented Brook.

"It may yet be untrue."

"But his passport would give his real address."

"It should do, but have you never heard of a faked passport? It shouldn't take long to prove that point, for I am under the impression that Alice Springs is far from being a big town. We'll get in touch with the police there and see what they know of Mr. Peyton. Then we'll start taking evidence from such persons as are available who were on the *Rantala* with Mr. Peyton."

4

IT WAS past midnight when Valerie McLean heard the sound of her husband's car outside their country cottage and, with a little sigh of relief, she rose from the couch on which she was resting, and put her hair tidy in the Chippendale mirror behind the couch.

A year of married life with a celebrated crime investigator had not yet lost its delightful novelty, but there were drawbacks difficult to reconcile with complete bliss, and the chief of these were the prior claims of Scotland Yard upon her very conscientious husband. One never knew at what time to expect him, or whether, at the last moment, she would hear over the telephone that he was compelled to spend the night elsewhere.

But this evening she had been left in no doubt, for it was the anniversary of their wedding and McLean had sworn he would be home no matter what happened to him. But he had warned her he might be a little late. In the silence she heard the garage door close, and a few moments later he entered the combined sitting- and dining-room, a little breathless and rather grimy.

"I daren't kiss you—until I've washed," he said. "Had a spot of bother with the car, and I'm filthy. What's this—a celebration of some sort?"

"You know darn well it is. One year ago today I made an honest man of you, and I've been sitting here like Penelope hour after hour wondering if some thug had coshed you."

"Thugs don't cosh, as you should know, being a policeman's wife. But I give you full marks for the dining-table—all those flowers and the pink candles. You've even polished up the candlesticks."

"You go and wash. I'm hungry. What goes with cold chicken? Is it red wine or white?"

"Who cares? What did Stevenson say? 'Home is the sailor—home from the sea, and the hunter's home from the hill.' "

"Are you going to get that oil off your face?"

"I go."

Valerie smiled as he left the room. She loved the little home which they had built together. Some of the furniture had come from her old home, and some from McLean's late flat. But other bits and pieces they had bought in antique shops, and at sales. The final result was all that she could have wished, and it was a joy to observe that her husband was absolutely happy in this new set-up, although there were disadvantages from his point of view, being so far removed from the main scene of his activities.

Within ten minutes he was back with her, having in that time completely altered and improved his appearance. He now administered his delayed kiss, and then quietly held her wrist and enclosed it with a plain gold clip-on bracelet.

"I just had time to raid a jeweller's shop," he said. "I'm sure you imagined I had forgotten the occasion, but your insistence that I should be home tonight rang a very loud bell. This is for completing one year of your life sentence."

"You darling," she crooned. "Oh, I do hope you haven't eaten?"

"Not so much as a biscuit."

"Then come and sit down."

They sat at the gaily-decked table, with no other light than that shed by the candlesticks in the centre, and revived the past, especially that part which led to their present relationship.

"I always knew it would happen one day," she said.

"I was not so foresighted," he replied. "Even now I can't think why you should be content to be a policeman's wife, with all it entails. You might have married some gay young dog who has social ambitions and a pocketful of invitations to cocktail parties. Or a budding politician with that gift of the gab which ensures a rapid elevation to the Cabinet——"

"Who's gabbling now?" she laughed. "Stop it, and tell me in mournful numbers how you have spent the day. Have you made any progress in the Peyton case?"

"Yes. It is established that he came to England a month ago on a ship called *Rantala*, which is on the India service. Fortunately for me the ship is in dock undergoing some repairs, so I was able to locate and question a number of her crew who live in the vicinity of the port. The sum total of information is scanty. Most of them were not able to recall the man at all, which is not at all remarkable in the circumstances, but I found two men who did remember him. One was the man who ran the cocktail bar, and the other a steward who was usually in attendance at the Bridge saloon. The first stated unequivocally that Peyton was a tremendous drinker, and most unsociable. There were several drinking schools but Peyton invariably took his drink alone, and kept himself much to himself. He never spoke about his past or about his future plans. The second man also mentioned Peyton's drinking propensities. He was not entirely unsocial as the first man would have me believe, but played Bridge regularly with three other men—whose names he gave me. It was those three men who kept me employed until this unearthly hour."

"You mean—you located them, and questioned them?"

McLean shook his head, and took a drink from his glass.

"What is this wine? It's very good."

"Sauterne. But tell me more—about the case."

"I had to go to Reading to see an Irishman named Murphy. He's an agent for an insurance company. His wife was at home, and informed me that her husband left yesterday by 'plane for Cyprus where his Company have business interests. That was disappointment number one."

"What about the other two?"

"One was an elderly tea-planter from Assam, named Winters. He was actually in London until two days ago, and now he's gone into the blue. The third is a younger man named Montague. My information was that he had gone to live temporarily with his married sister on a farm near Reigate. I found the farm—a gorgeous little place so far as I could see in the darkness, but I was unlucky from the start, because the sister and her husband had gone to London to see a show, and were not expected back until half past eleven. I decided to wait for them, and finally they arrived home. The woman was charming, but the husband seemed rather a sullen sort of fellow. I learned that Montague had been with them ever since he arrived in England, but recently he had bought himself a small car, and four days ago he had started off on a tour of Devon and Cornwall. They had no idea where he was, but expected him home for the week-end. That brings you right up to date, doesn't it?"

"Yes. So you really haven't got very far, have you?"

"As far as I expected to get—slightly farther. You see, this kind of case bristles with difficulties. The murderers covered their tracks most expertly. They left absolutely nothing to help us at this juncture. They tore away tabs and laundry markings from the dead man's clothing. They entered **his** flat and took away his baggage, leaving a note to tell the charwoman that Peyton had gone away for a few days. That was their one and only mistake—so far, if we exclude the presence of the bullet in the dead body, the extraction of which presented considerable difficulty."

"You mean you may be able to find the writer of the note
—later?"

"I hope so."

"Does that also apply to the owner of the weapon which
fired the bullet?"

"Yes—in a lesser degree, because knowing that the body
contained a tell-tale bullet I fancy that the owner of the gun
will lose no time in getting rid of it. My immediate task is to
find out something more about Peyton; what his business was
in London; why anyone should want to murder him. He gave
his address as Alice Springs in Australia, but that's just the
sort of address that a man might give who wanted to hold up
any enquiries about his way of life. I have sent a priority cable
to Alice Springs, and hope to get a quick reply."

"You mean that Peyton himself may prove to be a man of
mystery?"

"I think that is highly probable. On the ship he played the
part of a semi-recluse, except for the Bridge parties which he
seemed unable to resist. Now are you satisfied?"

Valerie helped her husband to a dish of peaches and cream,
and shook her lovely head.

"I'm never satisfied when a bunch of crooks keep you out
most of the night. Only today a police sergeant was shot to
death."

"I was hoping you wouldn't read that."

"Couldn't miss it. Bob darling, you will take care, won't
you?"

"My dear, I haven't the slightest intention of wilfully
leaving you a widow, existing mainly on the miserable pension
allotted to a comparatively low-ranking police officer. To tell
you the truth, I find life very desirable these days. Pass that
empty glass of yours. There's still some wine left."

Valerie helped him finish the wine, and was about to bring
in the coffee when the telephone bell rang.

"All right," said McLean. "It may be from the Yard. I
asked for any important message to be forwarded here."

He went to the instrument, and Valerie lingered while he
took the message. Finally he replaced the receiver, and came
back to his seat.

"It was from Alice Springs—by wireless," he said.

"Peyton!"

"About Peyton. He is back there after spending two months abroad——"

"But——"

"Wait a moment. While in India he lost his passport, and much time was lost in getting a fresh one. Exactly where and when he lost it he hasn't an idea. That mucks up my case rather badly, for I am now investigating the murder of a completely unknown man."

"But how could the murdered man use another man's passport?"

"It only needs another photograph, and some tinkering with the stamp of the issuing office. Not at all a difficult matter in these days of crookedness. Well, get the coffee, dear, and let's drop the subject for tonight. We have many pleasanter things to talk about."

5

HARRY MONTAGUE, driving back from the sunny moors and delightful coves of the West Country, had much to occupy his mind. In the first place he was not happy about his sister Helen. She was three years Harry's junior, and had married Arkwright two years previously, after a comparatively short engagement. Harry had never seen his brother-in-law until his arrival at Holbrook Farm, which Arkwright had inherited from his father about a year before his marriage.

He found a man about ten years older than Helen, with rather hard eyes and a stubborn jaw. He looked less a farmer than a city business man, for he was fastidious about his clothing, and obviously vain of his appearance. He welcomed Harry with some warmth, expressing his pleasure at meeting his wife's brother for the first time, and hoped that he would enjoy his stay at the farm.

In the days that followed Harry did enjoy his stay, for after the heat and dirt and poverty of India the neat farm with its pedigree herd of Guernsey cattle, the lush meadows, and the clear stream which wandered through them, were by comparison a kind of paradise. But he was soon aware that Arkwright played a very small part in the running of the farm.

It was Helen who did all the planning, and shouldered all the troubles. Arkwright was far more interested in civic affairs, and was already a town councillor and chairman of several committees, and a great amount of his time was thus occupied.

To Helen he was always scrupulously polite, but Harry, looking for signs of real domestic happiness, saw none. Helen had never been the kind of woman who wears her heart on her sleeve, and anyone but the brother who loved her deeply would have imagined that she was as happy and contented as any young married woman could be. But Harry was not to be misled by her light laughter, for it was a different laugh to the one he remembered. A fortnight was enough to convince him that things were not quite what they should be, for on several occasions Arkwright, taken off his guard by some incident of which he disapproved, revealed the true man behind the suave husband. At heart he was unremittingly Victorian, expecting his wife to adopt his point of view however silly it might be. His vanity too was quite childish, as Harry discovered when, in a moment of indiscretion, he proved Arkwright completely wrong in some argument.

There was another matter which disturbed Harry's peace of mind. He had expected to hear from Denise, but not a word came from that direction, and now he felt sure that he never would hear, and that she was as lost to him as were all the other persons who had shared that pleasurable voyage from India. How foolish it was to expect anything different. Such friendships were seldom lasting. He should have known better than take seriously her promise to write.

Yet if she had forgotten him he was far from forgetting her, and now he wished he had forced that friendship to greater significance—told her plainly that he loved her. At least he would have known where he stood. But it was only after she had left the ship that he realized just how much she had meant to him. From Naples to Southampton he had been bored. The Bridge party had been broken up by Peyton's absence, and Joe Murphy had got himself into a Poker school in which Harry had no interest whatever.

There was also the question of his next move, for he felt that he had outstayed his welcome at the farm. It was because Arkwright had made that so evident that Harry had engaged in the touring holiday. So far he had made no attempt to seek a post, but he now resolved to waste no more time, and to get down to facts.

Late in the afternoon he reached the farm, and saw Helen coming from the direction of the dairy with a large jug of milk in her hand. He dumped his single suitcase and went to meet her.

"The return of the Prodigal," she said. "And no fatted calf, my lad. You should have warned me. Well, did you have a good time?"

"Most enjoyable. Let me take that jug."

"And not even a postcard," she remonstrated. "Harry, you are the world's worst correspondent."

"No news is always good news. You would have heard from the police had I piled up the car—myself included."

"That's funny," she said.

"Why funny?"

"Because I have heard from the police. A very superior police inspector named McLean called here. None of your common or garden inspectors—but straight from Scotland Yard. He wanted to see you."

"What earthly interest can the police have in me?"

"He didn't say. Sure you came by that car honestly?"

"I came by it by the time-honoured method of paying hard-earned cash for it. But didn't he give you any idea of what he was after?"

"No. He asked me if you were Harry Montague who came to England recently on the *Rantala*. I told him you were, but that you were on holiday, and that I didn't know where to find you."

"Is that all?"

"Yes, except that he would be obliged if you would telephone him immediately upon your arrival. After which he gave me a telephone number and then wished me 'good day'."

"That certainly is queer," mused Harry.

"Are you really as innocent as you look?" laughed Helen.

"Quite. I wonder if I can have left something behind me— in my cabin, and that the Steamship Company . . . No, that can't be the reason. It's too long ago. The best thing I can do is to telephone Inspector McLean."

"I should think so, and tell him not to bring any handcuffs."

Having disposed of his suitcase and put the car into the garage Harry telephoned the number which Helen had given him. There was some delay and finally he was told that Inspector McLean was not available. He thereupon left a message and went back to Helen, who was preparing the late tea which was normal at the farm.

"He wasn't there," he said. "But I left a message. Where's Mortimer?"

"Gone away. Oh no, not absconded. He and some of his fellow councillors have gone to some kind of conference—at Liverpool, I think. They do that occasionally to get away from their wives. It's to do with sewerage of all things. That's a nice subject to get engrossed in. This is Amy's afternoon off, so you can help me lay the table. Take that tray into the sitting-room, and for Pete's sake don't drop it."

"Why should I drop it?" asked Harry.

"Heaven knows, but Amy has managed to do so a few times."

It was during tea that Harry burst his bombshell.

"I've had a most enjoyable time here," he said. "But on Monday I propose to change my quarters. I've got to start looking round for a job, and London is the best place for head-quarters."

"But, Harry—there's no great hurry, is there? You've only had a few weeks' holiday after years and years——"

"You forget the weeks I had on the ship. That was all holiday. No, I've made up my mind. I'll go up on Monday, stay at a decent hotel for a couple of nights while I hunt round for more modest diggings. Then I'll search the advertise-ment columns in the newspapers, and probably advertise on my own account."

"Oh, Harry, dear, I was hoping you would stay here—at least until you found a job. You know you're welcome."

"To you—yes, but—let's be honest. Mortimer has had a bellyful of me, and I can't say I blame him for that. If I were in his place I expect I should get tired of having a brother-in-law hanging round the house."

"But Mortimer hasn't suggested——"

"Oh no—not in so many words, but it's clear he'll be much happier when I'm gone. I shall miss the walks round the farm, and the smell of wood fires."

"And I shall miss you," she said. "There isn't much social life here, and the town is five miles away. Mortimer's heart isn't in farming, you know. It was his father who made the place what it is."

"And you who are keeping it like that. You're not very happy, are you, Helen?"

"Not as happy as I might wish to be. But the farm keeps me busy."

"What's the trouble?"

"We—we don't hit it off very well. I don't say all the fault is on one side. Perhaps I expect too much."

"What is there which you expect and don't get?"

"Just ordinary consideration—and companionship. We ought to be a team, but we're not. The men look upon him as the boss, but when the boss doesn't turn a hand the men think they are entitled to go slow. But what hurts me most is his lack of confidence. I've no idea what our financial position is, and if I press the point he puts on an act, pretending to believe that women are by nature utterly unable to understand matters of finance. I've always wanted an allowance of my own—no matter how modest—which I could spend how I liked. But my lord and master hates the idea. If I want a new hat, or a summer frock, I have to beg for it—and beg hard."

She spoke calmly and dispassionately, but Harry knew that the thing went very deep. The matter was dropped for the time being, and after tea Harry took a gun and went across the fields to a copse where usually there was a chance of getting a rabbit or two, but this evening his luck was out, and he moved on to the wood on the far side of the long meadow, in which the cattle were grazing peacefully. It was a perfect evening, and the sluggish little stream which cut across the corner of the farm reflected all the colours of the sky. He halted on the bridge and admired the sylvan view. London would be drab compared to this. He wished the circumstances were such that he could prolong his stay indefinitely, but finally he sighed and continued his perambulations. The wood was as bare of rabbits as the copse, but he sighted two pigeons in the top branches of a tree, preening themselves in the light of the declining sun. The gun stayed under his arm.

Finally he came back to the house to find a car standing outside. He gave a glance at it, and entered the house by the casement window of the sitting-room. As he did so the door leading to the hall was opened, and Helen entered with two men.

"Oh!" she ejaculated. "You're just in time, Harry. These gentlemen are police officers. Inspector McLean, this is my brother."

"Pleased to meet you, Inspector," said Harry. "I scarcely expected you so quickly. Excuse me a moment."

He unloaded the gun and put the weapon in the long corner cupboard.

"I've got something cooking," said Helen.

"No, don't go, Helen," pleaded Harry. "You'd better hear what this is all about unless the inspector would prefer——"

"I don't mind in the least," said McLean. "You may not be in a position to help me, but I hope you may."

"I hope so too. Won't you sit down?"

McLean and Brook occupied the two ends of the settee, and Helen took the opposite chair, Harry sitting on the arm of it. McLean wasted no time.

"You came to England on the steamship *Rantala* about a month ago?" he asked.

"Yes," replied Harry.

"Among the passengers there was a man named Robert Peyton."

"That's so. He left the ship at Naples."

"So I am given to understand. Will you tell me what you know about that man?"

"There isn't much to tell. I knew him chiefly by playing Bridge with him fairly regularly. He was a brilliant player. A man of about fifty, I should say, with——"

"You may skip the physical details. What do you know about the man himself—his past life, for example?"

"I know nothing about his past, and I feel sure nobody else does. We used to speculate on that very point, but we learned nothing. Soon it was quite clear to us that he had no intention of satisfying our curiosity. He was a tremendously heavy drinker, but on only one occasion did I see him under the influence of drink, and that was on his birthday—or so he said —when he invited me and two friends to his cabin late at night."

Harry was silent for a moment as he recalled what had happened at that celebration.

"Go on," said McLean.

"I can't," said Harry. "This places me in an embarrassing position. May I ask you a question before I continue?"

"Certainly."

"Is this man in trouble? Has he committed some—some misdemeanour?"

"This man, who called himself Robert Peyton, is dead. He was murdered a few days ago."

Harry gave an ejaculation of amazement.

"You didn't expect that?" asked McLean.

"Good heavens—no! And yet I see now that what he told us at a time when we thought he was too drunk to know what he was saying might well lead to this end."

"What did he tell you?" asked McLean.

"He said—it sounded fantastic at the time—he said that he was on his way to kill a man."

"Did he say it as if he meant it?"

"Yes, with the utmost seriousness. We made an attempt to laugh him out of the idea, but weren't very successful. Finally we got him to bed."

"Did he ever mention the matter again?"

"No. Nor did we—except among ourselves. We came to the conclusion it was an irresponsible statement—possibly some old hatred which boiled up when he wasn't himself."

"In the normal way was he given to boasting?"

"Far from it. I've never met a man so self-possessed. He never lost his temper about anything. If the luck went against him at cards he would remain completely unruffled. I noticed that when he had occasion to open his wallet it was stuffed with notes."

"So you know nothing about his life prior to his taking that trip?"

"Absolutely nothing."

"No evidence of any profession or calling?"

"None. Murphy, who was one of the Bridge party, thought he might be some sort of secret agent. But that was just a wild guess. Just now you hinted that his name was not really Peyton. Is that so?"

"Yes. He appears to have travelled on a false passport. I am much obliged to you, Mr. Montague, for your information."

42

"Wish I could give you more," said Harry. "I don't appear to have been of much help."

"Yes, you have. I am looking for motives, and it may be that you have helped in that direction."

"You mean that Peyton's dramatic statement may have been true, and that the tables were neatly turned on him by the man he was after?"

"That's plausible. Now I won't detain you any longer. Thanks again."

Helen, who had listened to the conversation in dead silence, gave a little gasp of excitement when the door had closed on the two visitors.

"You never told me a word about that, Harry," she said.

"No. I regarded it as inconsequential. Not a very pleasant subject—an old soak breathing murder and hellfire. Poor old Peyton—or whatever his name is! He wasn't a bad sort. Someone must have dealt him a raw deal to have brought him to that pass. I should like to know the whole truth of the matter."

"You may one day."

"I doubt it. The police have so little to work on. One unknown man is murdered by another—find the murderer. I don't envy Inspector McLean his job."

"He looks a very efficient sort of man," mused Helen.

"So apparently is the murderer of Peyton. Fancy me running into a real murder case! It proves that you never know what is waiting round the corner for you."

6

McLean spent two more days hunting down passengers and crew of the *Rantala*. Brook's personal and private opinion was that nothing new would emerge from this, but McLean was not the man to give up hope so early.

"There's Peyton's cabin steward," he said. "He must have seen a great deal of Peyton. I missed him at Southampton, but we've got his new address. Look up the list. I think his name was Izzard."

Brook referred to the list.

"Charles Izzard," he said. "Oh yes, that's the fellow who's

just had his appendix removed. The address I've got here is Charing Cross Hospital."

"Ring up and find out if he's still there."

The reply was in the affirmative, and McLean and Brook went along to the hospital. They found Izzard looking remarkably fit and cheerful after his operation.

"I remember Mr. Peyton quite well," he said. "He gave me a handsome tip when he left the ship at Naples. He didn't mix much with the passengers. Spent quite a lot of time in his cabin reading books which he borrowed from the library."

"What sort of books?" asked McLean.

"Just novels—mostly detective stories."

"Did he ever talk to you?"

"Not much. I talked to him at first, but he didn't appear to be interested. Sort of man who lived inside himself, if you know what I mean."

"Did he ever entertain friends in his cabin?"

"I can remember one night when he had a kind of binge. Three other passengers came. A Mr. Montague, and a wild Irishman named Murphy. I don't remember the name of the other guest."

"No other persons?"

Mr. Izzard reflected for a moment, and McLean got the impression that he was keeping something back.

"Why do you hesitate?" asked McLean. "I must warn you that this case involves murder."

Izzard blinked his eyes incredulously.

"You—you mean Mr. Peyton?" he gasped.

"Yes. Now—why were you hesitating?"

"If I tell you something, will it be absolutely private?"

"Of course."

"What I mean is that if I should have committed an indiscretion will it tell against me?"

"I can make no promises. It depends upon the nature of your indiscretion. But you would be a foolish man to withhold any information of value to this investigation."

"I'll take a chance," muttered Izzard. "Well, it was like this. One evening, about three days from Naples, I was coming out of a cabin about three doors from Mr. Peyton's when I saw a woman enter his cabin. She didn't see me, but I knew her although her back was towards me."

"Who was she?"

"A Miss Denise Rostan. She was a beautiful girl—not more than about twenty-five, and I had seen her a lot of times with Mr. Montague."

"Was Peyton in his cabin at that moment?"

"I don't know. I thought he had gone to dinner, but I can't be certain."

"Do you know how long Miss Rostan stayed in Peyton's cabin?"

"No. I was very busy, and couldn't hang about. But that isn't all. After we had berthed at Naples and Mr. Peyton and Miss Rostan had left the ship, I went to Peyton's cabin to tidy up. On the floor I found a piece of jewellery. It was an ear-ring. I couldn't question Mr. Peyton about it because he had left for good. Of course I should have handed it to the purser, but—well, I didn't. See what I mean?"

"Yes, I do," said McLean. "What did you do with the ear-ring?"

Izzard reached out and opened a drawer in the bedside table. He extracted a wallet, and from the wallet he produced a single pearl mounted in gold, and attached to a small screw clip.

"This is it," he said. "If Peyton had been there I should have told him, but——"

"But you decided to keep it. Have you any reason to associate this piece of jewellery with Miss Rostan?"

"Yes. When I saw her outside the cabin door on the earlier occasion I noticed the ear-rings. They were gleaming in the electric light."

"Was her cabin anywhere near Peyton's?"

"Yes—at the other end of the corridor."

"Had you at any time seen her with Peyton?"

"No."

"I shall have to take charge of this," said McLean.

"Yes, of course. But what's my position, Inspector? I don't want to lose my job with the Company."

"Since you have handed this to me voluntarily I think you have no cause to worry."

"Thanks a lot," said Izzard, his face brightening. "Honestly, I've never done such a thing before, and I'm not likely to do it again."

"You'd better not. Well, thank you for your information."

Back at his office McLean looked through the list of passengers on the *Rantala,* and found the name of Denise Rostan.

"Interesting," he mused. "Originally she booked a passage to Southampton, but some time later she decided to disembark at Naples. Did she do that after she discovered that Peyton was getting off at Naples?"

"No ultimate destination, sir?"

"None. Had she landed at Southampton we could have got that information from the immigration control. What they do at Naples in such circumstances I don't know, and it may take a lot of valuable time to find out."

"There is Mr. Montague," suggested Brook. "If Izzard saw them together a great deal he may be able to help."

"Yes. I had thought of that. It seems to be our best bet. We'll run down and see him again."

The subsequent visit to the farm took Harry by surprise, for having told the police all he knew concerning Peyton he had imagined that he would be left in peace.

"I'm sorry to trouble you again, Mr. Montague," said McLean. "But I am anxious to trace another passenger on the *Rantala* and I thought you might help."

"I will if I can. What is his name?"

"It is a lady—a Miss Denise Rostan. Did you know her?"

"Yes. I saw a great deal of her. But I can assure you she knows nothing about Peyton."

"I have reason to believe that she did. When did you first make her acquaintance?"

"Soon after we left Bombay. It might be the first or second day out."

"Did you know she was getting off the ship at Naples?"

"Yes."

"Did you know that originally she had booked a passage direct to England?"

"No."

"Did she tell you where she was going from Naples?"

"Yes. She told me she was going to stay for a few days with some friends in Rome, and then to travel to England overland."

"To any particular address?"

46

"No. She said she had given up her old flat and would have to make fresh arrangements when she reached England."

"Did you expect to hear from her again?"

"Yes."

"And have you heard?"

"No."

"Did she give you the name of her friends in Rome?"

"No. But, Inspector, I don't understand all this. I saw Denise almost every day, and I'm certain she never met Peyton. On one occasion she saw me playing Bridge with him, and asked me who he was, but I should be greatly surprised if she ever spoke a word to him."

"Did she tell you what she was doing in India?"

"Yes. She had been staying with her married sister, whose husband has a job at the airport at Karachi."

"Did she give her sister's married name?"

"No."

"Did you ever see Miss Rostan wearing ear-rings?"

"Yes—she often did in the evenings."

"Do you happen to remember what sort of ear-rings they were?"

"I seem to remember two kinds. One set was rubies—just single stones in a plain setting, and the other pearls. I remember that she shed one of the pearl set when we were having a drink in the bar, and I was lucky enough to see it on the floor. She said the same thing had happened before, and when she got ashore she was going to have the little screw clip overhauled."

"Could this be the article?" asked McLean, and produced the ear-ring from a small box.

Harry stared at it, and then picked it up and examined it.

"It—it's exactly like it," he said. "But where did you get it?"

"It was found in Mr. Peyton's cabin—after Peyton had left the ship at Naples."

"That's very strange," muttered Harry.

"It would be if Miss Rostan was the complete stranger to Peyton which you imagined her to be."

"But it might not be hers. I can't swear to it. There must be many bits of jewellery like that, and the ship was full of women. Even if it should be hers I fail to see what you are driving at."

47

"I am only suggesting that Miss Rostan must have known Peyton quite well, and because I am anxious to find and question anyone who knew that man I want to locate Miss Rostan. That's reasonable enough, isn't it?"

"Yes—I suppose so."

"If the lady should communicate with you, will you let me know?"

"I don't know," replied Harry. "I can't promise that."

"Why not?"

"I want to know what the legal position is. Besides, I have given up all hope of hearing from her."

"But if you do?"

"It's a matter on which I need advice."

"I can give you that advice free of charge. It is your duty not to withhold any information from the police in a case where murder is involved. This young woman may well be a perfectly innocent witness, but her evidence can be of the utmost importance to this investigation. I hope I have made the situation clear."

"Too clear. It's putting me in the position of a police spy."

"Not at all. She may be glad to give me some information, and get back the jewellery which she lost."

When McLean left, Harry was sunk in despondency—stunned by McLean's revelation. That Denise could be in any way associated with the murder of Peyton was absolutely incredible, and yet it seemed to be a fact that she had visited Peyton in his cabin, for he had little doubt that the ear-drop was hers. That McLean had assumed her ownership of it went to prove that he had information which he had not divulged. Why—why had Denise gone to that cabin?

In the sitting-room he found Helen with her returned husband. She had but to glance at his gloomy face to know that his second interview with McLean had not gone well.

"Something wrong?" she asked.

"Yes—in a way. I told you about the girl I met on the *Rantala*?"

"Denise?"

"McLean is after her. I told him I had no idea where she could be found—that she promised to write to me, but never kept her promise."

"But surely she is not under suspicion?"

"I don't know. He pretends that he merely wants to question her about Peyton."

"But why should that upset you?"

"Because he expects me to notify him if I hear from her. I don't like playing that miserable part."

Arkwright stiffened in his chair. He had already heard about McLean's first visit and he took a very poor view of his brother-in-law being mixed up in a murder case.

"It's no more than your plain duty, Harry," he said. "Apart from which there is such a thing as being an accessory after the fact."

"I'm no accessory," said Harry. "Why should I drag an innocent girl into the case, if she prefers to stay out of it?"

"How do you know she is innocent? What do you know about her, anyway? These chance acquaintanceships are most unreliable. For all you know she may be the most scheming adventuress. I hope you won't be foolish about this."

Harry frowned. He didn't like Arkwright's way of putting things, but wanted if possible to avoid any fierce passage of words for Helen's sake. And Helen, reading his mind, did her best to pour oil on the troubled waters.

"Cheer up, Harry," she said. "You may not be forced into an embarrassing position. A month has passed since you last saw the girl, and you have heard nothing from her. In all probability you will never hear."

That was poor comfort to one who, every day, watched for the arrival of the postman, but he blessed Helen for her intervention. In three days he was due to leave the farm, and he wanted to do so, adding to the difficulties with which Helen was already battling.

But Fate, in which Harry had no belief, was to set his plans at naught. On the evening before Harry's intending departure, Arkwright took a gun from the cupboard and announced his intention of getting a rabbit or two.

"Like to bring the other gun, Harry?" he asked.

"Thanks, but I don't think I will," replied Harry. "I've got a bit of packing to do, and a few letters to write. Good hunting!"

The excuse was not entirely true. Harry wanted a last heart-to-heart talk with his sister, and the opportunity could not be missed.

"Oh, dear!" sighed Helen. "What a shame it is that all nice things have to come to an end."

"That's nice of you, but the trouble with you is that you don't get enough social life. No woman can go on doing chores for ever, without a break."

"What do you recommend me to do—go on strike?"

"More or less. You don't stand up to him. You're working yourself to death, and he doesn't seem to notice it. Or, if he does notice it, he doesn't seem to care."

"You're wrong. He does care—in his strange undemonstrative way. I'll admit he's difficult at times, but I've got to live with him, and to start a real rumpus would do no good."

"I think it would. That woman who comes in for mornings only isn't enough. Get a good strong girl to come and live in."

"He won't hear of it."

"Then get an extra milker. That would relieve you of a lot of work."

"Too expensive."

"Nonsense! You can't be as hard up as that. Mortimer might economize on those expensive cigars he smokes. The business must be prosperous or he couldn't have afforded that new car. Why don't you insist that he tells you exactly what the financial position is? You've a right to know that."

"I don't want any quarrels, because——"

"Because what?"

"I'm at the end of my tether," she confessed. "Our marriage is near to being a failure. I don't want to do anything now which might precipitate matters. I love the farm. In different circumstances I could be sublimely happy here. There's still a chance that I may get him to see that I must be a person in my own right, and not merely the wife of Mortimer Arkwright."

"But the longer you let him walk over you the more he will feel that you like life that way. Really, Helen, you should have made a firm stand a long time ago. Since I have been here he's never taken you out on a single occasion. You can't go on like this. Look here—shall I speak to him before I leave?"

"No. You must leave this to me, Harry. I've thought a lot about it, and——"

The sound of a distant shot came through the half-open window.

"He seems to have got a rabbit," said Harry. "That should put him in a good mood. Now's the time to ask for a new dress. But what were you saying?"

"Only that I will deal with the matter in my own way, and in my own time. Now I've got to see to the cows, or they'll be bawling their heads off. You go and do your packing."

Harry's packing was of no great consequence, and the two letters he had to write were but brief epistles. He was sticking down the envelopes when he heard a banging on the kitchen door. He looked out of the window and saw Bill, one of the farm hands.

"Anything you want, Bill?" he asked.

"I—I want the missus," gasped the distraught man. "Something terrible has happened. It's the master."

"I'll come down."

A few moments later Harry was beside the trembling man.

"What has happened?" asked Harry.

"I was going across the fields to the inn when I seed the master on the further side of the bridge—lying on the ground, with his gun not far away. He—he must have slipped in the mud as he came off the bridge. He's covered with blood, and I think he's dead."

"Good heavens! Wait a moment while I telephone the doctor. Then I'll come with you. Go and find a hurdle."

With the telephoning done, Harry hurried with Bill to the river bridge. As they drew near the prone figure Harry could see some of the dreadful injuries which Arkwright had sustained. They were concentrated on his neck and face. He drew closer, leaned down and raised one of the closed eyelids. The pupil was turned upwards. Then he felt a pulse, and shook his head.

"I think you're right, Bill," he said. "Help me get him on the hurdle, but don't touch the gun, and mind that blood."

They bore the body back to the house, and Harry was glad to discover that Helen was not back from the dairy. The body was transferred to the couch, over which Harry had spread an old mackintosh.

"Stay here, Bill," he said. "I must go and break the news to my sister. The doctor should be here at any moment now."

Harry met Helen half-way between the house and the

dairy. She was carrying the usual house supply of milk, which he took from her.

"Harry, is anything wrong?" she asked, staring at his very grim face.

"Yes. Helen, I've got some very bad news."

Her keen eyes never left his face.

"Tell me," she said in a hoarse whisper. "Is it—Mortimer?"

"Yes. He had an accident with the gun. I think he must have slipped in some mud, and the gun dropped and went off."

"You mean he's badly hurt?"

Harry put his free arm round her shoulders.

"I fear he's dead," he said.

"Oh, Harry—Harry!"

"Steady, old girl!" he murmured as she dabbed a handkerchief to her eyes. "He didn't suffer. I think he died instantly. Bill and I carried him into the house. Ah, there's the doctor!"

The days which followed were tragic ones for the young widow. It did not take the police long to arrive at the obvious conclusion, and at the inquest a verdict of accidental death was pronounced. Three days later the body of Mortimer Arkwright was interred in the little churchyard not far from the farm, and after the ceremony Mr. Winton, the solicitor who acted for the dead man, came back with Harry and Helen, and read the very simple will.

"No complications at all, Mrs. Arkwright," he said. "You are the sole beneficiary. I am glad to find that the farm is completely unencumbered, and there are other assets in the form of War Loan and industrial stock to the value of about eight thousand pounds. I presume you will carry on the farm?"

"I don't know," said Helen. "I've scarcely had time to think about the future."

"No, of course not. Well, if I can be of any help you have only to ring me up. Until probate is through the bank will give you accommodation. I will see to that."

"Thank you," said Helen, tearfully.

Harry, who had booked a room in a London hotel, and then cancelled it, was wondering what his sister would decide to do, but the matter was not discussed that day. It was on the following morning that Helen divulged the trend of her thoughts.

"Are you absolutely resolved to stay in the engineering profession, Harry?" she asked.

"It's the one I was trained for."

"Yes, but you're young enough to make a change."

"For what?"

"Farming, for example."

"But I know absolutely nothing——"

"You'd soon learn. I want to run the farm, but not alone. Why not come in with me, on a partnership basis?"

Harry's eyes gleamed at the suggestion, but he shook his head.

"I'd be so much dead weight," he said.

"Oh no. I know what I'm saying. The advantage would be mine. The men have never worked well for Mortimer, because he set a bad example. But they'd work for you. We could spend some of that eight thousand pounds in more up-to-date machinery. We've always needed it, but Mortimer wouldn't listen. Say you will, Harry. It would make me very happy."

Harry reflected for a few moments.

"Tell you what I'll do," he said. "I'll try it for three months and see how I fit in."

7

McLean's quest for Denise Rostan was a laborious and thankless task. The airport authority at Karachi, where Miss Rostan was alleged to have a married sister, were co-operative, but unsuccessful. Newspaper advertisements brought no response, and no word came from Harry Montague.

"And there it is," said McLean to Valerie. "I'm left with an unknown corpse. Not even that, for it has been buried. Not a clue of any kind as to who did it or why. But some good work has been done on the clothing."

"Where it was bought?"

"Oh no. Nothing so helpful as that. But we had reason to believe that before the man was shot he was held prisoner, without food. Mixed with the blood on the clothing—the outer garments—were fine metal filings, and lubricating oil. They suggest Peyton, as we still continue to call him, was locked up in some kind of workshop and shot there before he was transported in a car to the spot where the body was found."

"I may be dull," said Valerie. "but I can't see how that helps."

"Everything helps. Those filings, for example, were from several rather uncommon metals. If, in the future, we should nail down a suspect, and that person should be associated with a workshop in which those rare metals were used, we should be supported in our suspicions. We might even find traces of blood on the floor, and if that blood was of the same group as Peyton's, again we should be supported."

Valerie smiled as she poured out the coffee.

"Too many 'ifs'," she said. "If you ask me anything I think you're on a dud case this time, and why you want to rush up to the office at half-past six in the morning is beyond my comprehension."

"Ever heard of the early bird?"

"Yes, also the worm. Oh, I've got an idea. I thought of it yesterday. Didn't Mr. Montague tell you that Miss who-is-it was going to spend a few days with some friends in Rome?"

"He did."

"Then use a Rome newspaper. The woman's friends might see the appeal and put you on her track."

"That, my adorable wife, was done days ago, without any result whatsoever."

"What a man! You think of everything."

"Not everything, only just a few of the obvious things. The fact is the girl is a liar. She had no married sister in Karachi, and no friends in Rome. She told young Montague that she did not know Peyton. At least she led him to believe that. But we know that she went at least twice to Peyton's cabin. When a young woman lies so fluently one is justified in believing that she has quite a lot to conceal. Hence my very strong desire to meet her."

"Do you know what she is like?"

"I shall know this morning, because one of the passengers on the *Rantala* whom I had previously questioned rang me up this evening to say that she had rather a good snapshot of a bathing party in which Denise Rostan figures, and it should be at the office by the first post."

"You didn't tell me that when you dragged me out of bed at the most ungodly hour this morning," protested Valerie.

"Fibber! I told you distinctly that I was quite capable of getting my own breakfast."

"How could I lie comfortably in my bed knowing that you would be spoiling my nice new frying pan? But why this indecent haste to look at the picture of a girl in a bathing dress?"

"Because I intend to adorn the British Press with the lady's photograph, in the hope that someone will recognize her and tell me where to find her. She is, at the moment, my chief hope in this case."

By the time McLean reached his office the letter containing the snapshot and negative arrived. It depicted a jolly party of about a dozen persons splashing about in the improvised swimming bath of the *Rantala*. One of the party was ringed round in ink, and in the margin was written *Denise Rostan*. Small as the print was, the details were remarkably clear in the brilliant sunshine which lit the scene.

"There she is," said McLean to Sergeant Brook. "The girl who left her ear-ring in Peyton's cabin. I want a dozen enlargements as quickly as possible—the girl only."

"Quite a beauty," said Brook, as he quizzed the print. "Not much in the way of a bathing suit."

"Never mind about that. Get a move on."

The enlarged prints were in McLean's hands in a very short time. They were excellent, and McLean's hopes rose as he scanned the girl's unusual beauty.

"When you're as lovely as that you can't expect to go unnoticed," he said. "I want these sent round to the Press by hand. I'll give you the list of papers."

The popular Press were quickly off the mark, and within four hours two evening newspapers published the very alluring photograph, with a caption to the effect that Scotland Yard desired to get in touch with the original. McLean waited for quick results, but somewhat to his surprise none came that night.

"We should do better tomorrow," he said. "Those two journals circulate mainly in the Home Counties. When the dailies appear it should be a different story."

On the following morning McLean was at his office even earlier than the day before, to find that Sergeant Brook had beaten him by a short head, and had brought with him a whole sheaf of morning newspapers.

"They've done us well," he said. "I wonder if the bathing dress had anything to do with it."

"What low ideas you have, Brook. But probably there is something in what you suggest. Let's hope someone will recognize her and put us on the scent."

By nine o'clock there had been three telephone calls in reference to the police appeal, but McLean placed no reliance on any of them, for in two of them the callers gave dates and places in southern England when McLean knew for a fact that Denise Rostan was at sea. The third one appeared to be from either an imbecile or a practical joker, and McLean cut him off short.

"What a lot of people there are running about who ought to be in strait-jackets," he grunted.

It was shortly afterwards that the surprise item came. Brook, who answered the telephone, made an ejaculation of astonishment and turned his head to McLean.

"Wonders never cease," he said. "She's downstairs."

"Who?"

"The woman we want—Miss Rostan. Mitchell says it's all right. He recognized her at once from the photograph."

"Very considerate of her to save us many fruitless journeys. Tell him to send her up."

Within a minute there was a rap on the door, and a clerk showed Denise Rostan into the room. She was dressed in a suit more suited to the country than London, and she looked breathless and flustered. McLean took one look at her, and knew that she was the genuine article.

"Please be seated," he said. "I am most pleased to see you, Miss Rostan."

"And I you," replied Denise. "If you are responsible for the publication of my photograph."

"I accept the responsibility. But I tried to get in contact with you by other means, and failed."

"I have been away in Scotland for over a week. I returned early this morning, and the first thing I saw on reaching London was this—this photograph."

She opened the folded newspaper which she was carrying, and indicated the large photograph of herself.

"That was provided by a passenger on the *Rantala*, the ship which brought you from Bombay to Naples. The position is, Miss Rostan, that I want to question you about another passenger on that ship whom I think you knew fairly well."

"What passenger?"

"A man who called himself Robert Peyton."

Denise met McLean's intense look without any visible perturbation.

"I remember Mr. Peyton," she said, "but I didn't know him very well, as you suggest. We met for the first time on the ship."

"What do you know about him?"

"Scarcely anything. It was just a casual shipboard acquaintanceship."

"Did you visit him in his cabin?"

"No. Certainly not."

McLean opened a drawer and took from it the pearl earring.

"Do you remember this?" he asked.

"It—it looks rather like one which I lost on the ship."

"In what part of the ship was it lost?"

"I don't know. I didn't discover I had lost it until after I left the ship."

"Did you make no enquiries with a view to getting it back?"

"No. It isn't very valuable."

"I am informed it is worth over twenty pounds. I should have thought you would have made some attempt to recover it."

"At first I thought of doing so, but by the time I reached England I had forgotten all about it."

"And you did not go to Peyton's cabin?"

"No. Why do you keep asking me that?"

"Because this ear-ring was found in Peyton's cabin—after both you and he had left the ship at Naples."

"Perhaps he found it, and intended to give it back to me, but forgot to do so."

"So you knew him well enough for him to be able to identify odd bits of your jewellery?"

"He may have noticed the ear-rings on one of the few occasions when I spoke to him."

McLean was getting tired of this fencing. He put the earring back in the box, and went into the attack.

"You are evidently determined not to help me," he said. "You see, Miss Rostan, I have other evidence that you did have occasion to go to Peyton's cabin. You were actually seen to enter it by one of the ship's company. I think I should warn you now that this is a case of murder."

For the first time Denise was jolted out of her complacency. She gave an involuntary start, and stared incredulously into McLean's grim face.

"You mean—Mr. Peyton has been murdered?" she gasped.

"Yes.

"Oh, but I know nothing about that."

"Then why give false evidence? Why deny that you did go to his cabin?"

"I—I didn't think it was important. He kept some very special sherry there, and I was fond of sherry. There was no more than that to it, but some people might think otherwise."

"On how many occasions did you go there?"

"Three or four, I think—usually before dinner."

"Did you not learn something about him—where he came from or where he was bound for?"

"No. We just gossiped about people in the ship, and the events of the day."

"Did you know a young man named Montague?"

"Yes—quite well."

"Did you tell him that you had been staying with your married sister in Karachi?"

"Yes."

"That she was married to a man who had a post at the airport?"

"Yes."

"Was that true?"

"No."

"Then why did you tell him that?"

"Because I didn't want to tell him the truth."

"What was the truth?"

"I am not prepared to discuss that. My private life can have nothing to do with this matter. Until a few moments ago I had no idea that Mr. Peyton was dead. It is all very distressing, but there's nothing I can tell you about him."

"We must leave it at that," said McLean. "It was very good of you to come. Are you living in London?"

"No. Until I can find myself a flat I am staying with my uncle at Raven's Court, near Maidenhead. I propose to catch the next train to Maidenhead."

"Then I won't detain you any longer," said McLean.

When she had gone Brook transferred her address to a card and looked across at McLean, who was doodling with a pencil on a writing-pad.

"Not much for all our labours," he said. "I suppose she's genuine?"

"It depends upon what you mean by genuine. It's significant that she didn't ask for the return of her ear-ring."

"Significant of what, sir?"

"Of her state of mind. Any woman, as innocent as she pretends to be, would have displayed some interest in the recovery of her ear-ring. I think she was shaken by the news of Peyton's death far more than one would expect in the circumstances."

"And she didn't want us delving into her private life."

"That's natural enough, but I'm afraid she is going to be disappointed. Young Montague, who clearly knew her well, was convinced she knew nothing about Peyton, so she must have kept from him the fact that she visited Peyton's cabin. I should like to know the real reason why she went there."

"You don't believe the reason she gave?"

"No. The only part of her evidence that I do believe is that she didn't know that Peyton was dead when she came here. If she had known that she would never have come. Since the ear-ring is undoubtedly hers I think I shall use it as an excuse to make a call on her at Raven's Court, to see what sort of a place her uncle keeps."

"It's all a bit puzzling," ruminated Brook. "If she has anything to conceal why did she come here at all?"

"Possibly to head off any hue and cry. She might reasonably plead that she never heard the broadcast or have seen the appeal in the Press, before we had the photograph, but she couldn't ignore that photograph without arousing the very deepest suspicion on our part. A very shrewd young woman, I should say, and with her shrewdness goes a quite deplorable disregard for the truth."

8

RAVEN'S COURT was well known to users of the Thames above Maidenhead. Dazzling white against a green background of well-selected trees, it made a noble picture seen from the river across an acre or two of velvety lawns, and blazing flower-beds. Here and there, set in floral arbours were some excellent pieces of statuary, brought in the past from Italy and Spain, and cunningly placed, amid some weeping willows, was a miniature pagoda.

In the past the place had belonged to a royal personage, who had spent fantastic sums of money on it, but now it was the residence of Cedric Mannering, a middle-aged gentleman, who, according to gossip, had made a vast fortune out of oil in the Middle East. He had bought Raven's Court at an auction some five years previously for the proverbial song, and, with a young and beautiful wife, lived a somewhat secluded life among his books and pictures.

Neither he nor his wife was seen much in the neighbouring town, for most of their requirements came direct from the larger London stores, but occasionally he was on view in the pleasant upper reaches of the river, at the helm of a small but lavish motor launch, with his wife reclining amid a mountain of colourful cushions. It was inevitable that a man so blessed with this world's goods should be the subject of gossip, started by persons who had occasion to visit Raven's Court, and the most succulent item was the allegation that he and his wife were nudists, and practised their cult in the sunken garden on the western side of the house, where there was a swimming pool, and a direct entrance to the house through two green walls of dense yew which took in the sunken garden, and shielded the nudists from the vulgar gaze. But how the Peeping Tom contrived to get a glimpse of what went on inside the considerable palisade was not divulged.

Some efforts had been made by well-meaning neighbours to enlist Mannering's interest—not to say purse—in social welfare, but all in vain, for Mannering through his foreign-looking butler made it quite clear that he did not wish to be bothered about such matters. The Rector, who believed there was a soul there worth saving, had braved the barrage on one occasion, but had been so impudently received by the saturnine butler, on his master's behoof, that he registered a silent vow to see the owner of Raven's Court in hell before he repeated that indiscretion.

But there were others, notably some workmen who had been called in to understake some repair work, who gave rather a different picture of Mannering. For their 'elevenses', which actually started at about ten o'clock, and went on for a long time, they were provided with beer and cheese, and were cordially treated by Mannering whenever he came upon the scene of their activities.

McLean knew nothing of these contrasting pictures of the man when, in due course, he and Sergeant Brook motored down from London, and entered the long winding drive through the heavily timbered grounds. He had never heard of Raven's Court, other than from Denise Rostan, and the first sight of the sprawling house, with its lawns and gardens, and the delightful view of the river beyond, caused him to catch his breath. The lodge at the entrance gates had suggested a fairly opulent residence behind the belt of trees, but he had not imagined anything like this.

"Quite a personage—the girl's uncle," said Brook. "Unless she was kidding us."

"That we shall soon be able to decide."

Arriving on the wide terrace, McLean was better able to appreciate the lovely scene which the house commanded, and he stopped for a few moments to admire it. Then he and Brook went to the handsome entrance door, where McLean pushed the bell-button. The left-hand side of the double door was opened, and a swarthy middle-aged man in a neat dark suit scrutinized the callers.

"Is Miss Rostan at home?" asked McLean.

"I am not sure, sir. What name shall I give?"

"Inspector McLean, of Scotland Yard."

The effect of this announcement was nil, for the dark

countenance seemed to be the essence of immobility. The owner of it ushered them through another door, and into the interior hall, which was a spacious affair, and magnificently appointed.

"If you will kindly wait . . ." he said, and indicated a wide settle.

McLean nodded and watched him vanish up the passage by the side of a broad staircase.

"French?" whispered Brook.

"I doubt it. The slight accent savours of the Near East. Well, we may as well sit down."

It was some minutes before the manservant reappeared.

"I regret I cannot find Miss Rostan," he said. "I think she may be somewhere in the grounds. But Mr. Mannering—Miss Rostan's uncle—told me to ask you if there is anything he can do."

"Possibly," said McLean. "I should like to see Mr. Mannering."

"Certainly, sir. This way, please."

They were conducted along a passage that was broad and well lighted from the roof. It was little more than a picture gallery, and McLean, who loved good pictures, was entranced by what he saw. At the second door their conductor stopped and knocked. A deep bass voice was heard from within and then the door was opened for the visitors to enter.

It was a large library, well stocked with handsomely bound books on three sides. The fourth side was composed almost entirely of casement windows through which could be seen the lovely garden leading down to the water's edge. Two of these were wide open, and standing between these and the large central table was a thick-set man of about fifty years of age, with a large head of iron-grey hair and a chest that would have done credit to a bull.

"Good morning, gentlemen," he said. "I have sent the gardener to search for my niece. In the meantime I am at your disposal. I am, in fact, anxious to know just what my unpredictable niece has been up to. Yesterday I was shocked to find her photograph vulgarly displayed in the daily newspapers. I was about to get in touch with you when my niece rang up to say she had seen you and would explain everything when she saw me."

"Then there is nothing I need tell you."

"I'm not so sure that she told me everything. You see, Inspector, I know very little about her. Until yesterday I hadn't seen her for three years, nor had I heard of my poor sister's death in Algeria. Rostan, the man she married, died some years ago, and I understood that he had left her well provided for. Denise was an only child and seemed to have inherited her father's adventurous spirit. At one time he had a great deal of money, but he frittered it away in expeditions to most ungodly places, looking for buried treasure and vanished civilizations. He called himself an archaeologist, which is fashionable these days. I too have spent a lot of my life abroad, but unlike my brother-in-law I had to work damned hard. Frankly, I don't quite know what to make of the girl."

"In what way?" asked McLean.

"She's so secretive about her life since her mother died. I know that she has been in India, but for what purpose I haven't a notion. I gathered from her that she met a man on board the ship she travelled home in, and that your enquiries were in respect of this man. What was his name?"

"Peyton."

"Oh yes—Peyton. What is the position exactly? I feel I should know because she is staying with me, and I have a sense of responsibility."

"Naturally. The position is that your niece was wanted for questioning because it was in evidence that she knew this man. She came forward voluntarily as soon as her photograph was published. I had hoped to get in touch with her before publishing the photograph, but according to her statement she was away in Scotland, and did not hear the broadcast appeal or read the same appeal in the Press."

"That is so. She telephoned me from Scotland to ask if she could stay here for a short time while she was finding a flat. I too missed the broadcast, but I seldom listen to the radio. But please continue."

"Her statement was satisfactory as far as it went."

"You think it should have gone farther—that she had some knowledge which she was reluctant to reveal?"

"I may be wrong, but I think that is so."

Mannering stroked his big jaw, and looked worried.

"She swore to me that she knew nothing about that man,"

63

he said. "There is no reason why I should doubt her word, but as I told you just now I know so little about her. As a young girl she gave her mother a great deal of trouble, but it was never suggested she was a liar."

"What sort of trouble?" asked McLean.

"I never got the whole truth, but there was a man involved, and Denise was absent from home for several days. My sister was always reluctant to discuss the matter, but I believe the man concerned was later proved to be a most unmitigated scoundrel, and was charged with forgery and sent to prison. It's all very perplexing. I presume you wish to question her again?"

"No. She made it quite clear to me that she had nothing more to say."

"Then why are you here?"

"Merely to return an ear-ring which she lost on the ship, and which came into my possession."

"Oh yes—she told me about that. It is very good of you to bring it in person."

"Not at all. I should have returned it to her before she left my office. I should like to hand it to her personally, as I need a signed receipt."

"Of course. I'm sure she isn't far away. May I offer you some refreshment while you are waiting?"

"Thank you—no." McLean looked round at the full bookshelves. "You have a very nice collection, Mr. Mannering."

"Yes. I go about very little now, and books and pictures are my hobbies. The whole world seems to be in an unholy mess and I have no desire to see much more of it than what I see from this room and my bedroom above. Ah, here comes my niece—with my wife."

He pointed through the open window, and in the distance, across the sloping lawn, McLean saw a punt being propelled by means of a pole towards the landing-stage, adjacent to the boat-house. He was just able to recognize the punter. It was Denise, clad in a white frock and wearing a jumper which enhanced the beauty of her form. The passenger reclined amid cushions, with a gaudy sunshade protecting her head. He noticed that Denise used the pole with all the skill and grace of an expert.

In a few moments the punt was tied up and the two women stepped ashore and began to walk towards the house. Mannering now stepped outside and beckoned them, whereupon they changed their line of progress and were very soon inside the library. Denise was flushed from her exercise, but her companion was as pallid as an ivory mask, yet strangely beautiful, with her mass of dark hair and slanting eyes. McLean thought she might be forty but she contrived to look much less.

"My wife," said Mannering. "Zolta, this is Inspector McLean."

Mrs. Mannering smiled, and McLean gave a little bow. Denise also smiled, and looked from McLean to her uncle.

"I have been trying to find you everywhere, Denise," said Mannering. "I had no idea you were on the river."

"I persuaded her to take me for a little excursion," explained Mrs. Mannering, in a pleasant lisping voice. "You do not mind, Cedric?"

"Of course not. But the inspector has been kept waiting quite a time. He has something to give you, Denise."

"Is it—my ear-ring?" asked Denise.

"Yes. I should have given it to you before, but I overlooked it. I shall have to ask you for a receipt."

"Of course. I'm very glad to have it back."

McLean produced the ear-ring and the official receipt form, and handed them to her. She looked round for a pen, and Brook swiftly produced one from his pocket.

"If you will please excuse me . . ." said Mrs. Mannering. "I have a hair-dressing appointment."

"Certainly," laughed Mannering. "That hairdresser charges for every minute he is kept waiting."

Mrs. Mannering bowed to McLean and Brook and passed through the interior door. Denise handed the signed receipt to McLean.

"Is that all?" she asked.

"Yes, unless in the meantime you have remembered anything about Peyton which might be useful to my investigation."

"No," she said. "I wish I could help."

Here Mannering took a hand in the matter.

"Denise, you are not keeping anything back, are you?" he asked sharply.

"Why should I keep anything back?" she replied, as if she resented the question.

"I don't know. But it would be very foolish if you did."

"I know that. I wanted to help the police, or I should not have gone to Scotland Yard. I think it's a little unkind of you to suggest——"

"My dear, I'm not suggesting anything. But you were in India, and this man—Peyton—boarded the same ship at Bombay. What were you doing in India? What reason had you for going there at all? You have no friends there, have you?"

Denise was silent for a moment.

"Well, have you?" repeated Mannering impatiently.

"I had, but he died there. Oh, why, why do you ask me these painful questions? I don't want to speak about it. Is there no privacy at all in this world? I can't——"

She produced a diminutive handkerchief, dabbed her eyes and then left the room.

"There it is," muttered Mannering. "One cat out of the bag, but it doesn't appear to help matters. I'm sorry, Inspector."

"I'm sorry too. Well, I won't keep you any longer, Mr. Mannering."

Back in the car Brook expressed himself in his usual forthright manner.

"Looks as if we're getting nowhere," he complained. "Or is the beauty queen still lying both to us and her uncle?"

"She could be."

"And the wife! What a woman! Looks as if she escaped from Bluebeard himself. She's a foreigner, isn't she?"

"Yes, possibly Persian or Armenian."

"I got the idea she didn't like us," said Brook.

"Why should she? We weren't invited to call. Mannering didn't like us either, but he contrived to cover up his antipathy. As for his niece—she spoke her part beautifully."

Little more was said during the journey back to London. Brook was ready to say a lot, but it was clear to him that McLean was more ready to think than gossip. When they reached the office McLean was informed that a man had been waiting to see him for over an hour.

"What's his name?" he asked.

"Mr. Harry Montague."

"I'll see him," he said.

"Come to tell us where to find Miss Rostan," laughed Brook.

Harry Montague entered the office a few minutes later, and McLean waved him into a chair.

"Sorry you had to wait so long, Mr. Montague," he said.

"That's all right. I didn't expect to see you at once."

"What's the trouble?"

"I saw the photograph which you published of Denise Rostan."

"Well?"

"I presume that by now you know where she is?"

"I have a very good idea. Why do you ask?"

"Purely personal reasons. I want very much to get in touch with her. Will you help me?"

"What do you want me to do?"

"Tell me where I can find her."

McLean reflected for a moment and then shook his head.

"I don't think I can do that," he said. "It would be rather an abuse of my position. You told me on a previous occasion that you had given her your address. Does that address still hold good?"

"Yes."

"Then it is fairly clear that she does not want to renew that old friendship, or she would have communicated with you."

"That may not be the case. She may have mislaid my address. Or she may have written and the letter got lost in the post."

"No," said McLean. "I am certain she had no intention of writing to you. If I were you, Mr. Montague, I should try to forget all about her."

"I have no intention of doing that. If she's in some sort of trouble I want to help her."

McLean looked at him shrewdly.

"Do you happen to be in love with her?" he asked.

"Yes—if you must have the truth. I didn't quite realize it until she had left the ship, but I know now. If you think you would be abusing your position in giving me her address, there is still something you can do for me. Will you forward a letter to her if I address it care of yourself?"

"Yes, but you had better send it to my private address. This is it."

He scribbled his address on a sheet of paper and handed it to Harry.

"Thank you," said Harry. "At least it will give me a chance to tell her that I haven't forgotten her."

"Well, I wish you luck," said McLean. "But I am inclined to think you are wasting your time."

"I would rather waste it this way than any other. Thank you again, Inspector."

McLean gave a little sigh as Harry left the room.

"Wonderful thing—love," he mused. "It blinds one to a lot of painful facts."

Harry certainly lost no time in carrying out his project. The next morning Valerie McLean answered the postman's knock, and came into the dining-room with two letters in her hand.

"One for me from my precious brother, after a silence of six months," she said. "And one addressed to Denise Rostan, care of Robert McLean, Esquire. Why, she's the bathing girl with the exposed bosoms! Now why on earth——?"

"Calm yourself, Mrs. McLean! I promised to do something for a young man who has nothing but the most honourable intentions, doomed, I think, never to be realized. Give me that letter."

Valerie handed him the heavy missive, which he weighed in his hand reflectively.

"Reams of it," he said. "All the things that Romeo told Juliet, with more beside. I might as well burn it for all the good it will do him."

"You think she's a no-good sort of girl?"

"No. I think she loves something else more than she loves Harry Montague. But just what it is, I confess I don't know."

"But you mean to find out?"

"I have hopes in that direction. Now may I remind you that those eggs have been boiling for close on four minutes."

9

HARRY MONTAGUE found his new mode of life absorbing enough, and in his sister he had a patient and competent tutor. Hitherto he had had no inkling of the part played by cows in farm economics, and was amazed at the intricacy of the laws governing the production of milk worthy of the name. He had in fact never stopped to realize that calves and milk went hand in hand, and that young bull calves in the main were not worth their keep, and were hustled off to market as soon as possible after their unwelcome appearance in this world.

"It's no use your getting sentimental," said Helen. "You've just got to get used to the idea. They're like the drones in a beehive. They have to go before they eat us—or drink us—out of house and home. How's the ploughing going?"

"Very well. Now there's a straight-forward job. Give me a ten-acre field and a tractor, and I can go on until the cows come home. Of course Bill shakes his head when he looks at what I've done, but he's been doing it for thirty years. Now tell me about milk yields. How much do you expect to get?"

"What I expect and what I get are two different things. Cows that yield less than seven hundred gallons in one lactation are not worth their keep, yet we have kept a lot of them in the past because I couldn't induce Mortimer to sell them for a knock-out price. But now it's going to be different. I'm aiming at a thousand gallons, and that means selective breeding, and ruthless weeding out. What about those twelve acres of scrub?"

"Bill says we must hire a bulldozer."

"Well, get moving. It's later than you think."

Harry did get moving, and within a short time the farm was as busy as a beehive. While he and Bill were busy with the ploughing, the man with the bulldozer played havoc with the scrubland. Helen was no less active, doing her drastic weeding out, and replacing the uneconomic beasts with young pedigree Guernseys in calf.

"Lovely, aren't they?" she asked.

"So they ought to be at eighty pounds a head."

"They're worth every penny of the money."

The change in Helen was joyful to observe. With extra help in the house she was able to give her whole heart to the job she loved. The colour came back to her cheeks, and she was more like the carefree girl of her youth.

"It's a grand life, isn't it?" she asked.

Harry agreed that it was, and meant what he said, but Helen was not entirely misled by his enthusiasm. At times she would find him reflective and serious of face. The cause was not far to seek, for she knew of the long letter which had taken him hours to write, and was conscious of his anxious wait for the postman each day. The fact that the letter had been written immediately after his return from an apparently purposeless trip to London led her to draw correct conclusions.

"That girl again?" she asked quietly.

"How did you guess?"

"Not very difficult. You found her address?"

"No, but McLean did. He promised to forward a letter if I wrote it."

"Did you expect to get a reply?"

"It was the least she could do."

"Not after she had shown you by her silence that the affair meant nothing to her. Did it mean so much to you?"

"Yes."

"There are many good fish in the sea, Harry. There is, for instance, Ruth Preston, who loses no opportunity to find an excuse to call on me. I can't help wondering at this sudden interest on her part in our humble holding."

"What nonsense!" he protested.

"You don't really think so. Ruth is a charming girl. You should be less frosty to her."

"Frosty!"

"Well, more observant. She's deeply in love with you, and you treat her as if she didn't exist. Too bad, when she's our next-door neighbour."

Harry laughed it off, but it made no difference to his inner yearning to see Denise again. He recalled those days on the ship, the nocturnal promenades, the delicious thrill of holding her close to him when the ship was executing strange antics. The passing days did not dim those memories, but strengthened them. Her lovely face and form hung constantly in his mind's eye, and was the one disturbing thing in his new life. But as the days passed, and the significant silence continued, he realized the folly of mere wishful thinking, and gave his whole mind to the job to which he had set his hand. No longer did he take any interest in the postman's arrival, and his observant sister noted the fact with silent pleasure. It looked as if, at long last, her brother had accepted the situation.

"You should take a holiday, Harry," she said. "Why not run up to London and visit the Dairy Show? You'd see some of the finest cattle in the world, and it's all in the line of business. Besides, you might buy a few useful gadgets."

"Why not go together?"

"I can't. I've got two of the new cows due to calve at any moment. Can't risk taking any chances."

"Good lord—what can you do about it?"

"You'd be surprised. But do go. You'd enjoy the change, and you could do a couple of theatres in the evenings. Everything is going along splendidly here."

Harry thought the matter over and decided to adopt the suggestion. The next morning he went by car, taking with him a list of dairy utensils needed by Helen.

Having got himself fixed up at a hotel he went to the show, and was soon fascinated by all he saw. It was natural that he should be chiefly interested in the wonderful display of new and ingenious machinery, and he went from stall to stall watching demonstrations and collecting brochures by the dozen. It was whilst watching the judging of some cattle that he became interested in a tall thin man, whose whole attention seemed to be given to the judging. Somewhere he had seen the man before, but in very different attire, and then suddenly he knew where. It was on board the *Rantala*, and the man himself was Captain Loveday, who had caused him the first pangs of jealousy, through his intimacy with Denise.

He moved closer to the man, and waited until the judging was over. Loveday was moving away when Harry touched him on the arm. He turned and stared into Harry's face.

"Pardon me," said Harry. "But I think we have met before."

"Yes, I think we have. But I can't think——"

"It was on the *Rantala*. Miss Rostan introduced me to you. My name is Montague."

"So it is, by gad! I had no idea you were interested in this sort of thing. Denise told me you were an engineer."

"That was true. But I'm a farmer now, and liking it very much."

"Good! I too have changed my occupation. But my people always have been stock-breeders, so I slipped into it naturally. Have you seen Miss Rostan lately?"

"No. I suppose you have?"

"Not I. I live in the wilds of Scotland. But I had a card from her a few weeks ago."

"I should like to get in touch with her," said Harry, attempting to appear casual. "Do you know where I could write?"

"Yes. Let me think now. It was some house near Maidenhead. Her uncle's place, I think. Something 'Court'. Yes, Raven's Court was the name."

"Thanks a lot," said Harry.

A friend of the captain's came along, and Harry chose the opportunity to slip away. The wonderful cattle, the ingenious machinery, Helen's dairy utensils—all were forgotten. He went into the restaurant, bought himself a drink and wrote down the address lest by some strange freak of memory he should forget it. Within an hour's motor ride was Denise. Would it be folly to make an attempt to see her? Would she thank him for breaking in upon her privacy and attempting to renew an acquaintanceship which possibly she preferred to be at an end? He had indeed accepted his dismissal, but now he was able to persuade himself that he could have been mistaken by her silence—that perhaps McLean had not kept his promise, and that she had never received that long letter in which he had laid bare his heart. Or perhaps the postal service had been at fault. At least he could ask to see her, and if she refused that would indeed be the end.

Another long drink helped him to make up his mind. He would go there and risk a rebuff. It could scarcely be worse than the uncertainty which now tormented him. Yes, he would make this final attempt and risk the outcome. He rose and went to the car park where he had left the car. In the door pockets were some road maps, and he plotted his course.

A few moments later he was away, with his heart beating almost painfully. Periodic traffic delays in the London area tried his patience, but finally he extricated himself and made good speed through the suburbs and on the rolling highway. On approaching Maidenhead he realized he had chosen an awkward time to make an unannounced call, for it was close upon one o'clock. He decided to have some lunch and enquire about Raven's Court at the same time.

The waiter at the hotel which he chose had never heard of Raven's Court, but explained that he was new to the district, which fact seemed borne out by his Lancashire accent. But he promised to make enquiries. By the time Harry got through the first course the enquiry bore fruit.

"It's about two miles up river, sir—towards Marlow. The chef says you can't miss it. There's an entrance drive from the main road, on the left-hand side. It's a fairly big house with grounds that go down to the river."

Harry thanked him, and lingered over the remainder of his meal, so that it was past two o'clock when finally he entered his car and resumed his journey. It was almost exactly two miles on the speedometer when he came upon the wide open gates of Raven's Court and turned the car into the drive, passing a well-built, attractive lodge on his left. Within a minute or two he came out of the heavy timber and saw the house ahead of him.

It was imposing enough to cause him to catch his breath and again question his audacity. He had not imagined anything like this, and he now disliked the idea of driving right up to that noble pile as if he were the honoured guest. A bay in the drive, made for the convenience of traffic, caused him to use his brakes, and to bring the car to a standstill inside the bay. Yes, it would be better to continue on foot.

Leaving the car he walked to the wide terrace, hesitated for a few moments as he saw the main entrance door, and then taking his courage in both hands he went to the door, and was about to ring the bell when he saw Denise herself. She was ascending the few steps which gave access to the garden, and she appeared to see him at the same moment as he saw her, and stopped as if deeply surprised. He turned from the door and hurried across the terrace, coming face to face with her at the top of the steps.

"Harry Montague!" she gasped. "I—I could scarcely believe my eyes."

For a moment he was speechless, for there were changes in her which puzzled him. Her face looked thinner, and her eyes sunken.

"Forgive me," he said. "But I had to come."

"Had to come!"

"Yes. You got my letter, didn't you?"

"No. I received no letter—not from you."

"That's strange. I wrote you a long letter—about three weeks ago."

"But—how could you—how could you know where I was?"

"I didn't. The letter was forwarded by . . . someone else."

She looked uneasy in her mind, and stared towards the big house.

"We can't talk here," she said. "Come with me. There are some quiet spots in the garden. No, not that way."

She conducted him to the western end of the terrace, and then down some steps and through a rosary, to a little arbour where there was a bronze statue of Mercury, and a small circular pond alive with colourful fish. They sat on a rustic seat just above the pool.

"Now," she said, "tell me about the letter. Who offered to forward it?"

"I don't think I should tell you that."

"Was it Inspector McLean?"

"I won't say it wasn't."

"He had no right," she said angrily. "I did not——"

She stopped abruptly, and Harry winced at the significance of her unfinished sentence.

"You did not want to hear from me?" he asked.

"No."

"Then you got your wish, since the letter never reached you."

"I asked for that," she said, with a wan smile. "It's true I did not wish to hear from you, but all the same I'm glad to see you—now."

"Isn't that a little inconsistent?"

"Yes, it is. But things have changed. It's difficult to explain. When I left you at Naples I meant to write, but afterwards I changed my mind. There were reasons."

"What reasons?"

74

"I can't tell you. You mustn't ask me that."

"But I must. That letter of mine would have told you why. Do you want to know the gist of it?"

For a moment she hesitated, and then she shook her head. "No. It doesn't matter."

"To me it matters a great deal. I told you in the letter that I had been a fool to let you leave the ship without telling you that I loved you."

"Harry!"

"Is that unpleasant to hear? Do you mean you regret that friendship on the ship, which we built up until—until it over-flowed. If I had told you then would you have listened?"

"Yes—I would have listened."

"Then what has happened since? Why do you look so drawn and anxious? Are you ill?"

"No—just worried. You mustn't question me—not yet. Tell me about yourself. Have you found a job?"

"Yes. I am farming with my sister, at the address I gave you. Her husband died suddenly, and she asked me to go in with her. It's a beautiful little farm, and we are getting along very well together."

"That's splendid. I've always envied people with farms."

"That comes strange from you, living in this wonderful place."

"I'm only a guest here. It belongs to my uncle, who is putting me up until I can find myself a home. But how did you know where to find me?"

"I ran against a friend of yours—Captain Loveday. You wrote to him."

"Yes, I did. Don't frown like that. I know what you're thinking. I kept my promise to him, but not to you. But in his case there was no reason why I shouldn't write. He was no more than a friend."

"And I was?"

"Much more. But I dared not write because it would have caused you to believe that . . . Oh, can't you understand?"

"No. There is so much I don't understand. Your friendship with Peyton, for example, when you led me to believe you were not even on speaking terms with him."

Denise stared at him.

"I wasn't," she said.

"But Inspector McLean . . . No, I oughtn't to mention that. I'm sorry."

"Inspector McLean may be a clever man, but he can be mistaken about some things," she said with some bitterness in her voice. "I had no idea he wanted to see me about the death of that man until I saw a newspaper with my photograph blazoned across three columns. I went at once to Scotland Yard. Harry, you must trust me. I need a friend just now, more than ever before in my life."

"I do trust you," he said, staring into her earnest eyes. "But how can I help you unless I know just what is troubling you?"

"Give me time—time to know what to do for the best. I'll keep in touch with you. This time I mean it."

She reached out and touched his hand. In an instant it was enfolded in his own, and all his doubts about her miraculously vanished.

"Why not come to the farm and stay with us?" he asked. "My sister knows about you and would welcome you. I'll not plague you with questions until you are ready to confide in me. Will you do that?"

"I'll think it over."

Suddenly she withdrew her hand, and Harry heard a woman's voice from not far away.

"You had better go," she whispered. "That's my aunt, talking to the gardener. I promised to take her on the river. I'll go and join her. If you go back the way we came you are not likely to meet anyone."

He nodded and rose. Then suddenly he drew her close to him, and kissed her on the lips. For a moment she returned his embrace, and then pushed him gently out of the arbour. With fast-beating heart he hurried back to the car, and having turned it, shot out of the drive like a rocket.

How different were his spirits now! The cloud that had hung over him for so long had been magically lifted, and the kiss which she had given willingly still tingled on his lips. She had begged for his trust and he was willing to trust her till the end of time.

Arriving at his hotel he decided to spend the rest of the day celebrating his good fortune, dining later at one of the most expensive restaurants, and booking a seat for the ballet. The following morning he visited the Dairy Show again, and on this occasion carried out all Helen's commissions, overspending the sum which she had allocated for the purpose. By mid-day he was on the road again, eager to get back to the farm.

Helen, about to start her solitary lunch, was surprised to see the little car shoot up the drive and stop outside the front door. In a minute or two Harry was in the kitchen, sniffing at the pleasant smell.

"Just in time," he said.

"You'll be lucky if there's enough to go round," she said. "But I expected you to stay in town a few days."

"No need. I've done all the shopping. The stuff will come along later. Gosh, it's good to be back. London's all right, but I can't stand the noise and the crush of people. I'd better lay myself a plate and knife and fork, before you swipe the lot. What is it?" ·

"Curried mutton."

"Just the job. I'm as hungry as a horse. Rotten breakfast they served me. An egg from Poland, and two square inches of bacon, all fat."

Helen was amazed at his high spirits. She had not imagined that two days in London could produce such results. But during the meal Harry shed light on the matter.

"Helen, would you object to my having a friend down for a day or two?" he asked.

"I should be glad, if he's not a fussy sort of man."

"It's a woman—Denise Rostan."

Helen nearly choked at this admission.

"You mean—you've seen her?" she asked.

"Yes, by accident. At the show I ran into a man I had met on the boat. He told me where Denise was staying, and I ran down to see her."

"I see. Apparently she received you well?"

"Yes. The fact is she never got my letter. Had she done so I should have heard from her. She's not very well, and I suggested she might spend a little time here."

"And she accepted?"

"She said she would think it over."

"Of course she's welcome."

"Thank you."

During the next few days Harry flung himself into the work

on hand with all the enthusiasm of a young boy. The new utensils arrived and Helen enjoyed herself junking the old battered things with which she had had to put up with for so long. Then she turned her attention to the house, and room after room was turned out, dusted and scrubbed.

"If you go on like this," said Harry, "Amy will be giving you notice. There's an antagonistic gleam in her eye."

"Amy knows which side her bread is buttered. I'm paying her far more wages than she can get elsewhere. Now you run and play."

"Play! If you call muck-spreading play you've got a strange idea of entertainment. There's no need to touch the dining-room. It's as clean as a new pin."

But Helen was not to be deterred, and by the time she had finished she was satisfied with her achievement.

"Now we're fit to receive visitors," she said. "If indeed she ever comes."

Harry looked at her sharply.

"You don't think she will?" he asked.

"I wish I knew definitely. Can't you write and suggest a date?"

But Harry had no need to do this, for that evening the telephone-bell rang, and Helen went to answer it. It was Denise, and Helen beckoned Harry to the instrument. He spoke for a minute or two, and then hung up the receiver with a joyous expression on his face.

"She's coming tomorrow afternoon," he said. "We are to expect her round about four o'clock."

"Good! That's what you've been praying for, isn't it?"

"Yes. Now admit you were wrong."

"I admit it. Well, I shall be pleased to see what sort of a woman she is, to be able to stir up your emotions so tempestuously."

10

INSPECTOR MCLEAN was not at all pleased with life, in its professional aspect, however satisfactory it might be domestically. It was inevitable that occasionally he should be 'stumped' in an investigation, but in the Peyton case he began to feel that he had been clean bowled. The weeks had passed and nothing new had emerged. The Press had entirely forgotten the matter, and some of his colleagues were of the opinion that nothing more would ever be heard of it. Even Valerie, who took the greatest interest in her husband's cases, and had the deepest respect for his genius, was prepared to admit that the Peyton case had proved too much for him.

"Better luck next time, darling," she said.

"You talk as if I were engaged in a game of pitch and toss," he protested.

"There's bad luck and good luck in every kind of human activity, isn't there?"

"I suppose there is, but when the results are in our favour we are inclined to ascribe them to our intelligent actions. When they are unfavourable we blame the Devil and all his works. But you talk as if the Peyton case was closed."

"Well, let's agree it isn't paying any dividends at the moment. I had imagined that you would wring some information out of the bathing beauty, but presumably she turned out to be just another dumb blonde."

"Very dumb. A curious woman that. She lies when it suits her purpose, and rather expertly too. I dare say that in some countries she would be put on the rack, but we do things rather differently here. All I can do is keep my tabs on her."

"Is she still staying with her uncle?"

"Yes."

"Suppose she decides to leave her present address, and disappear into the blue?"

"She has freedom to do so. Now shall we discuss pleasanter things? It's Saturday afternoon, and the world is ours. Where would you like to be taken, Mrs. McLean?"

"Oh, anywhere. You know all the nice spots. Help me wash up, and then I'm all yours. It's a beautiful day, and we'll stay out to dinner, at some nice old remote inn."

But this innocent and attractive programme was doomed to be unfulfilled. McLean was actually getting the car ready for the excursion when the telephone-bell rang, and Valerie called to him through the casement window.

"The office," she said. "I don't like the smell of it. I almost said you were away from home. Hurry up!"

McLean spoke on the telephone, and the tone of his voice

was enough to convince Valerie that it was business, and urgent business at that. When he hung up the receiver his face was uncommonly grim.

"One of those coincidences," he said. "Denise Rostan is dead."

"You—you don't mean murdered?"

"I don't know. Head office naturally suspect a link between this business and my unfinished case."

"Where did it take place?"

"Her body was found in a punt on the river—some miles above where she was staying. There's been no time to get a medical report. I am to proceed to Maidenhead at once. Brook is to join me at Raven's Court, where the body is resting for the time being. The quiet dinner at the remote inn of your imagination is definitely off."

"Blast!" said Valerie, under her breath. "Can't we even have a week-end together?"

"Only by the approval of Providence. But come as far as Maidenhead, and you can amuse yourself in the town. Later I may be able to pick you up, but at the moment I can't promise."

"I'll come. This is a bad blow, isn't it?"

"In a way—yes. I had still hoped to extract something from that girl. On the other hand, the murderer—if it is murder—may have made a less perfect job of it. But we shall see."

McLean drove the little car at speed, and finally dropped Valerie close to a famous riverside restaurant.

"It's three o'clock," he said. "I'll ring you up here at five o'clock, and give you some idea of my movements. We might even be able to go home together, but don't hold me to that."

"I won't. Best of luck, dear."

McLean drove on to Raven's Court, to find that Sergeant Brook had not yet arrived. He found instead an inspector from the County force, named Adams, who welcomed him and took him across to the summer-house where the body lay. There McLean saw the doctor whom the police had called in. He was sitting beside the corpse, reflectively smoking a cigarette, but rose as McLean entered and flung the stub of the cigarette out of the window. Adams introduced McLean, and the doctor nodded.

"I've done all I can do for the time being," he said. "I

suspect poison taken by the mouth, but there must be a post-mortem. My tests suggest that she died about three hours ago."

"That would be about noon?"

"Yes, I think so."

McLean moved closer to the corpse. Her face was extra-ordinarily composed, and she looked as if she were sleeping. She wore a white linen frock, and a woollen pullover, the sleeves of which were rolled above her elbows. On her feet were canvas shoes with rubber soles.

"In what circumstances was she found?" McLean asked the local inspector.

"In a punt about two miles up river. There's a little back-water up there, and a very pleasant mooring spot under over-hanging willows. According to her aunt it was her favourite spot to lounge and read. She set off in the punt about eleven o'clock, without saying where she was going. At half past twelve two lads in a row-boat saw her lying back in the punt. At first they thought she was asleep, but a little later one of them had occasion to pass close by her and became suspicious. He called his companion and they took fright and ran to the nearest telephone. I motored to the spot with a colleague, and saw at once that she was dead. In her handbag I found a letter addressed to her here, so we brought the punt back, and took what evidence was available. I understand the girl was a niece of the owner of this place, and was on a visit."

"Yes, I know the circumstances," replied McLean. "What did you do with the handbag and the punt?"

"The punt is locked up in the boat-house, exactly as I found it, with the handbag and a few other items. I looked for any-thing which might explain the girl's death, but found nothing. On reporting to my chief later I was instructed to do nothing further as the C.I.D. had an interest in this matter. The doctor came along, and since then I have been waiting for you. Here is the key of the boat-house."

McLean took the key and turned to the doctor, who had been listening intently.

"Have you any observations to make, Doctor?" he asked.

"No—not until after the post-mortem. A short time ago I telephoned for an ambulance, and it should be here at any moment. I shall wait until it arrives."

"In that case I'll take a look at the punt."

Inspector Adams led him to the building, which was of considerable size, and from which a slipway led down to the water, where Mannering's motor-boat was moored. It was a cabin cruiser of the latest design, and it made a pleasant picture with its shining brass and bright paint.

Inside the building were several small boats, all of excellent construction. The punt was close to the sliding door, and the larger of the many coloured cushions in the stern still showed the impressions made by the last occupant.

"There it is," said Adams. "Exactly as I found it. The hand-bag was on her lap, and the book beside her, with her right hand resting on it. The punt pole was rammed into the river-bed to stop the punt from swinging out. I put that back in its slings, and used the paddle to bring the craft here, as I don't know how to use the pole."

McLean nodded and picked up the handbag. It contained some articles of toilet, a purse in which was some odd cash and two one-pound notes, and a letter from a London firm in reference to an enquiry about dress material.

"That's the letter which gave me her address," said Adams.

McLean then took up the book and scanned the title. It was *Mathematics for Fun*, and was of recent publication. The contents covered magic squares, acrostics, and other problems.

"Queer reading for a young lady," mused Adams.

At that moment Sergeant Brook appeared, his broad face red from hurrying, and his breath short.

"The doctor told me you were here, sir," he panted. "I got here as quick as I could."

"You must have exceeded the speed limit," replied McLean. "This is Inspector Adams of the County Constabulary."

Brook nodded and Adams reciprocated.

"I want everything removed from the punt," said McLean.

While Brook started to carry out this order Adams looked at his watch.

"I have to get back to headquarters," he said. "Unless you want me for anything, Inspector?"

"No, I don't think so. Oh yes—the position of the punt when you found it. I may need to go up there."

"Of course. I made a sketch, and the site is indicated on the bank by two wooden pegs. Here is the sketch."

He produced a folded sheet of paper from his note-book, on which the exact spot was clearly indicated by features on the river bank. McLean took it and nodded his appreciation.

"Quite a good artist," mused McLean as he transferred the drawing to his own note-book. "But I fancy he rather resents our butting in. You know what has happened?"

"I didn't, until I saw the corpse just now. I was simply told to contact you here. Knocked me flat, as you might say. Is it connected with the Peyton job?"

"I hope so, because it might have the effect of putting us back on a lost trail. What's that?"

Under one of the cushions was a small paper cup, with crinkled sides. Brook retrieved it and handed it to McLean, who opened the crushed sides and restored it to its original shape. Then he smelt it, and finally wetted a finger, touched the inside of the cup and put the finger to his tongue.

"Sweet," he said. "I think this came from some sort of confectionery. Jellied fruits, probably."

"I think you're right, sir."

"See if you can find any more."

Bit by bit the rest of the cushions and the floor carpet were removed, and finally the gratings, but there were no more paper cups; only a matchstick and traces of cigarette ash.

"That's interesting," mused McLean. "She carried no cigarettes or matches. We must find out if the punt was cleaned out just before she used it."

"Well, there's nothing else here. Am I to replace the cushions and other things?"

"Yes. Then we'll take some evidence."

"Poisoning, isn't it?"

"Apparently, but it might be unwise to anticipate the finding of the post-mortem."

"She didn't look the sort of girl who might poison herself," said Brook.

"What do they look like when they have such an intention?"

"Yes, I guess that was a silly remark," said Brook. "What I mean is why should she poison herself?"

"Better still—why was she poisoned?"

"You haven't arrived at that already?"

"Not quite. Yes, I'll take possession of the handbag and the book."

Brook passed the two articles, and as he did so the book fell off the handbag, and a piece of paper fluttered from its pages.

"Sorry, sir," he said.

Brook picked up the book, but McLean retrieved the sheet of paper. It had been torn from a diary, but was evidently one of the spare pages provided in some diaries, for there was no date on it. Drawn on it in light blue ink, obviously by a pen of the ball-pointed type, was an acrostic:

"I remember that from my school days," said McLean.

"What is it, French?" asked Brook, peering at the words.

"No—Latin. It's fairly well known, and I expect she copied it from the book. But we'll see."

For a few minutes he was busy turning over the pages of the book. But that particular acrostic was not included in the examples given.

"Curious!" he muttered.

"Does it mean anything?" asked Brook.

"Yes, unlike most acrostics it makes some sort of sense. It means 'Ploughman Arepo holds the works and the wheels.' Very ingenious."

"But what a waste of time."

"Some people have a passion for this kind of problem and Denise Rostan was one of them. She must have seen it somewhere, and copied it."

"What are the little ticks against all the letters?"

"I don't know. Now we'll get across to the house."

As McLean was locking the door the ambulance arrived, and two men with a stretcher came across the lawns towards the summer-house, but McLean left that matter to the doctor and continued on his course. His ring at the bell was answered by the manservant whom he had seen on his previous visit. He looked very depressed.

"Mr. Mannering told me to show you into the library," he said. "He told me you would probably wish to see him."

When they entered the library Mannering was pacing up and down, sucking at a huge cigar.

"Ah, Inspector!" he said. "This is a terrible business. I am utterly bewildered. When I was told . . . But I mustn't hold up your investigation. Please go ahead."

Sergeant Brook drew up a chair and sat down at the table, with his note-book open.

"I understand that your niece went on the river at about eleven o'clock?" said McLean.

"Yes. I didn't actually see her leave, but my wife did."

"Did you see her at all this morning?"

"Yes. She came down to breakfast about her usual time. Later I saw her in the garden. I think about ten o'clock. I never saw her after that."

"Was she accustomed to taking out the punt alone?"

"Oh yes—almost every day. She loved the river, and was quite expert with a punt."

"When I was here last, in regard to another matter, you told me that she was very reluctant to talk about her past life."

"That is so."

"Did she continue to behave like that?"

"Yes. You will remember that on that occasion she was brought to admit that there had been a man in her past, and that he had died in India?"

"I remember that."

"She never referred to the matter again, and she showed by

her attitude that she would not welcome any probing on my part, or my wife's."

"Did she not find the flat she was seeking?"

"No. She went to London once or twice, and saw a number of places, but none of them seemed suitable. I told her there was no hurry so far as I was concerned. As my sister's daughter she was welcome here."

"But you never really got on together?"

"No. I must confess I felt a little hurt about her lack of trust in me. My wife was a little more successful in gaining her confidence, but not to any great extent. Her reticence in respect of her earlier life was most exasperating. Nor would she discuss her financial situation, although she appeared to have considerable funds."

"How did she employ her time here?"

"She read a great deal, but seldom went out to any place of entertainment. She seemed to enjoy the garden, and her trips on the river."

"Had you any reason to believe she was interested in a man?"

"No. There was scarcely any mail for her, and only an occasional telephone call."

"Was she interested in acrostics, word squares, and so forth?"

"Yes, and in chess problems. I don't play chess, so I don't know how far her knowledge of the game went. But she used to attempt the chess problems in a Sunday newspaper."

"This book was found in the punt," said McLean. "Did it come from your shelves?"

Mannering looked at the book which McLean produced, and shook his head.

"She must have bought it," he said. "I have no books of that type here."

"Was she fond of sweets?"

"Sweets?"

"Confectionery."

"I really don't know. She certainly seemed quite partial to the sweet courses after her meals, and always ready for a second helping."

"I presume you saw the body when it was first brought here?"

"Yes."

"Did the doctor tell you anything about the probable cause of her death?"

"No. He said he was not prepared to make any sort of statement, but the fact that he did not bring the body into the house led me to suspect that he did not think she had died from natural causes. Is that the case?"

"We don't know—yet. There is to be a post-mortem. Now I should like to see Mrs. Mannering."

"Yes, of course. She has taken this matter rather badly, and is lying down in her room. I will send the maid for her."

He pushed a bell, and a rosy-cheeked girl entered the room.

"Emily," said Mannering, "will you tell the mistress that the inspector would like to see her here. She is in her bed-room."

"Yes, sir."

It was some minutes before Mrs. Mannering entered the library, and she looked a somewhat pathetic creature in the black dress which she had donned. She wore considerable make-up, possibly to cover up the traces of her woe. Mannering was prepared to stay and see her through her ordeal, but McLean said he would prefer to question Mrs. Mannering alone.

"Certainly," said Mannering, rather huffily.

"Please be seated, Mrs. Mannering," said McLean, when the door closed on her husband. "I am sorry to be so much trouble, but you will appreciate that there are a number of routine questions which I must put to you."

"I understand."

"When did you last see your niece?"

"It was a few minutes to eleven o'clock. She was waiting for the gardener to finish washing out the punt."

"Oh, so the punt was thoroughly washed out before she used it?"

"Yes."

"Did you actually see your niece leave?"

"No. I went back to the house. She asked me if I would go with her, but I had some letters to write."

"Did you notice what things your niece had with her?"

"Yes. She had a red handbag—quite a small one, and a new book which had arrived by post that morning."

"Nothing else?"

Mrs. Mannering thought for a moment.

"No. I am sure there was nothing else."

"Is this the book?" asked McLean, and produced the volume which he had found in the punt.

"Yes. I laughed when I saw it, because I thought it was a curious book to buy, when there were so many others."

"But you knew she was interested in the subject?"

"Oh yes—anything mathematical."

"Were you and she on good terms?"

"Yes. I liked her. She could be very amusing, although at times she had moods."

"What sort of moods?"

"She would avoid me, as well as my husband. Perhaps for two days on end she would scarcely say a word. Then it would all be over and she was charming again."

"Do you know any cause for the moods?"

"No—not definitely. But there was a man in her life who died. I don't know who he was or what her relationship with him might have been. I think in time she might have told me the whole story, but, alas, I shall never know now."

"Was she particularly fond of confectionery?"

"Yes. I have been with her when she bought sweets, and sometimes I gave her my sweet ration."

"Any particular kind of sweets?"

"Mostly chocolates—in boxes, but sometimes fruit jellies with sugar on them."

"Did she always buy them at the same shop?"

"I don't know where she bought them."

"Had she independent means?"

"Yes. But I don't know what they were. She told me that her mother had left her well provided for."

"I presume she had a banking account?"

"Yes, somewhere in London. But it was only an accommodation account. I think her main account was in Algiers, and there was some difficulty in getting money transferred. I lent her fifty pounds until her permit came through."

"Do you think she was the sort of woman who, in a moment of deep depression, might take her own life?"

"Oh no—I can't think that. She had beauty, health, money, freedom. What else could a young woman want?"

"Happiness, perhaps."

"She was happy most of the time."

"Do you think she was seriously looking for a flat to live in?"

"Yes. I have seen letters which she had from a London house agency, and she went to town twice, I think, to look over some available flats."

"Had she close friends in this country?"

"She never mentioned any, but there were one or two telephone calls which she did not attempt to explain."

"Would it be an exaggeration to describe her as a mystery woman?"

"No. My husband has often said the same thing."

"Had you met your niece before her recent visit here?"

"No. My husband had spoken of her, but I had never seen her. I think that my husband had not seen her for years. We were surprised when she telephoned to say she was in England, and would like to spend a short time with us."

"How long have you been married, Mrs. Mannering?"

"Five years. I met my husband in Persia, where he had business interests. But we came to England six months later, and he bought this place.

"But you are not Persian, are you?"

"No. I am an Armenian by birth, but my mother was English."

"Thank you. I think that is all for the moment. Now I should like to see the room which your niece occupied."

"I will show you."

They followed her into the main hall and up the broad staircase to a room which had a fine view across the garden towards the pagoda. The divan bed was made, and the whole place was scrupulously tidy.

"I will leave you, unless you require me . . ." said Mrs. Mannering.

"Thank you," said McLean. "I will see you before I leave."

"You will find me in the lounge."

As soon as she had gone McLean commenced his search. The wardrobe was full of frocks, coats and shoes, and the drawers packed with expensive-looking underwear. In a trinket box McLean found a quantity of jewellery, but nothing which looked really valuable. He took out a pair of pearl earrings and showed them to Brook.

"One of those must be the one you brought to her," said Brook.

"Yes. That point was never satisfactorily cleared up. Try those drawers under the dressing-table. I'm looking for a diary from which that torn page might have been extracted, also a ball-pointed pen."

But search as they might neither of these articles came to light, nor were there any letters or documents. But one quite unexpected article came to light. It was concealed in a riding boot which McLean tipped upside down. It was a fully loaded automatic pistol.

"Golly!" ejaculated Brook. "Peyton was shot with a pistol!"

"Hold your horses!" said McLean. "Peyton was shot with a pistol of quite different calibre. All the same, it gives us a new angle on Mademoiselle Rostan."

"Certainly does," said Brook.

"Then there's the matter of that acrostic drawn on the sheet of paper. It looks as if it did not originate here, and raises the question—how did it get into her hands?"

"That applies also to the paper cup."

"And the matchstick and cigarette ash."

"But she did smoke," said Brook. "There's a cigarette-case half full of cigarettes, and also a petrol lighter."

"She left them behind her. Remind me I want to see the gardener to check up on the cleaning of the punt. If it was thoroughly washed and cleaned then we have to presume that the girl was not alone in the punt all the time."

The search went on for some time longer, and finally he came upon something which was of first-class importance. He opened a leather writing-pad, and found inside a few envelopes and several sheets of notepaper, bearing the address of the house.

There was a comparatively new sheet of blotting paper on the pad, and it bore a fairly good impression of reversed writing, done with a thick ordinary pen. He held this up before the mirror, and read slowly what was legible.

My dear Harry,
  *This is a difficult letter . . . since I saw you . . . realize
how troubled . . . better if you forgot . . . lied to you . . . very happy
days . . . so far away now . . . heart was sad when I got off at
Naples. . . . Now about Peyton. I feel you should . . .*

"There it stops," said McLean. "There is no sign of her
having blotted any continuation of the letter—if there was any
continuation; and there's no date at the top. It's probably a
reply to the letter which Harry Montague sent her through
me. She is evidently trying to explain her conduct in regard
to Peyton. If the complete letter exists it might explain much
to us."

"Shall I get him on the telephone?" asked Brook.

"Yes, but not yet. Run into the garden and try to find the
gardener, before he knocks off. No need to bring him here if he
swears positively that he cleaned out that punt this morning,
and left nothing in it."

Brook was absent for a few minutes, during which time
McLean turned out the books from the small bookcase, and
examined the labels on various empty suitcases which he
found in an otherwise empty cupboard. Then Brook returned.

"Just caught him on his way home," he said. "He is quite
sure the punt contained nothing but the cushions and floor
carpet when he had finished with it."

"I thought as much. Well, now we'll see the manservant.
Round him up."

The swarthy young man was soon sitting in a chair facing
McLean across the library table.

"What is your name?" asked McLean.

"Achmed Knullah. I am a Syrian."

"How long have you been with Mr. Mannering?"

"Five years. He engaged me soon after his marriage, while
he was on his honeymoon."

"In what capacity?"

"He told me he was coming to England to set up a permanent home, and he needed a trustworthy butler, but there
were other reasons."

"What reasons?"

"He is studying Arabic, and I am able to help him. Also

he is fond of Arab dishes, and sometimes I prepare them for him."

"Tell me about this morning. Did you see Miss Rostan go out on the river?"

"No, sir."

"Did you see Mr. Mannering during the morning?"

"Yes—most of the morning."

"What do you mean by that?"

"I took his newspapers to him after breakfast, and for an hour he read them in the library. Then at half past ten he rang for me and told me he wanted his hair cut. For years I have done that for him. He does not like to go to a public hair-dresser, and is satisfied the way I do it."

"How long did that take?"

"About an hour, because he also had a face massage. After that he went into the garden, and a little later Madame joined him. They stayed together in a seat along the terrace until it was time for lunch. I sounded the gong for them at half past twelve, and they came into the dining-room. They were at lunch when the bad news came."

"What happened then?"

"The Master went with the police officer to identify the body, but Madame was so distressed she went straight to her room."

"Did you have much to do with Miss Rostan?"

"No, sir. I regard myself as Mr. Mannering's valet. That was understood when I took the position."

"But you must have seen a good deal of her."

"Yes—about the house."

"Was she of a happy disposition?"

"No, sir. Always she seemed to be brooding over something. It was a happy house until she came, but she cast a sort of gloom over it."

"Did not she get on well with her aunt?"

"Yes. But Madame is very easy to get on with. I think she got the impression that Miss Rostan had had a bad deal some-where, and that she needed sympathy and companionship."

"Did you ever see Miss Rostan before her recent arrival here?"

"No, sir."

Subsequently the two female resident domestics were

questioned. They were both very nervous, and their evidence was of no value except as corroboration of what McLean already knew. By the time McLean had done with them it was five o'clock and he remembered his promise to Valerie.

"Brook, I want you to ring up this number, and ask for my wife. She is expecting a call from me. Tell her I'm going to be delayed, and that I suggest she should make her way home under her own steam."

While Brook carried out this order McLean took a closer look at Mannering's bookshelves. It was indeed a most interesting collection of books, ranging from travel to philosophy, with a good representation of modern physics. Two long shelves were full of works in Arabic, together with an English-Arabic dictionary, and these bore out Achmed's statement. So far as he could see there was no volume dealing with the subject which had intrigued the dead girl. But there was a leather-bound set of *Encyclopaedia Britannica*, in which McLean found a fairly comprehensive article on Acrostics and Magic Squares. Somewhat to his surprise the 'Sator-Arepo' example was not given. Then Brook returned.

"It's all right," he said. "Mrs. McLean says there's a bus which will take her most of the way. She wishes you luck."

"I shall need some. But at least we have made a little progress."

"Have we?" asked Brook.

"Don't be so dismal. In the case of the spurious Mr. Peyton we never succeeded in identifying him, nor discovering just where he was murdered, but here we have a mass of information. The result of the post-mortem is a foregone conclusion. She was deliberately murdered by someone she knew intimately. Someone who, like herself, was interested in acrostics. It was, I believe, this unknown person who entered the punt after she had left this place and, noticing the book which she was reading, wrote that acrostic on a page torn from his diary, while she was enjoying some sweets which he had given her. The doctored sweets brought coma, and finally death. He cleaned up the punt afterwards, removing all the sweet wrappings but one, which had got under a cushion, plus a matchstick and a little cigarette ash."

"And the acrostic."

"Yes. That was not noticeable, because she had slipped it inside the pages of the book."

"What about those ticks against the letters?"

"There I am beaten for the moment. It looks like some sort of checking process, but against what?"

Brook had no reply to that, and at McLean's request he read through the evidence that had been taken, to refresh McLean's memory on certain points. They were in the middle of this when there was a knock on the door and Achmed entered.

"Excuse me, Inspector," he said. "There is a man on the telephone asking for Miss Rostan. I did not know what to tell him, so I asked him to wait for a moment."

"Did he give any name?"

"Yes. He said his name was Montague."

"I'll speak to him."

II

AT THE farm everything was ready for the expected guest. Helen gave a last look round the best bedroom, rearranged the bowl of freshly cut flowers on the table near the window, and made sure that the bed was properly aired. Then she went downstairs to lay the table for tea. Harry adopted an air of complete imperturbability, but was far from feeling that way, and every few minutes he gazed at the clock.

"Did she say by what means she was getting here?" asked Helen.

"No. I forgot to ask her."

"You should have done. If she comes by train it may not be easy to get a taxi."

"I presumed she was coming by road, as she never said anything about trains or buses."

"Has she got a car of her own?"

"I should imagine so. Helen, you shouldn't have done all this cooking. There are enough cakes to feed a dozen."

"We can use what are left over. It was time I had a good cake-make."

By the time the table was fully laid, and the kettle boiling, it was half past four. Harry, sitting in the window recess with a book, stared up the vacant road, and put down the book.

"You're like a cat on hot bricks," laughed Helen. "You'd better go out and stroll up the road. You may meet her."

Harry took his stroll and came back about a quarter of an hour later, shaking his head.

"I suppose you haven't muffed the day or time?" asked Helen.

"No, of course not."

"Then she's a very unpunctual lady."

"There are such things as mechanical breakdowns."

"Also such things as telephones, through which she could inform us of any trouble."

Harry watched the hands of the clock moving round the dial. Five o'clock came and by that time Helen's patience was almost exhausted.

"I think we should start tea," she said.

"No. Give her ten minutes more."

Helen nodded, and the ten minutes passed.

"I'm going to ring up Raven's Court and find out what time she left," said Harry.

"But have you the telephone number?"

"No. I can get that through 'Enquiries'."

He was absent for a few minutes, and then came back to Helen with a face that was ashen.

"Well?" she asked. "Harry, what's the matter?"

"The most dreadful and horrible thing has happened," he said brokenly. "She—she's dead."

Helen stared at him incredulously. She waited for him to speak again, but he seemed incapable of doing so, and slumped into a chair, to stare fixedly into space. She came and sat beside him.

"I'm sorry, darling," she murmured. "Was it some sort of accident?"

"I don't know. McLean wouldn't tell me."

"Inspector McLean? Did you speak to him?"

"Yes. A servant answered first, and was very mysterious. He told me to hang on, and then McLean came to the 'phone. He—said he was sorry to tell me that Denise died suddenly, and that he wished to ask me some questions. He's coming here later this evening."

"But didn't he tell you how she died?"

"No. I asked him that, but he evaded the question."

There was silence for a moment or two and then Helen faced up to the situation.

"If there had been an accident there would be no good reason for him to behave like that. It must be something worse. You realize that, don't you?"

"Yes—yes, I do."

"Then it's either suicide—or murder."

"Helen!"

"Better to be prepared, Harry. I think the inspector was trying to soften the blow."

"Yes, you're probably right. I—I think I'll go and rest for a bit."

"No, stay and have some tea. I don't feel like eating alone. Won't you?"

Harry nodded, and Helen went out and came back almost immediately with a pot of tea. It was inevitable that the goodly array of home-made cakes should remain almost untouched, but the tea was acceptable, and the pot was refilled before they had finished.

Then came the long wait for further information, which was ended as darkness settled down, and McLean and Brook arrived and were shown into the sitting-room where Harry was walking to and fro with fretted nerves.

"If you will excuse me . . ." said Helen.

"I have no objection to your staying if you wish, Mrs. Arkwright," said McLean.

Helen looked across at Harry.

"Yes, do, Helen," said Harry.

"Very well."

She sat down opposite Harry, and watched McLean draw some papers from a brief-case. Among these was the sheet of blotting-paper which he had removed from Denise's writing-case.

"I'm sorry to be the bearer of bad news," said McLean. "The dead body of Miss Rostan was found in a punt a mile or two up the river above Raven's Court, round about noon today. She appears to have died by poisoning, but I am awaiting a fuller medical report as a result of a post-mortem which will take place this evening. Whether the poison—if it was poison which killed her—was self-administered has yet to be proved. I understood on the telephone that you expected her here this afternoon?"

"Yes," replied Harry. "She told me to expect her round about four o'clock."

"When did she tell you that?"

"Yesterday—on the telephone."

"Had you invited her here?"

"Yes. Some weeks ago when I saw her."

"So she responded to the letter which you sent her through me?"

"No. She denied ever having received that letter, and I doubted whether you forwarded it to her."

"I sent it immediately I received it as I promised to do."

"Well, she denied all knowledge of it."

"Then how did you know where to find her?"

"From a man who was aboard the *Rantala*. I met him quite by accident."

"Did you see her at Raven's Court?"

"Yes."

"How did you find her?"

"Unwell. At least, that was the impression I got. It was a brief meeting, in the lower garden. I did not go into the house as she did not seem keen for me to see her relatives. I begged her to spend a few days with us here, and she promised to think it over. I thought she had no intention of coming when I failed to hear from her. Then, yesterday, she rang up and said she would like to come today."

"You say you heard nothing from her after that visit until she telephoned you yesterday?"

"That is so."

McLean produced the sheet of blotting-paper and passed it to Harry.

"If you hold that before the mirror you will find the beginning of a letter intended, I think, for you. Please read what you can of it."

Harry got up and did as he was bade. In a few moments he turned round to McLean, his hand shaking badly.

"I never got such a letter. I never heard a word from her."

"That's a pity," said McLean. "I was hoping it might enlighten us as to her real relationship with Mr. Peyton."

"At that meeting she swore there was no sort of relationship."

"Did you believe that?"

"Yes."

"Do you believe it now?"

"Why not?"

"This letter which she started makes it clear that there was some sort of relationship, and she was going to tell you what it was when, presumably, her courage failed her, and she destroyed what she had written."

"When was that written?"

"I don't know, but I should think it was quite recently—just before she decided to come and stay with you, perhaps with the intention of confiding in you, rather than entrust her secret to pen and paper."

"It might be so," agreed Harry thoughtfully. "But why do you drag in the Peyton affair?"

"Only because the two events may have a connection."

"Do you mean that you suspect Denise was involved in that dreadful murder?"

"I do."

"But it's unthinkable! She was a most charming girl, kind and gentle in actions and speech. I can't imagine her doing anything brutal or dishonest. Peyton was a man old enough to be her father, and he hated women. All the time we were on that ship I never saw him talk to a single woman."

"Yet this woman was in his cabin on more than one occasion. She also changed her port of disembarkation after leaving Bombay. Could it have been due to Mr. Peyton, who got off at the same port—Naples?"

"Are you trying to poison my memories of her?" asked Harry, with bitterness in his voice.

"Not at all. I have no doubt that she had many saving graces but she lied to you on many occasions, and when she wasn't lying she was concealing information most important to me in my investigation. Now she's gone, and I've got a double murder on my hands. Who was the man who told you where to find Miss Rostan?"

"A Captain Loveday, late of the Indian Army. I don't know his address, but Denise knew it because she wrote to him. You should be able to find it in her diary."

"So she used a diary?"

"Yes. I saw her writing in it on several occasions while we were on the ship."

"What sort of a diary was it?"

"Quite small—about three inches by two."

"So far I have been unable to find it. Tell me more about this Captain Loveday. I think he must be in the list of passengers, but I cannot remember taking any statement from him. Did he also get off the ship at Naples?"

"No. He told me he lived in the wilds of Scotland, and is now helping in his father's stock-breeding farm. He was exhibiting at the Dairy Show recently held in London. That's where I ran into him."

"He's in the passenger list, sir," said Brook. "I think he lives in Perthshire."

"Yes, I think you're right, Brook. Mr. Montague, did the captain appear to be an old friend of Miss Rostan?"

"No. I think they met on the ship for the first time, but they became very friendly during the voyage."

"Did Miss Rostan drink to any extent?"

"You mean alcoholic drinks, of course?"

"Yes."

"No. She and I went to the bar on occasion, but she always had soft drinks."

"It is in evidence that she went to Peyton's cabin on several occasions, ostensibly to drink some old sherry which he kept there. What do you say to that?"

"I don't believe it. Whenever I invited her to have a short drink she always declined."

"But it was Miss Rostan herself who made that statement," said McLean.

Harry was taken aback. He had either to believe that Denise was a secret drinker or had gone to Peyton's cabin for some other purpose, and he liked neither of these alternatives.

"I'm puzzled," he said. "I wish I could help you more, but I can't."

"Then I won't trouble you any more at the moment. I had hoped that you might have received the letter she started and presumably did not finish. It might have helped considerably."

"I wish I had," said Harry. "I want to think well of her,

and I'm sure she would have explained everything to my satisfaction. As it is I'm left in horrible doubt. When is the inquest to be held?"

"The day after tomorrow, I think."

"At Maidenhead?"

"Yes."

"I think I shall attend."

McLean nodded his head, put the papers back into the brief-case, and then left with Brook. A moment or two later the car could be heard making up the long drive.

"Oh, dear!" sighed Helen. "Why did this have to happen just when we were so happy?"

Harry took her hand and pressed it.

"It's clear I've got to forget her, somehow, by some means," he said.

"There's the farm," she said. "Waiting for our undivided attention. Work in itself is a magical panacea."

"I think you're right," he replied with a smile. "But don't ask me to believe she was as evil as McLean seems to imagine."

"If she had been you wouldn't have loved her, Harry."

"Thanks for that. Now I think we've got some book-keeping to do."

12

LATE that evening McLean heard the result of the post-mortem. It was that Denise Rostan had died from poison taken by the mouth, and the contents of the stomach indicated that the poison had been introduced through the medium of sweet-meats of a gelatinous nature. Almost simultaneously McLean received a laboratory report on the paper wrapping which he had found in the punt. It was negative.

"Question is who gave her the sweets," mused McLean. "And the answer isn't easy."

"Will the verdict be murder?" asked Brook.

"On the evidence it can be nothing less. I didn't expect to find poison on the paper wrapping. Any person planning murder by such a means would almost certainly inject the poison into the centres of the sweets."

"Do you think it was done to prevent the girl from going to stay with Montague?"

"That's pure hypothesis, but it might be the case if it was suspected by some interested person that she might open her mouth too wide about certain events in the past. If she proposed to spend a few days with Montague and his sister it is only natural that she should tell someone at the house. We will go into that matter tomorrow. There's one more thing I want you to do before we pack up, find Captain Loveday's address, and get his telephone number."

Ten minutes later McLean was through to the Loveday estate in Perthshire, but on asking for Captain Loveday he was informed that Loveday was in London, and was staying at the Caledonian Hotel.

"Our luck is in," he said to Brook. "Find me the telephone number of the Caledonian Hotel."

The subsequent telephone call was successful, and after a minute or two of delay he was speaking to the captain, who informed him that he was leaving for Scotland by the night train, but would be pleased to see McLean at the hotel if he could come fairly soon.

"I'll be with you in a quarter of an hour," replied McLean.

Later, the hotel being very busy, McLean and Brook were taken to Loveday's bedroom, and found there the tall and aristocratic-looking man, who was yet in the dark regarding the object of the visit.

"This is the only place I could think of to have a private talk, Inspector," he said. "Downstairs it is like a circus. I should like a few shares in this hotel. Now, sir, what have I done wrong?"

"Nothing, I hope," said McLean. "But the matter is rather serious. It concerns a Miss Denise Rostan, whom I think you knew."

"Yes, but it was only a passing acquaintanceship—a few weeks on a steamship. I hope nothing is wrong with her?"

"Her dead body was found this morning, in a punt near her home."

"Good gracious! How very sad. I am indeed tremendously sorry. She was such a charming girl, and I got to like her enormously. But am I to presume that the circumstances of her death call for an enquiry?"

"Yes. Will you tell me what you know of her connections?"

"I know very little. I seem to remember that she told me she had been staying with some relative in Karachi."

"That was untrue."

"Indeed!"

"What else did she tell you?"

"She said she was getting off at Naples to stay with some friends there, and then going to England overland. I understood her to be without parents, and not engaged in any kind of business. When we parted she promised to write to me, and later I had a letter from her. She told me that while she was trying to find a place to live in she was staying with her uncle at a place near Maidenhead. Curiously enough I met a man at the Dairy Show who recognized me as having been on the same steamship, and asked me if I could put him in touch with Miss Rostan. I was able to remember the address."

"I know about that," said McLean. "Mr. Montague has already made a statement. Did you know a man on the ship named Peyton?"

"Yes, but not to speak to."

"Did you ever see Miss Rostan talking to him?"

"No, but she did comment upon him once, when he passed us on the promenade deck."

"What did she say?"

"She said, 'There's a man who arouses my instinctive dislike', or words to that effect."

"Did she give you any reason for her instinctive dislike?"

"No."

"Did she see a great deal of Mr. Montague?"

"Yes. I teased her about that, but stopped when I realized she was quite serious in that affair."

"You think she was in love with him?"

"That was my impression."

"And you—forgive the question—were you also in love with her?"

"I don't mind the question at all. The answer is definitely no. I liked her. She was excellent company, but I have recently lost my wife, and have no intention of falling in love again—so soon."

"Was Miss Rostan addicted to drinking?"

Loveday shook his head emphatically.

"On the contrary, she never drank at all, except insipid soft drinks."

"Did she never say anything about her parentage?"

"I understood that her mother was English and her father French. Her father had been an explorer or something like that, and had died before her mother. She was certainly bi-lingual, for a French woman whom we met on the boat told me that her French was perfect. Her English, as you possibly know, was impeccable."

"Is there anything else you can tell me about her past?"

"No, I can't think of anything."

McLean thanked him, and a few moments later he and Brook were outside the hotel.

"Now I think we will call it a day," said McLean. "I'd drive you home if it wasn't so late, but I have a wife whose week-end has been completely spoilt, and when she knows I have to go to Raven's Court again tomorrow she'll probably start throwing dishes at me. By the way, I can spare you tomorrow if you have something to do."

"Not me, sir. I'd just as soon be at Raven's Court as anywhere else. Will ten o'clock do?"

"Make it eleven. After all, Sunday is Sunday."

"Very good. Did you get any grist out of the captain's statements?"

"Yes. They confirmed the fact that the girl didn't drink, and that her excuse for being in Peyton's cabin was a lie. So her visits there were for another purpose. Oh no, Brook, not that sort of purpose."

"Sorry. But what other purpose is there?"

"Information about him. It is significant that she went there when most persons were in the dining-saloon."

"But wouldn't she find the door locked if he wasn't inside to let her in?"

"I don't know, but at any rate she went there, and I'm certain it wasn't by invitation on his part."

"Mr. Montague would be glad to know that."

"He would, but her object there may be no less reprehensible than that which some people would impute."

"Just a cheap low-down spy?"

"We'll leave it at that for the moment. See you tomorrow morning. Sleep well!"

McLean arrived home to find his wife sitting up, reading. She looked at him from under her long lashes.

"You're a nice sort of husband!" she said.

"I'm just the sort of husband you knew I was. But I'm sorry all the same. It's been ding-dong ever since I left home. Apart from the work at Raven's Court, I had to go down the river to look at the site where the punt was found. Afterwards I had to see young Montague, and when I thought I had really finished I had to see another man."

"I know—I know. And I bet you haven't had a bite of food since I last saw you."

"As a matter of fact, I haven't. But I'm too tired to worry about food. I'll have a drink instead."

"You won't," said Valerie, getting up. "I'm getting expert at keeping meals hot. Sit you down, my lad. It's all laid on."

McLean's alleged indifference to food was soon proved to be the flimsiest invention, for he found no difficulty in finishing every morsel of the meal which Valerie had prepared for him during which she shot questions at him with the rapidity of a machine-gun.

"So it's murder?" she said, finally.

"Yes."

"And where do you go from here?"

"Tomorrow morning I——"

"Oh, Robert—no!"

"Sorry, darling. But that's how it is. On Monday the inquest takes place, and I have a lot of things to do before then. But we'll make up for it—later."

"Jam tomorrow," she said. "Well, if I'm going to be a grass widow until you solve this mystery I may as well take up painting again."

"You have already. I can smell that filthy palette of yours."

"That's right. I've been cleaning it. I think you were intended to be a bloodhound, with a nose like that. Coffee, or will it keep you awake?"

"Nothing will keep me awake."

"That sounds as if you are satisfied with progress."

"I am. I'm back on the trail again after having wandered in the wilderness for many weeks. Frankly, I began to despair of making anything of the Peyton case, but now the outlook is brighter. By the way, Miss Rostan packed a gun."

"In plain English she carried a pistol?"

"Yes—hidden in a riding boot. It is certainly not the weapon which killed Peyton, but it makes one think."

"It makes me think that the whole world is mad, with the exception of you and me, and sometimes . . ." Her eyes gleamed mischievously. "Sometimes I have doubts about you."

She escaped before McLean's raised hand could administer a corrective, and was soon back with the steaming coffee. They sat for some time talking of things other than McLean's immediate problems.

On the morrow McLean met Brook at Raven's Court. It was a beautiful morning, with a bright clear sun shining from a peerless sky and throwing into wonderful relief all the attractive features of the place. No one, ignorant of the facts, would have sensed tragedy so close at hand. Brook, to McLean's surprise, had spent the early morning transcribing his shorthand notes of the previous day, and these he handed to McLean with a smile of self-satisfaction.

"Good work!" said McLean. "You must have got up very early."

"I did. Can't let all this evidence pile up on me. You'll find one or two discrepancies. I've noted them in the margins."

"You're right. There are far too many discrepancies. We'll deal with some of them this morning. Now for Mr. Mannering."

On this occasion Emily answered McLean's ring at the bell, and gave him a sunny smile.

"Is Mr. Mannering in?" asked McLean.

"Yes, sir. Will you wait in the hall while I tell him?"

She was absent for a minute or two and then came back to conduct them to the big lounge, where Mannering was sitting, reading a newspaper. McLean noticed that he was now wearing a dark suit and a black tie.

"Good morning, gentlemen," he said. "I have just heard over the telephone that the inquest is to be held tomorrow, and that I may be needed to give evidence."

"That is so. Mr. Mannering, I'm sorry to worry you again, but there are one or two points I want to clear up. After I left here yesterday I saw a man named Harry Montague, who was on friendly terms with your niece. Have you met him?"

"No. Denise never mentioned him."

"They travelled on the same ship together, from Bombay."

"I had no idea of that."

"Mr. Montague has stated that he was expecting Miss Rostan to stay with him and his sister this week-end. Did she not tell you that she would be spending the week-end elsewhere?"

"No. I don't think she could have told my wife either, for she would have mentioned it to me if she had known."

"When I examined Miss Rostan's room there was no sign of anything being packed, although according to Mr. Montague she was expected at his home round about four o'clock. One would have expected her to pack something since she would have to leave here soon after lunch."

"Yes, I suppose that would be natural. But I know absolutely nothing about the matter."

"Then again, I have failed to find the passport which she must have possessed when she came to England, or any sign of a cheque book, which I presume she must have had, since it is in evidence that she had a drawing account on a bank in London. Both these things are important to the case."

Yes, I suppose they are. But I have no idea where she kept them."

"My impression is that she intended to leave the house without telling you——"

"You mean for good?"

"That is my impression, but I may be wrong. Had she a car of her own?"

"No. She could drive a car, and sometimes used mine."

"It is scarcely likely she would have taken your car, so presumably she intended to go by train, and that would mean ordering a taxi to take her to the railway station."

"Yes, she would certainly not be able to walk to the station laden with suitcases. But I don't quite see the gist of this, Inspector."

"If, as I suggest, she intended to leave secretly, it is possible that she did pack a bag with essential articles and leave it somewhere in order to pick it up later."

"But why should she leave secretly? She must have known that far from my wanting to prevent her going, I should have been relieved. But for my wife I would have suggested her leaving long ago."

"Mrs. Mannering was fond of her?"

"Yes. They were together a great deal. My wife sensed a tragedy in the girl's life, and thought she could be of service to her. I can think of no reason why Denise should want to run away. It doesn't make sense."

"A great many things do not make sense," replied McLean. "She seems to have lived in fear of someone, for in her bedroom I found a pistol."

Mannering stared at him incredulously.

"That's amazing," he said. "Was it loaded?"

"Fully loaded."

"Well, I give up!" Mannering thought for a moment. "But doesn't that spoil your theory about running away? If she intended to do that, wouldn't she have packed the pistol along with the other things which appear to be missing?"

"She may have desired to slip that into her handbag at the last moment. It was quite a small pistol."

"The whole business gets stranger and stranger. If she had the pistol why did she poison herself? She could have——"

"She didn't poison herself. She was deliberately poisoned by someone else."

"You—you mean—there will be a verdict to that effect?"

"I think it is certain."

"That is shocking—simply shocking. Such a possibility never entered my mind. Inspector, have you any idea who could have done this thing, and why?"

"If I did I should scarcely be asking you all these questions. Your niece has made statements to me and to other persons which were mainly untrue. What I need is trustworthy information about her life prior to her leaving India. You have stated that her mother died three years ago in Algiers."

"That is so."

"Can you give me the address at which her mother was living at the time of her death?"

"No. I only heard of her death from my niece when she came here."

"But did your sister never write to you, prior to her death?"

"Very infrequently, and very long ago. I remember getting a letter when her husband died, and while I was in Persia. I wrote back to her, but I can't remember the address."

"Had she any other living relatives at the time of her death?"

"No. She and I were the only children of our parents, and my sister had but one child—Denise."

McLean then asked to see Mrs. Mannering, and Mannering pushed a bell, which brought Emily into the room. She went in quest of her mistress, and a little later Mrs. Mannering entered. She, like her husband, had gone over to semi-mourning, and she looked very attractive in it.

"Good morning," she lisped. "I am sorry to be so long, but I was in the garden."

McLean smiled and waited for her to be seated.

"Mrs. Mannering," he said. "First of all, some bad news. I am afraid that the verdict at tomorrow's inquest will be one of murder."

"Oh no!" she cried. "Surely—surely not!"

"I thought it would be kinder to prepare you for that."

"Thank—thank you," she whimpered, and then searched vainly for a handkerchief. Mannering rose and went to her, offering a large cambric square, into which she sobbed for a few moments.

"Steady, my dear," he said.

"I'll be—all right—in a moment."

Finally she sniffed and returned her husband's handkerchief with a murmur of thanks.

"I am puzzled about some features of this case," said McLean. "Certain things which I expected to find here are missing. Are you familiar with your niece's belongings?"

"I think so. I was in her company a great deal."

"And in her bedroom?"

"Yes."

"Then will you go through her effects and try to tell me if any things are missing?"

"Yes. But if you mean jewellery I do not know what she possessed, except for the few things she wore on occasion."

"I do not mean jewellery in particular, but items of clothing such as she might pack if she proposed going away for a few days."

"Yes. I will do that. Do you wish me to look now?"

"Please."

Mrs. Mannering was absent for about a quarter of an hour,

during which time her husband showed McLean some interesting Venetian books which he kept locked up in a small safe. They were obviously of great value, and Mannering turned over the pages with all the care and love of the born bibliophile, apparently forgetting the grim purpose of McLean's visit. Then Mrs. Mannering came back.

"I cannot discover that anything is missing," she said. "All the clothing which I can remember is there, except what she was wearing. She had four suitcases when she arrived here, and they are also there."

"Then I must be mistaken," replied McLean. "Did you ever see her passport?"

"Yes. She used to keep it in the top drawer of the dressing-table, where she kept her handkerchiefs."

"Is it there now?"

"No, I'm sure it isn't. That's rather strange."

"Strange and disappointing. It might have given me some clue to her movements in foreign countries."

"Hm!" grunted Mannering. "It looks as if she didn't want us to know just where she had been, and deliberately destroyed it. Probably other things too. Well, it was a bad day when she came here to——"

"Cedric!" expostulated Mrs. Mannering.

"I'm sorry, my dear, but it's true. She has caused us nothing but trouble. If she had been more trusting we might have been able to help her. Now, unfortunately, it is too late."

"It may not be too late to bring the person responsible to justice," said McLean. "I should like to have another look at Miss Rostan's bedroom."

"Certainly," said Mannering. "You will find me here if you want me again."

McLean and Brook went up the staircase and into the bedroom. It was exactly as they had seen it the previous day, except that Mrs. Mannering had left some of the contents of the drawers in a state of untidiness.

"So she really did search!" muttered McLean.

"Mrs. Mannering? Did you think she wouldn't?"

"I thought that quite possible—if she knew more about her niece's intentions than she is willing to admit."

"But you accept her conclusions about nothing being missing?"

"I accept nothing. There are the four suitcases. There may have been five."

"But why should she lie?"

"Why does anyone lie except to cover up the truth. It may be that they are just as eager to cover the girl's tracks as I am to find them. Lovely view from this window."

He was standing at the main window looking across the sunlit garden, when suddenly his shortening gaze fell on something wedged between the top sash of the side window and its frame. It was an envelope folded up several times, and clearly used to prevent the loosely-fitting window from rattling in a strong wind. It was addressed in typewriting to Miss Denise Rostan, and on the back of it was the name of the sender.

"From her bank, in Leadenhall Street," said McLean. "That is worth coming here for. If we can find the source of her money we may learn quite a lot. Unfortunately we can't go into that until tomorrow morning, when the bank opens. I don't think we need spend any more time here. We'll go down and take a look at the grounds."

They left the house by a side door which gave access to the terrace on the western side. Here they descended a few steps and were soon among rosaries and flowery arbours, away from the main open lawns. Some of the statuary was remarkably good, and obviously imported from foreign parts, and from time to time McLean stopped to admire it. Finally they came out into a formal garden which appeared to have been neglected, and beyond this was a tall yew hedge, above which they could see the top part of an old building. Farther along the hedge was a wrought-iron gate, giving access to the building. There were curtains at the windows, and it had the appearance of being occupied.

"Gardener's cottage?" asked Brook.

"I shouldn't think so. I can see a lane behind the building. It's possibly not part of the estate at all."

Behind the yew hedge to the right was a large greenhouse, and to McLean's surprise a man was working inside it. Brook recognized him as the gardener, and as they approached the mass of glass he came out and touched his cap.

"Overtime?" asked McLean, with a smile.

"Kind of," he replied. "It's the heating stove. It won't last out over the week-end, so I usually come along on Sunday morning to give it a rake out and some more fuel. Got some nice orchids in there, and can't afford to take any risks."

"Did you see much of Miss Rostan while she was here?" asked McLean.

"Yes, sir. She spent a lot of time in the garden, and on the river. Very nice young lady she was."

"Did you ever see her with anyone outside the members of the family?"

"No, sir, except Mr. Cartland who lives at the Pavilion."

He pointed to the building beyond the yew hedge.

"Is that part of the estate?" asked McLean.

"Yes, sir. In the old days it was used for dancing and garden fêtes, but when Mr. Mannering bought the property he had it converted into a bungalow residence, and let it to Mr. Cartland. He's a lame gentleman, and I think he was once in the Church. He's away at the moment, but will be back this evening. He sent me a card and asked me to light a fire for him in the Pavilion. He'll be horrified to hear about Miss Denise."

"Has he been away long?"

"Since last Wednesday. He came to my cottage and handed me the key of the place. He always does when he goes away."

McLean stared across at the pagoda.

"That's rather unusual," he said.

"Yes. I was told it had been there for over sixty years, and that it came from Siam."

"Is it locked up?"

"No. There's nothing in it now. But in winter I use the bottom room to store garden chairs. There's another room above, but the stairs which lead to it are very unsafe. I told Mr. Mannering the other day that he ought to get the stairs seen to, and he said he would."

McLean thanked him and then moved on in the direction of the pagoda. Seen at close quarters it was an admirable piece of work, built entirely of some sort of foreign hardwood, with a great deal of ornamentation. McLean tried the door and found it unlocked. Inside was an octagonal room. There were still some articles of garden furniture in it, including two broken statues, one of which was an angel minus one wing.

The stairs to the upper room were, as the gardener alleged, very unsafe, and complained noisily when McLean ascended a few steps, but he persevered and finally reached the upper room. It was like the lower one, but rather smaller, for the building narrowed considerably towards the top.

"Do I risk it?" shouted Brook from below.

"No. I don't want to be sued for damage. There's nothing up here, except a very fine view. I'm coming down."

Finally they completed the tour of the garden, coming back to the house by the swimming pool where, as rumour had it, Mannering and his beautiful young wife engaged in nudist practices. But McLean knew nothing of this, and was enchanted by the setting.

Entering the house they found Mannering pouring himself a drink from a decanter, but Mrs. Mannering was not present. Mannering invited them to join him in an aperitif, but McLean declined politely.

"Lovely garden you have here," he said.

"Too big. Much too big for one gardener, and with income tax at its present ridiculous level I can't afford more help. So I concentrate on this central piece, and let the rest go hang. In the old days it was different. They had an army of servants."

"At least the one gardener you have is enthusiastic. You won't find many who will work on Sundays."

"That's true. Donaldson is a good chap. If he left me I should have to find two men to replace him."

"The Pavilion is also part of the estate?"

"Yes. I was glad to get rid of it or at least to find a tenant for it. He's quite an interesting fellow—a missionary who was repaid for his good work in some god-forsaken spot by being beaten-up and severely injured by a gang of witch doctors who didn't like competition. Now he spends his time keeping bees, and pottering around."

"Does he live alone?"

"Yes. Does all his own chores including the cooking, and seems to enjoy it. He keeps the place like a new pin and pays his rent on the dot. So I have no complaints."

"Did your niece meet him?"

"Not to my knowledge. She may have seen him across the boundary hedge, but if so she never mentioned it."

McLean did not linger much longer, but had no intention of returning home at once.

"I should rather like to see the retired missionary," he

said to Brook, when they were back in the car. "Miss Rostan appears to have met him without her uncle's knowledge, if we can trust Donaldson's statement. What about going down to the coast and breathing some sea air? We could get there in time for a late lunch, and perhaps see the reverend gentleman on our way home."

Nothing was more to Brook's liking, and very soon they were making south in the bright, warm sunshine.

13

IT WAS quite late in the evening when McLean and Brook arrived back at Raven's Court after their very pleasant excursion to the sea, but instead of entering the drive McLean turned into the lane about a hundred yards farther on, believing that this would bring him direct to the entrance of the Pavilion.

This proved to be true, and very soon the squat building was seen in the twilight, lying across a fairly large garden at which the narrow lane terminated. From two of the windows there came beams of light, which led McLean to conclude that Mr. Cartland was back.

"Shall I drive in?" asked Brook.

"You'd better if you want to turn the car round."

Brook finally brought the car to a standstill outside the modest front door, and then both of them got out. McLean pushed the bell-button, and there was a minute or two of delay before the door opened, revealing a man of about fifty years of age, who leaned rather heavily on a stout stick. He had rather a fine head, and features, with a good crop of stiff grey hair, and he quizzed the visitors over the rims of a pair of reading glasses.

"Are you Mr. Cartland?" asked McLean.

"Yes."

"We are police officers, and I should like to ask you a few questions regarding a certain matter."

"Ah, I think I understand. Mr. Donaldson, with whom I left my key, told me some most unpleasant news. Do come in, gentlemen."

He led them down a short passage to a very pleasant and well-furnished room, in which a wood fire was burning. On a table close to the fire was a tray, on which were two plates, some cutlery, and the remnants of a meal.

"Please excuse the untidiness," he begged. "I have just finished a meal, and this place lacks a dining-room. Won't you be seated?"

McLean and Brook sat down on a small divan, and watched Cartland reoccupy the chair he had left, which he did with some difficulty, after which he pushed his stick into a recess between the fireplace and a bookcase.

"Now, gentlemen, I am at your disposal," he said.

"So Mr. Donaldson told you about Miss Rostan?"

"Yes. It's shocking."

"Did you know her very well?"

"No, I don't think I am entitled to say that, but I have chatted with her on a few occasions at the little gate which gives access to the grounds of Raven's Court. That is my boundary line, and I am bound by a gentlemen's agreement to stay on this side of it. You see, I am a tenant of Mr. Mannering."

"So I understand. When did you first see Miss Rostan?"

"I think it was about three weeks ago. She told me that she had come from abroad and was staying with her uncle and aunt for a short time."

"Did she say exactly where she had come from?"

"Not then, but later, when we had another chat, she mentioned India."

"Any particular place?"

"No. I gathered that she had relatives there, but she did not seem inclined to follow that line of conversation."

"Did you get the impression she was happy?"

Cartland stroked his long square jaw reflectively.

"On the whole—yes," he said. "Yet I could not help feeling that she was labouring under some emotional upset. In the middle of a conversation she would lose interest, as if her mind was not concentrating."

"When was the last time you saw her?"

"The day before I went away. That would be Tuesday. I told her I was feeling a bit stale and was going to run down to Devon in my little car. She displayed some interest, but there was still that far-away look in her eyes."

"Did you ever discuss her with Mannering?"

"Yes, but once only, for I have only seen him once since his niece arrived. I passed some complimentary remark about her beauty."

"What did he say to that?"

"He said she was like her mother in that respect, and just about as unpredictable. Then he changed the subject so abruptly that I was bound to conclude that further discussion would be unwelcome."

"Have you been here long?"

"Just over four years. I was looking round for some place to settle in when I was told that Mr. Mannering was converting this building into a residence. I saw him and asked him if he had a tenant fixed up and he said he hadn't. I asked him if he would consider me, and after a long talk about terms and conditions, he agreed to give me a lease. In about a month the job was finished, and I moved in."

"Is the furniture yours?"

"Only partly. He told me that he could not let me the place unfurnished because if he did he would lose all control of it, and it would ruin his chances of selling the whole estate at some future date if he wanted to. Of course I saw his point, and agreed to his leaving a few items of furniture here. But in the matter of rent he was most considerate, knowing that I have to exist on a very small pension. Actually I was very lucky to find an anchorage so much to my liking."

"Mr. Mannering told me you kept bees."

"Just a couple of hives—more for study than for profit. I find them delightful creatures to live with, and there's always something one can learn from them."

"Such as patience and self-sacrifice.?"

"Exactly. If humanity were less self-seeking, and more devoted to the welfare of the community—I mean world community—we should not be constantly living on the brink of war, as we are now. The policy of every man for himself and the devil take the hindmost is the policy of Hell itself. But forgive me for my garrulity. You did not come here to listen to a sermon."

"That's true," said McLean. "But I find it difficult not

to agree with you. Reverting to Miss Rostan—did you notice any change in her health during the time she was here?"

"I got the impression she was not so well on the last occasion that we met as on the former ones. She seemed more listless, and quite pallid. But when I asked her if she was well she assured me she was."

"Did she ever come in here?"

"No. As a bachelor, living entirely alone, I scarcely dared suggest such a thing."

"Did she ever mention any of her friends—apart from the family?"

"No."

"Did she tell you she was looking for a place of her own to live in?"

"Yes. She said she wasn't very successful, as people were asking the most exorbitant rents for furnished flats. I knew that to be true from my own experience."

"Then there is really nothing you can tell me about her past life?"

"Nothing at all."

"Then I think that's all."

"I wish I could help. Inspector, am I to understand from your enquiries that there is some doubt about the cause of her death?"

"There is considerable doubt. One thing is certain—she did not die from natural causes."

"You—you mean she may have taken her own life?"

"That is for the coroner to decide."

"So there is to be an inquest?"

"Yes. Tomorrow at noon."

Cartland shook his head sorrowfully.

"How true it is that one half of the world does not know how the other half lives," he said. "Some love affair, I presume, for it is difficult to imagine any other cause that would drive a beautiful and cultured young girl to such a desperate deed. Her uncle and aunt must be distracted. And one feels so helpless in such circumstances. But I'm keeping you."

He rose, taking his heavy stick as he did so.

"Don't trouble," said McLean. "We can let ourselves out."

"It's no trouble. This old leg of mine is more stiff than painful. It does good to exercise it."

"Not a permanent disability, I hope?"

"I'm afraid so. At one time I thought it would have to come off, but fortunately I was spared that. It was an assegai which caused the trouble. Had it been a foot higher I should have left my bones in an African jungle. So really I count myself lucky."

He hobbled with them to the door, and then bade them good night. A minute or two later they were driving through the darkness, Brook to the railway station, and McLean to his long-suffering wife.

Early the next morning McLean drove to the office, and after an hour's intensive work on the new evidence he and Brook called at the bank in Leadenhall Street. The bank manager did not know Miss Rostan, but he sent for one of his staff who brought details of the dead girl's account. McLean was a little surprised to learn that it was an entirely new account, and that only one sum of money had been paid into it, and that about the time when Miss Rostan had come to Raven's Court. It was in the sum of two hundred pounds paid by cash. This had been drawn upon until it was exhausted, leaving a debit balance of two pounds. Later this overdraft was settled by a payment in cash, and the account was ruled off.

"I remember writing her the routine letter informing her that the account was overdrawn," said the bank manager. "I presume this envelope which you have was the one which contained my letter."

McLean nodded and went through the cancelled cheques drawn by the dead girl. Many of them were in favour of London dress shops, and the rest were to 'Self' and cashed either at the bank or through the post.

"I understood that Miss Rostan was expecting a remittance from her bank in Algiers," said McLean.

"I have no knowledge of that," said the manager. "I was away when the account was opened, and never even saw her. But if she was expecting a remittance to the bank direct from some other account she certainly never advised us."

"Is her present address the only one she gave you?"

"Yes."

McLean finally left the bank, disappointed by the poor

result of his enquiry. He had hoped that here at least he would forge some link with the girl's past.

"What a tangled skein of falsehood and evasions!" he said. "She has covered up her past as effectively as did her friend, the spurious Mr. Peyton. Later I will get in touch with our French colleagues in Algiers, and see if they can tell us anything about the Rostan family. Now we'll get along to the inquest, but I want to see the coroner first."

The subsequent inquest went as McLean had prognosticated. There was no question as to the direct cause of death, and little doubt as to the method employed to introduce the poison into the victim's body. There was some evidence to show that the girl was emotionally upset, but nothing to support the theory of suicide. The fact that she had arranged to spend the week-end with the Montagues weighed against this ill-founded hypothesis, and then there was the fact of the loaded pistol in her possession which suggested strongly the existence of a deadly enemy, unless she had at first proposed to use it on herself, but subsequently chose another method. There was just a chance that the jury might return an open verdict, but after a forceful and brilliant summing-up by the coroner a verdict of murder was returned. McLean had drawn attention to the presence of cigarette ash and the matchstick in the punt, after it had been thoroughly cleaned out, neither of which could be traced to the girl, but for reasons of his own he omitted the discovery of the sheet of paper bearing the acrostic.

"It may yet prove to be a clue to the murderer," he said to Brook. "And I have no intention of publicizing it for the murderer's benefit. The newspapers would seize on to it like leeches."

Among the public admitted to the court McLean recognized Harry and his sister, also Mannering's tenant—Mr. Cartland. The latter saw McLean before he left, and expressed his surprise and horror at what had been revealed.

"I didn't expect that," he said. "It's quite incredible. And what a crush! I had the utmost difficulty in getting into court."

"Blame the Press," said McLean. "They were there in droves. Tomorrow Denise Rostan will be front-page news—all the more so because she was young and beautiful. Then, in a few days, she will be forgotten, to make way for the next human tragedy."

Cartland nodded and then went to find his car. After a brief chat with the coroner, McLean did the same.

"Well, we've got that out of our way," said Brook, when they were on the road back to London. "Now we shall have time to breathe."

"Shall we? I doubt it. Somewhere there must be persons who know a lot about the girl's past, and it is in the past that all hope of solving this case lies. We may have to go to North Africa. I can't say until I get a report from Algiers. We'll get moving in that direction as soon as we reach the office."

Two hours later McLean spoke over the telephone to the Gendarmerie at Algiers, giving the details of the information he desired. He was promised full co-operation, and he hung up the receiver with a little sigh.

"You wanted time to breathe, Brook," he said. "Better take it now. Close up that desk and beat it, before something happens to prevent it. I'm leaving too."

14

VALERIE McLEAN, doing a little work in the garden of her cottage, stared with astonishment to see her husband's car enter the gate, and pull up outside the porch. She came across the small lawn, with a garden-trowel clutched in a gloved hand, and surveyed him as he stepped from the car.

"Don't tell me you've got the sack?" she said.

"No. I've sacked myself—for a few hours. Throw away that implement and go and make yourself look pretty. I've got you on my conscience."

"Rot! You've never had a conscience."

"Then I've a very effective substitute. We'll have tea here and then take the open road, to any den of vice you care to name. How does that appeal to you?"

"Very much. I hope you've got plenty of cash because I feel reckless."

"All I have in my pockets are moth-balls."

"Then I must lend you the housekeeping money. You are going to take me up to town."

"Havers! I've only just left the place."

"It won't be beyond your capabilities to tootle up there again—after you have booked the seats."

"What seats?"

"The ballet at Covent Garden. It's the last time they'll do *Scheherazade* this season."

"But I'll never get seats at this late hour."

"Not the cheaper seats, but I don't want a cheaper seat. I want to dress for the occasion and sit in a box."

"But my dear Valerie——!"

"All right! Let's call it off and go to the movies. Two seats at one and ninepence, and fish and chips afterwards."

McLean laughed and kissed her on the ear.

"You win," he said. "I can't compete with you along those lines. I'll see what rude remarks the box-office have to make."

"Play fair," said Valerie, brandishing the trowel. "I'll go and see about the tea."

McLean got his small box, to Valerie's great delight, and they were having tea when the telephone-bell rang. McLean was about to answer it when Valerie forestalled him.

"It may be the office," she said. "If so—you're not at home. I haven't seen you and have not the slightest idea where you are."

"You can't . . ." complained McLean, but Valerie already had the receiver to her ear.

"Hullo?" she said. "No, we are not 2047. You must have dialled the wrong number. What fools people are," she said, hanging up the receiver. "That's the third time this afternoon."

"You mean the third time someone has dialled the wrong number?"

"Yes."

"Did it sound like the same person each time?"

"It was a man each time. Why do you look so reflective?"

"Was I looking reflective?"

"Oh, I get it," said Valerie. "You think it might have been someone trying to discover if anyone was at home?"

"It's a very old dodge. If anyone rings again, before we leave, don't answer it, and we'll see what happens."

But the telephone did not ring again, and finally Valerie appeared in her 'burning best', looking as radiant as a rose. In her excitement she had forgotten all about the telephone, and after putting her husband's bow-tie straight, and dusting the lapels of his dinner-jacket with her hands, she pronounced herself ready.

They reached London in time to pick up the box ticket and eat a sparse meal before the ballet was due to start, and after that all was forgotten in the thrills of the moment. The big theatre was packed out, and Valerie, who had brought a small pair of opera glasses in her handbag, spent a long time quizzing the larger boxes for persons of notability before the curtain went up.

"Well, I'm blessed!" muttered McLean.

Valerie removed the opera glasses from her eyes.

"What are you blessed about?" she asked.

"I could swear . . . Lend me those glasses."

Valerie was passing the glasses when the lights were lowered and the curtain went up. After that it would have been sacrilege to utter a word, and Valerie at least was so entranced by the wonderful music and dancing that nothing else mattered and, apart from an occasional exclamation of appreciation, no conversation passed between them until the interval, when the curtain fell to a tempest of applause.

"Oh, glory!" sighed Valerie. "That was worth leaving home for. Do we go and find a drink?"

"In a moment. Lend me those glasses."

"Oh yes, you were in the throes of some excitement just before the lights went out. Here you are."

McLean focused the glasses on one of the larger boxes near the stage, where a couple were seated, the woman in full view, but her male companion slightly in the background. McLean had some difficulty in getting a view of the male features, but when he did he made a little ejaculation, and handed the opera glasses back to Valerie.

"Well?" she asked. "Who is she?"

"She is Mrs. Mannering of Raven's Court."

"Oh, Robert—she can't be!"

"But she is."

"Give me the glasses."

Valerie altered the focus a little and stared at the beautifully dressed woman.

"She's lovely," she said. "I had noticed her before, but now I can see her more clearly. Who's the man?"

"That's where scandal creeps in. The man is her husband's butler and valet."

Valerie took the glasses from her eyes and stared at him.

"Are you sure?" she asked.

"Quite sure."

"But you can only see his profile. It might be Mr. Mannering."

"Mannering is at least fifteen years older than either of them, and he has iron-grey hair and a big square head. I think it is not by accident that Achmed is keeping rather in the shadow. Do you still want that drink?"

"Of course I do."

"Then prepare to be pushed about, for there is a very big exodus—and all with the same object in view."

They left the box and made their way to the bar, which, as McLean had foreseen, was packed to excess. McLean tried in vain to find a seat for Valerie.

"Never mind me," she said. "You go in to the attack while I defend your rear."

It was some minutes before McLean got his drinks and fought his way back to Valerie, with some of the liquid spilling over the tops of the glasses. Valerie took her gin and lime from him, and then switched her gaze to her right. McLean took the cue and came face to face with Achmed Knullah. He was immaculately attired, and McLean could have sworn that his sallow cheeks had a trace of cosmetics on them.

"Oh, good evening!" said Achmed. "This is what one might call a coincidence."

"It is indeed," replied McLean. "Two minds with but a single thought presumably."

"I am very fond of ballet. Not often do I get the opportunity to indulge my taste."

"Nor I. I hope you are enjoying it."

"Who could fail to do so. Oh, there goes the warning bell, and I seem to be no nearer getting my drink than before. Well, I would rather miss the drink than the dancing. Excuse me."

He turned and made his way out, with many others who suffered the same disappointment, and McLean and Valerie were not long in following his example.

"What a butler!" said Valerie. "But somewhat remiss as a

cavalier—leaving his lady alone while he goes to get a drink. But he's attractive enough in a vulgar sort of way. You certainly caused him some embarrassment. I'll bet he's wondering whether you saw his companion."

By the time they reached their box the lights were down again, and everything outside the brilliantly lighted stage was in darkness. But when finally the curtain fell, and the auditorium became lighted, the box which had contained Achmed and his companion was empty.

"Taking no chances," said McLean. "It would be interesting to know what his employer is doing at this moment. I think I'll find out."

"You surely don't propose going to Maidenhead?"

"Oh no. Bow Street is just across the way, and the telephone will serve my purpose."

"But, Robert, what business is it of yours if Mrs. Mannering chooses to spend the evening with one of the servants?"

"Everything that happens at Raven's Court is very much my business. You can wait in the car outside, and I'll tell the night officer to keep an eye on you."

"Don't be absurd. Do you think someone might kidnap me?"

"I shouldn't blame anybody on that score, and that's meant to be a compliment, Mrs. McLean."

When McLean had collected his car from the garage where he had left it, he carried out his project. He was absent for only a few minutes and then came back, and drove away.

"Well?" said Valerie. "Was he at home?"

"Yes. He answered the 'phone himself. I recognized his voice immediately, and pretended I had got the wrong number."

"You didn't expect that, did you?"

"No, I did not."

"Then what do you make of it?"

"I don't know—yet."

"But if he's at home isn't it obvious that he knows his wife is out, and that his valet is also out? Doesn't it appear that he has no objections to that curious state of affairs?"

"Not necessarily. He may have set a trap for them."

"Pretending he was going to stay the night somewhere, and then waiting to catch the guilty couple?"

"That's possible. But there are other possibilities. Whatever the truth is, it will emerge in due course."

"Why should it?" asked Valerie.

"If it was a trap deliberately set by Mannering, then it has succeeded, in which case Achmed Knullah will not remain long at Raven's Court. We shall see."

"And does it help you in the least?"

"It may do. It depends which way the cat jumps."

"Robert, you can be aggravatingly vague when you choose. I want to know more about this Rostan murder."

"So do I, but theorizing can be overdone. One ounce of fact is worth a ton of theory. Now let's talk of pleasanter things. This was intended to be an evening of pleasure."

Valerie snuggled up close beside him.

"It has," she said. "I've still got that delicious music going through my mind. I think I could go to the ballet every night and never tire of it. Now why didn't I think of becoming a ballerina and wearing tights up to my thighs, not to mention being the Sultan's favourite wife, and the envy of the entire harem——"

"To finish with your head being chopped off."

"I shouldn't complain about that."

"You wouldn't be in a state to complain."

"No, I suppose not. But it would have been nice while it lasted. Oh, dear, I'm quite tired," she yawned.

In a few minutes the rhythmic note of the car sent her to sleep, and McLean looked down at her face and pulled the rug closer round her knees, for the night air was cold, and the car had no heater. After that he drove swiftly in the bright moonlight, and subsequently finished up inside his own garage. The sudden silence caused Valerie to open her eyes.

"Oh, did I nap?" she asked.

"More than nap. We're home."

"Surely not!"

Valerie staggered out of the car, and waited while her husband locked the garage door. They went across to the cottage and straight into the lounge. McLean switched on the light and then stared at the drawn curtains.

"Did you draw the curtains before we left?" he asked.

"No. It was broad daylight."

"Then—— Wait a moment."

He went out to the back door and found it unbolted. This, in view of the fact that he had bolted it himself, was illuminating. In the kitchen he found a broken pane of glass close to the inner latch. Valerie, who had followed him, stared at the hole in the window.

"We've had burglars!" she said.

"Yes. Remember those wrong telephone numbers?"

"Oh, the brutes! And we fell for it!"

"In a way. But——"

"Yes, I know. We might have caught them but for my determination to see the ballet."

"No recriminations. Let's see what is missing."

A swift examination of the place, and their comparatively few valuables, revealed no loss of any sort. But in the two bedrooms drawers had been opened, and the contents disturbed a little. In McLean's room the disturbance was the more obvious, for his discarded lounge suit was not exactly where he had left it.

"Not ordinary burglars," he said. "The silver in the dining-room could have been whipped into a bag in a few moments. The interest taken in my wearing apparel signifies much. I think it is possible someone was after my official pocket-book."

"Was it in your coat?"

"No. It is locked up in my desk at the office."

"Would it have been of any use to anyone?"

"It would, to some extent, have revealed the range of my enquiries in the Rostan case."

"What are you going to do? Inform the local police?"

"No. Nothing would be gained by that. Far better to let the matter lie, and take steps to guard against a repetition."

"But how?"

"Would you like a nice dog, trained to deal with un-invited guests? We have such animals, and I know one who would be just the fellow for our need. His name is Rex, and he's good to look at, and as gentle as a lamb to his friends. I think I could persuade him that you are a friend of mine."

Valerie's eyes gleamed.

"That's a wonderful idea," she said. "At times it is a bit lonely here, and I—— Yes, Robert, get him as quickly as you can."

15

THE abortive invasion of his private residence afforded McLean food for reflection. It was significant that it had occurred almost immediately following the coroner's inquest, with its sensational verdict, and it went to show that certain persons were not entirely happy about that verdict, and were not prepared to lie quiet and let matters take their course. Brook, when informed of the incident, bristled like an ill-treated dog.

"What a neck!" he growled. "And how did they know where you live?"

"I may have been followed after the inquest, or even prior to that. One thing seems certain. They think I know a great deal more than I do. That act was an act of fear. On the face of it it appears to be a silly move—not worth the risk involved, but we should be foolish not to take the matter very seriously."

"You mean the cold war may be over?" said Brook.

"I think so. I've got permission to borrow Rex while the emergency lasts, and I hope to take him home tonight. You might get me a few pounds of horsemeat."

"A few pounds! You'll need a hundredweight."

The dog was acquired and taken home in the car that evening. He was a handsome Alsatian, with intelligent brown eyes, and a set of very useful gleaming white teeth, and he won Valerie's heart at sight. The introduction was successful, and within an hour he was eating out of Valerie's hand.

"He's beautiful," she said. "But far too docile."

McLean smiled. He had seen the docile creature in action, and had no doubts about him.

"Don't mistake discipline for docility," he said. "And don't fondle him. He'll try a lot of sentimental stuff on you, but keep him in his place—as you do me."

It was two days later that a report came from the Algerian police, respecting the family of Rostan, so far as they were able to discover. McLean read it aloud for Brook's edification.

"Henri Rostan, son of Arnaud Rostan, date of birth unknown. Settled in Algiers 1901 where he assisted his father in an antique business, until the latter's death in 1912. Joined the French Army in 1914, and returned to Algiers in 1918, where he made some success as a painter of pictures. Married in 1922 to an English woman, who had been governess in an Algerian family. Died in 1938 from alcoholic poisoning, leaving a young daughter named Denise. Madame Rostan ran her house as a *pension* and sent her daughter to England to be educated. She died in Algiers in 1948, leaving no estate. The daughter is believed to have taken a post as governess, but later married the son of a wealthy Hindu in Paris, where the young man was studying medicine. It is believed he died in India some months ago, and that his wife, who had been estranged from him for some time, travelled to India to see him before he died. No trace of her since then."

"So the story that she was left well provided for wasn't true," said Brook.

"Apparently not. But at least we know why she went to India."

"But why should she conceal that reason from Montague?"

"It may be because she wasn't legally married."

"And where does the man who called himself Peyton come into it?"

"At the moment that is anybody's guess. That man is even more mysterious than she is, but I am convinced he played a very important part in her life, and that she could have told us exactly what happened to him had she wanted to."

"And was murdered because she could not be trusted to hold her tongue?"

"I can't think of any other reason."

"And what now, sir?" asked Brook.

"I think we'll run along and see if Achmed Knullah is still at Raven's Court."

"You think he may have been sacked?"

"If he isn't it will suggest that his master condones his queer conduct. But we shall see."

It was dark when they reached the house, and McLean's ring at the bell brought Emily to the door.

"Is Mr. Mannering at home?" asked McLean.

"Yes, sir. If you will come inside, I will go and tell him. He is having dinner."

Emily was absent only a few moments, and came back to

usher them into the lounge. It was empty, but a minute or two later Mannering came in.

"Good evening, gentlemen," he said. "I'm sorry to have kept you waiting."

"Not at all," replied McLean. "I hope I haven't interrupted your meal?"

"I had just finished. But what can I do for you?"

"My visit really concerns your servant Achmed Knullah. May I see him for a few moments?"

"I'm sorry, Inspector, but Knullah is no longer in my service. He left yesterday."

"That was rather sudden, wasn't it?"

"Yes. I sacked the swine."

"May I ask the reason?"

"I should prefer not to discuss the reason. It was a personal matter, which caused me both pain and anger. I did a lot for that man, and trusted him implicitly. He abused that trust, and caused me to regret that I ever set eyes on him."

"Have you any idea where he has gone?"

"None whatever. They went off——"

"They!"

"Yes. Oh, you may as well know. My wife was involved. How long it has been going on I don't know. But I came home unexpectedly after telling them that I should be away for the night. I found the house empty except for the servants, who had gone to bed. At close upon midnight Knullah came back with my wife. The swine tried to brazen it out. The mistress wanted to go to London, and there was no convenient train, so he had taken her in the car, and brought her home. But he didn't attempt to explain why he should have to dress himself up like a prince to perform that duty. I sacked him on the spot, but allowed him to stay the night in view of the late hour. The next morning he had gone, before I was up and, God forgive her, my wife had left with him. That's the whole beastly story."

"Did they leave in one of your cars?"

"No. I found both the cars in the garage. Emily told me that a taxi arrived very early and took them away."

"You did not expect that?"

"Expect it! Would any man expect such a miserable deception? A servant in my own house, and she a highly

128

cultured woman of good family! Women are a constant enigma."

"Where would they be likely to hire a car?"

"I don't know. I can't remember an occasion when there has been need to use a hired car."

"Had your wife money in her own right?"

"Yes. There was a marriage settlement. She wanted it that way, and I thought it was reasonable enough, for a modern woman likes to feel a bit independent. But I'm damned if I like the idea of my money being used to support her lover."

"Do you propose to start any action?"

"I don't know. I want time to think. It knocks all my plans sideways. I had intended to spend the winter abroad— Bermuda or some other sunny spot, but now . . ."

He shook his head and produced a large cigar from a case abstractedly, rolling it round in his fingers and making no attempt to light it.

"I wish I could help you," he said. "But I don't imagine I shall hear from Achmed again, or my wife. Is there anything I can tell you about him?"

"I think not, but you will appreciate that it is necessary for me to keep in touch with him while this investigation continues."

"Of course, but all the same, I don't think he can help. He had very little to do with poor Denise, and was as surprised and shocked as we all were. Still, I see your point."

"If you should hear from him or your wife, I should like to know immediately."

"I will bear that in mind. But much as I have reason to hate and mistrust Achmed, I must confess that I have always found him gentle and kindly. It is impossible for me to think he could be involved in any way in the cruel murder of my poor niece. The cause of what happened to her must lie in the past, and no one here had any share in that past."

McLean nodded his head, and then asked to see Emily. The subsequent questioning took place in the kitchen, where Emily was busily engaged. The cook, she said, had gone out for the evening, and was not likely to be back before half past ten.

"There are one or two questions I should like to ask you,"

said McLean. "They concern your mistress and the manservant who, I understand, left here early yesterday morning. Did you see them before they left?"

"No, sir. Cook and I were here when the hall bell rang. It was about half past seven. I was going to answer it when Achmed called out from the hall that it was for him, and that it was a taxi which he had ordered."

"Did you see the taxi at all?"

"No, sir, but I heard it go off a few minutes later."

"So you don't know where that taxi came from?"

"No, sir."

"Have you known Achmed to order taxis on any other occasion?"

"Yes—several times. He hated walking to the station. He used to ring up Gorringes in the town. It's a garage, but they have a number of hire cars."

"Tell me about the night before. Did you see Achmed go off with Mrs. Mannering?"

"No, sir, but he told me earlier he was going to drive Mrs. Mannering to a Bridge party, and would probably wait to bring her back, as it was a long way from here."

"Did you hear him come back?"

Emily hesitated for a moment.

"N-no," she stammered. "But I heard a kind of a quarrel later. For some reason I couldn't sleep, and I went to the bathroom to get a glass of water. I heard the master almost shouting at Achmed. I couldn't help hearing because the bathroom is near the head of the stairs, and the lounge door was open."

"Did you hear what he said?"

"Some of it. He said that Achmed had behaved like a lunatic and that he would have to go. Then Madame said it wasn't entirely Achmed's fault and that she had encouraged him. Then the door closed with a bang and I couldn't hear any more. At least I couldn't hear any words, but I could still hear angry voices."

"Did the cook also hear?"

"No. But I told her afterwards."

"Did Achmed often take Mrs. Mannering in the car to keep appointments?"

"Not often, but I think she didn't like driving at night."

"Did Mr. Mannering explain the situation after they had left in the taxi?"

"He—he said that Achmed had gone for good, and he would have to replace him, but he never said a word about Madame."

"Naturally he was upset?"

"Oh yes. When I went to Madame's room later I found that she had taken many of her personal things, including her toilet set, and then I knew she was not coming back."

"Had you any reason to believe that something like this might happen?"

"Oh no. I thought the master and mistress were devoted to each other, and that Achmed was devoted to Mr. Mannering."

McLean did not detain her any longer. His main purpose had been, if possible, to trace the taxi which had been hired, and to attempt to locate the refugees. After a final word with Mannering he and Brook drove into the town and found Gorringe's Garage. The main part of it was closed, but the hire service office was open. McLean disclosed his identity, and the man in charge was duly impressed.

"I want to find out if you sent a taxi to Raven's Court early on Wednesday morning," he said.

"Yes, Inspector, we did. I was on duty that night, and the call came about seven o'clock in the morning. I think it was wanted at seven-thirty."

"Is the driver available?"

"I think he has just come on. If you'll excuse me a moment I'll try to find him."

He was absent for a few minutes and then came back with a ruddy-faced middle-aged man.

"This is Summers—the driver of the taxi," he said.

"That's right," said Summers. "I picked up a lady and gentleman at Raven's Court at seven-thirty and drove them to the railway station."

"Did they have much baggage?"

"Three suitcases in all."

"Have you any idea where they were going?"

"No, sir."

"Did they give their baggage to a porter?"

"Yes. He's an old chap we call 'Charlie'. Must be nearly

sixty years old. Everybody knows him. But he won't be on duty this time of night."

McLean thanked them both and then tried his luck at the railway station. Charlie was not on duty, but the station-master was, and he gave McLean the man's address, which was but a short distance away. Within a few minutes McLean was talking to Charlie himself.

"I remember them, sir," he said. "I took their baggage to meet the London train which left at seven-fifty, and put it into a first-class compartment."

This was disappointing news, but McLean rewarded the old man for his information, and then got back into the car.

"She would have to be London," grunted Brook. "But if they registered anywhere under their right names we ought to be able to find them."

"You take too much for granted," said McLean. "One can go anywhere from London. Still, we can try."

"Back to London, sir?"

"You for London—me for home. You can drop me there. It isn't much out of your way."

For half an hour or so the car moved swiftly down the main road, and then Brook cut off to the right with a view to carrying out McLean's instructions. Here there was scarcely any traffic, and it was a relief to get away from the blinding headlights of oncoming cars, but speed was reduced by the inferior road surface, and the many tortuous bends. It was a region of large country houses, hidden behind extensive private grounds, with only a lodge to indicate that they existed at all.

"How people manage to keep up such places beats me," complained Brook. "I thought the country was broke. Any-way, who wants a twenty-roomed house and ten acres of grounds?"

"There's someone wanting to pass us," said McLean.

"I'm not stopping him," replied Brook. "I've given way to him twice. It's a motor-cyclist, and I think he likes following our rear light."

"Well, slow down and let——"

He did not finish the sentence for at that moment there came the distant sound of several reports and the nearer noise of splintered glass and reverberating bullets. McLean ducked,

132

and Brook let loose a howl of mingled pain and anger. The car pulled up with a jerk, and Brook was seen holding his left arm down which blood was streaming on to his hand.

"He got me," he growled.

McLean swung round and stared through the back window. He saw the headlight of the motor-cycle move round to the left and disappear. In a moment he was out of the car door and round on the driving side. Brook moved along the seat and McLean took the wheel.

"Are you all right for a bit?" he asked.

"Yes, I can manage."

McLean swung the car round with a couple of rapid reverses, and then put his foot down hard, and slewed round the turning down which the gunman had turned. The powerful headlights showed half a mile of straight empty road. Changing gear he let the car full out and reached the bend in a matter of seconds.

"There he is!" cried Brook.

McLean had but a momentary glimpse of the vanishing rear light, but that was enough. On rounding the next bend he had the motor-cycle in full view, with an open road as far as his headlights would reach. On full throttle the car fairly annihilated space, and the distance between the two vehicles narrowed every moment.

"Feel in that door pocket," said McLean. "There's a gun behind the maps."

Brook found the automatic and slipped it into McLean's coat pocket.

"When I corner him you'd better stay here," said McLean.

"Not me," growled Brook. "I'm feeling pretty good. Ah, this will do."

He had opened up the tool container, and produced a tyre-lifter, which he held fondly in his right hand.

"Cornered rats are dangerous."

McLean was now almost abreast of the motor-cyclist and forcing him towards the deep ditch on his left. A scared face was turned momentarily, and then the fellow braked hard. McLean did the same, and finally brought the car to a standstill, with the motor-cycle neatly trapped on the verge of the ditch, and the long bonnet of the car across its line of progress. In a second Brook was out with the tyre-lifter swinging in his right hand, and a moment later McLean was with him, pistol levelled.

"Hands up!" he snapped.

The order was obeyed instantly, and Brook went through the fellow's pockets.

"Nothing here, sir," he said.

"All right. Get him inside the car."

Brook opened the rear door, and the man left his machine on its side and entered the car. McLean switched on the roof light, and surveyed the prisoner from the front seat, while Brook sat beside him. He was a man of about thirty-five, clad in a short waterproof coat, a driving helmet, and leather gloves. He was breathing heavily, but showed little sign of fear.

"What's the game?" he demanded. "I've nothing worth pinching."

"What did you do with the gun you had?" asked McLean.

"I don't know what you're talking about. It's you who've got a gun, not me. Who are you, anyway?"

"You know well enough. But I'll deal with you in a minute. Brook, I'd better have a look at that arm. Can you get your coat off?"

While Brook wrestled with his coat McLean produced lint and a bandage from his first-aid set. Fortunately the wound was superficial, the bullet having been deflected by passing through the back of the car, and the bleeding was now reduced to a trickle.

"You're lucky," said McLean, as he fixed the bandage. "A few inches to the right and it might have been a different story. How's that?"

"Much more comfortable, thank you, sir."

McLean turned again to the scowling prisoner.

"This is going to set you back a bit," he said. "Where did you throw that gun?"

"You're mad. I know nothing about this. Do you think I cycle about the country shooting people up for fun?"

"Hold your tongue!" snarled Brook. "Except to answer the inspector's questions."

"Inspector!"

"All right, Brook," said McLean. "He knows. I'll take the number of his machine, and then we'll drop him at the nearest police station and come back and search for the gun. That arm of yours may need a shot of penicillin. Look after him while I get the bike off the road."

McLean was back again in a few moments, to take over the driving-wheel, and a quarter of an hour later the prisoner was lodged at a police station, where Brook had his arm properly attended to. When they left two constables in a van accompanied them.

McLean's guess was that the gun had not been disposed of until the sniper realized that he was being pursued, and so he started the search for it at the spot where his machine had come to rest, working backwards to the road junction, with the headlights of the cars floodlighting the ditches on either side.

But although no weapon was found on the road itself, no less than five cartridge cases were recovered, and these were all scattered over a distance of a hundred yards, just before the road junction was reached, and where McLean expected to find them.

"Nicely planned," he said. "He shot just before he reached the turning on his right, with the full intention of using it as an escape route. We shall have to try the other side of the hedges for the gun itself."

A further hour was spent on this, but without success, and finally McLean had to call off the search until the next morning. Back at the police station the car damage was examined in detail. There were three punctures in the rear of the car, and two holes in the triplex glass window. The two higher bullets had gone through the driving window, but the three remaining bullets were in the car. Two of these were embedded in the backs of the front seats, and the third was lying on the floor in a very battered condition. When the two bullets were extracted from the backs of the seats one of them was found to be in almost perfect condition. McLean examined this carefully through a magnifying glass.

"Mighty like the one we took from Peyton's body," he said. "I think we'll get back to London, and take the prisoner with us. I'll question him in the morning when I know more about this bullet."

16

EARLY the next morning McLean had the firearm expert's report on the bullet, and it was such as to raise his hopes considerably.

"A nine millimetre bullet, probably fired from a Luger automatic," he said to Brook. "In every detail similar to the one which killed Peyton. Clayton is ready to swear that both of them were fired from the same weapon."

"My hat!" ejaculated Brook. "That's progress with a capital 'P'. No doubt now that the two crimes were connected."

"There never was a doubt. We have every reason to congratulate ourselves, but——"

"But what, sir?"

"I'm not happy about the man we took last night. But we'll have him up and hear what he has to say."

The detained man was subsequently brought to McLean's office. He looked as if he had not slept all night, but he managed to put up a bold front."

"What's your name?" asked McLean.

"George Colby."

"Address?"

"No. 9 Duke Street, Greenwich."

"Trade or profession?"

"Engineer."

"Place of employment?"

"I'm self-employed. I've a workshop behind my house."

"Where were you going when we ran you down last night?"

"I was going home?"

"From where?"

"Windsor."

"You wouldn't be on that road if you were going from Windsor to Greenwich."

"I was going to make a call at my sister's house, which is in Godalming."

"Why did you go to Windsor?"

"I know a young woman there. I often go to see her."

"What is her name and address?"

"Maud Coombes. She lives over the little café which she keeps. It is called the 'Corona', in South Street."

"Why did you fire at our car?"

"That's a lie. I've never owned a firearm. Besides, you can't use a a firearm while riding a motor-bike, as you ought to know."

"We saw you coming up behind us."

"It was somebody else you saw—not me. I never even saw your car. I had turned into that road when a fellow on a powerful bike passed me in a jiffy. He must have been doing over sixty miles an hour."

"A nice story," said McLean. "Why did you attempt to get away from us when we came up behind you?"

"I didn't try. If I had wanted to get away from you I could have done so easily. My bike will do eighty miles an hour and more."

"That's just about what you were doing," said McLean. "You were gonged, but you still went on."

"I never heard any gonging. I didn't even know you were police officers until you told me. Why should I shoot at you? It doesn't make any sense."

"Where is your driving licence?"

Colby felt in his pocket and produced a wallet. From this he took his licence and handed it to McLean. It was in date, and McLean handed it back to him.

"Are you a married man?" he asked.

"Yes, but my wife left me two years ago. I don't know where she is now, and don't care."

"You realize what this may mean to you?"

"I realize that you are making a damned awful mistake. I know someone shot you up, and injured the sergeant, but it wasn't me. I've got a clean sheet and you can't find any reason why I should want your blood."

"Don't be so sure of yourself. Suppose I tell you that the bullets which hit the car, and wounded Sergeant Brook, were fired from a pistol which killed a man a short time ago?"

"I should say—find the man who owned the gun. Look here, Inspector. I've no doubt you really believe it was me who did that shooting, because I was unlucky enough to be behind you when it happened. But you couldn't have seen the face of the man in that darkness. It's all an assumption. I've a good reputation and you can't put me in the dock on a charge like this."

"Suppose I can prove that you were associated with a man who called himself Robert Peyton?"

"But you can't. I've never heard of the man."

"Or a woman named Denise Rostan."

Colby shook his head vigorously.

"No use you shooting off these names at me. I tell you you're barking up the wrong tree."

McLean looked at him fixedly.

"You might help yourself a little by telling the truth," he said. "You must have been trailing us for some time. Who put you on to that?"

Colby put out his hand despairingly.

"We don't talk the same language," he complained. "I tell you I know absolutely nothing about the shooting, and that's my last word, until I see my lawyer. Now, maybe, you'd like to charge me."

"Not yet. I'll talk to you again later—when I have found the gun."

Colby was taken away, and McLean shrugged his shoulders.

"Cocky!" said Brook. "I suppose he knows that there won't be any finger-prints on the gun—if we find it?"

"There may be."

"But how? He was wearing gloves."

"Yes, I've got the gloves. They are very thick wool-lined gloves. I don't believe it would be possible for him to press the trigger of any automatic while he was wearing the gloves. But we shall see, if we have any luck."

The subsequent search for the weapon, in broad daylight, with the help of several men, was ultimately successful. It was found on the further side of a hedge, lying in a puddle. This was disappointing since it removed all chance of finger-prints on the butt. It was, as the firearms expert had prognosticated, a Luger. To test out his conclusions McLean put on the thick glove, and tried to insert his trigger-finger into the trigger-guard, but there was insufficient room.

"You see—he had to take off the glove," he said.

Brook nodded and then shook his head.

"Pity it fell in that puddle," he said, "and got garmed up

138

with mud. We might have got him good and proper. Every time this arm of mine nags I think of him—most unlovingly."

"We may scare him a bit. He can't possibly know the weapon is useless from the point of view of finger-prints, and he may change his tune when he thinks he is in a tough spot."

Before seeing Colby again McLean handed the pistol over to the firearms expert. Every effort was made to bring up finger-prints which might still be under the coating of mud, but the work met with no success. But one fact was established. The pistol was proved to be the one so long wanted by the police. It had killed Peyton, and had been used in an attempt to put an end to McLean's activities. This latter business puzzled Brook deeply.

"Can't think what good it would have done him to have killed one or both of us," he said. "He was sticking his neck out a long way for no appreciable gain. Can you put me wise on that?"

"No, I can't—unless it was panic. Panic-stricken persons don't behave reasonably. It's on a par with the break-in to my cottage. Some person, or persons, are living in a state of deadly fear. They may imagine they can put the same sort of fear into us. But let us see how Mr. Colby takes this discovery. We'll take his finger-prints first."

When this was done, and the results photographed, the prisoner was brought again to McLean's office. He looked just a little less truculent now, and his glance went to the table on which were lying the fresh prints from the photographs. McLean opened a drawer and drew out the automatic pistol which was now clean and shining.

"Look at this pistol," he said. "Have you ever seen it before?"

Colby gave it a stabbing glance.

"No," he said.

"It is the pistol which was used last night, in an attempt to cause one, or both, of us grievous harm. It was also used with more success on a man known as Robert Peyton. There are two distinct charges—one of deliberate murder, and the other of shooting with intent to kill. It may be that you will be charged with the less serious offence only. But if you are obstinate you may be charged with both. Now think carefully before you answer. Where did you get this pistol?"

Colby was unmistakably shaken by McLean's grim expression and tense words, and for a moment it looked as if he were on the point of blurting out something. Then suddenly his whole attitude changed.

"I've told you a dozen times I've never handled any pistol in my life. That's my last word."

Here at least he spoke the truth, for McLean's next question was met with a stony stare, and McLean finally had him taken away.

"That's that," muttered Brook. "Can we keep him?"

"I'm not sure that we can. You and I may be reasonably sure that it was he who fired those shots, proving it is another matter. I think we'll run along to Windsor and see his girl-friend."

When McLean and Brook reached the Corona café they found it to be a dingy little place in a mean street, with some sad-looking cakes in the window, and a few customers taking morning coffee at marble-topped tables, and waited on by a young girl who looked as if she couldn't care less. McLean asked her if Miss Coombes was on the premises, and the girl jabbed her thumb towards a staircase farther along the narrow shop, at the bottom of which was a printed card bearing the word 'Private'.

They mounted the stairs, and finally reached a door which was clearly the entrance to Miss Coombe's living quarters. McLean rapped on this and in a few moments it was opened by a middle-aged woman with a mass of untidy red hair. She stared at the two visitors.

"Are you Miss Maud Coombes?" asked McLean.

"Yes. What do you want?" she asked bluntly.

"We are police officers and I should like to ask you a few questions concerning a man named George Colby."

"Oh—him," she said. "Well, you'd better come inside. You'll have to excuse the mess. I'm doing a bit of tidying up."

She led them through a passage into a room over the shop, where things were indeed higgledy-piggledy, flung off the apron round her waist, and pushed her hair into shape.

"Not bad news, I hope?" she asked.

"It depends upon what you call bad news," said McLean. "When did you last see Colby?"

"Last evening. He came down to see me, just after six

140

o'clock. We had a bit of food together, and a drink, and then he left."

"At what time did he leave?"

"I didn't notice. But it must have been about eight o'clock. I closed the café at seven o'clock, and then I fried some eggs and bacon. Yes, it must have been a little after eight o'clock."

"Did he come to see you on any particular business?"

"No. He often drops in unexpectedly, to have a yarn. I knew him before I bought this little business three years ago. He's an engineer."

"What sort of an engineer?"

"Search me! I know nothing about machinery."

"Do you know any of his friends?"

"Can't say I do. I used to know his mother, but she died. I don't think he's got many friends. He's a very reserved sort of man."

"Was the waitress here when he called yesterday?"

"Not her. Nothing in the world would induce her to stay after six o'clock. They're like that these days."

"So you have no one to corroborate that he was here last evening?"

Miss Coombes' face grew red.

"You mean I'm a liar?" she said.

"Not at all. But in these matters corroborative evidence is always desirable, and in this case it is very important."

Miss Coombes shrugged her plump shoulders.

"I can only tell you what I know," she said.

"Naturally. How was he dressed?"

"Dressed?"

"What kind of suit and hat?"

"I didn't take much notice of his clothes, but I think it was a dark suit, and brown felt hat."

"Where did he park his car?"

"I—I didn't see any car. I thought he had come by train."

"Didn't he tell you?"

"No."

McLean looked at her fixedly, and she seemed to wilt a little under that intense stare.

"Just now you were indignant because I appeared to doubt your word," he said. "Well, I have greater cause to doubt it now. I suggest you never saw Colby last evening. Had you done so you would have noticed that he was wearing a short waterproof coat, with a driving helmet. In fact he would have come by motor-cycle, because at half past eight he was involved in an incident ten miles from this place. Are you prepared to repeat your former statement on oath?"

"Yes."

"Very well. I must ask you to come with us."

"I—I can't leave my business. That girl is not capable of looking after it."

"It won't take long. I hope you fully understand that perjury is a very serious offence. If you would like to withdraw your former statement you had better be quick about it."

Miss Coombes was now in a state bordering on panic, her ample bosom swelling and deflating rapidly.

"I—I was only trying to help him," she stammered. "He told me he might be in a spot of trouble, and I could help him if I said he came here."

"When did he tell you that?"

"About seven o'clock—on the telephone."

"Do you know where he telephoned from?"

"No, but he was all out of breath, as if in a hurry."

"Why should you do this for him? Has he any hold over you?"

"In a way."

"What way?"

"He lent me two hundred quid when I bought this business. I still owe him over a hundred. You can see how I was placed, can't you?"

"I can see that you behaved foolishly. Have you any other relations with him apart from business?"

"No. You've no right to suggest——"

"I'm not suggesting anything. Do you know anything about his sister who lives at Godalming?"

"No. I never knew he had a sister."

"When did you last see him?"

"It must be two months ago. He called here to see how things were going with me, and asked me if I could let him have fifty pounds off the debt. I hadn't that amount of spare money, but was able to let him have twenty pounds."

"On that occasion did he come by motor-cycle?"

"No. He had a car—a very old one, which he said he was trying to sell."

Finally McLean warned her not to leave her present address without informing him, and then went with Brook back to the car, satisfied with what had emerged.

"Strengthens our case considerably," he said. "At seven o'clock when Colby put that telephone call through to his girl-friend we were at Raven's Court. Obviously he had been following us for some time, waiting for darkness before he put his plan into execution. Clever of him to fake an alibi in the event of the plan going wrong—as it did."

"But was it an alibi?" asked Brook.

"Not bad. Had he given Miss Coombes fuller details I couldn't have tripped her up about his clothing, and then the case against him would have been weak, for it would have been inconceivable that he should have found us by accident. When he knows that Miss Coombes has given him away he may change his tune a bit. But before I see him again I want a search warrant on his house."

Later in the day McLean got the warrant and armed with a bunch of keys taken from the prisoner he and Brook made their way to Greenwich, and finally located Colby's abode. It was a small house in a bad state of repair, not far from the river. By the side of it was a yard at the entrance to which was a board which bore the legend 'G. Colby—Engineer', and through the locked iron gates McLean could see a rough work-shop built of cement blocks, with a corrugated-iron roof. Strewn about in the yard were sundry bits of machinery, including some old ships' propellers, broken anchors and whatnot.

"There's an entrance to the workshop from the house," said McLean. "We'll go that way."

Various keys were tried on the front door, and eventually the door was opened. It was now nearly dark and McLean switched on the electric light in the narrow hall. The whole place was damp and uninviting, and such furniture as was there was broken-down and cheap. The front room on the ground floor was used as an office. It was equipped with a telephone and gas fire, and a lot of space was occupied by a large table-desk, on which was a telephone receiver and some files. McLean opened some of the files and found them full of receipts for raw materials supplied, and correspondence relative to various jobs of work done for firms in the neighbourhood.

"Seems to be a jack of all trades," said McLean. "Repairs to marine engines, phosphor-bronze bearings, winding an armature, but nothing of recent date. No private correspondence of any kind."

Brook bent down and retrieved a small piece of paper that was lying under a chair.

"Here's something," he said. "Looks like a telephone number. T.B. 21756, scribbled in pencil."

McLean took the slip of paper and scanned the writing.

"Yes. T.B. Could be Temple Bar exchange. Let's check that up."

He reached out for the telephone receiver, and then dialled the exchange and number. Immediately a woman's voice was heard.

"Is that Mrs. Hopgood?" asked McLean.

"No, sir. You must have the wrong number. This is Brayton Court Hotel."

"I'm sorry," said McLean, and hung up the receiver.

Brook had already reached out for the first volume of the London Telephone Directory.

"Was it Brayton or Drayton, sir?" he asked.

"Brayton, I think."

Brook turned over the pages, and then ran his finger down the BR's.

"Here we are," he said. "Brayton Court Hotel, Lexford Street, Holborn."

"We'll go into that later."

Brook entered the address and telephone number in his note-book, and McLean continued his search. Colby appeared to keep no books of any kind, but McLean found an old bank statement which showed a very small credit balance, but the last entry was three months old. The payments into the bank were very small and infrequent, and McLean got the impression that up to three months previously he had been living from hand to mouth. There was nothing to indicate that he had any other means than those provided by his profession.

There was another small reception room downstairs, which appeared not to have been used for a long time, and an old-fashioned kitchen and scullery, both in filthy condition. From the scullery there was a recently built narrow passage which gave access to the workshop. Before investigating the workshop they went upstairs, to find there three bedrooms, only one of which was in use. The other two were completely empty. The used bedroom was the only tidy room in the house, and was moderately clean and comfortable. By the bed was a small bookcase, filled with books—mostly novels of a 'sexy' type. McLean investigated the dressing-table and the drawers under it, but nothing of any importance came to light. The wardrobe was full of clothing—mostly well-worn suits. McLean went through all the pockets, and in one of them he made a small discovery. It was a slip of paper on which was written in pencil:

Calling tonight with car. Be ready round about midnight.

"No date, no signature," mused McLean.

"Looks very much like dirty business," said Brook.

"Yes. A date might have helped a lot. Now we'll take a look at the workshop."

They went downstairs and made their way through the kitchen and into the workshop. It was a fairly large room, with a long bench on one side, and a good modern electric lathe on the other. The cement floor was stained with oil and covered with metal filings, especially around the lathe. In some bins were metal rods and bars, and in racks above the lathe were numerous drilling and cutting tools. McLean picked up a handful of glittering dust from a metal tray, and gazed at it reflectively.

"I think we may have something here," he said. "Remember Peyton's clothing when we found his body?"

"You mean that metal dust sticking to the blood on it?"

"Precisely. He could have picked it up in a place such as this. I saw a broom in the scullery. Run and get it."

Brook came back with the broom, and McLean took it and began to sweep the floor carefully, collecting all the metal dust into a single heap. It was about a yard from the lathe that he uncovered a dark stain on the floor, which was certainly not oil.

"Blood?" ejaculated Brook.

"We mustn't jump to conclusions, but it looks remarkably like blood, and some of the metal dust is covered with it.

Collect some in that tin, and we'll have it examined. If it is blood, and the ingredients of the metal dust correspond with that removed from Peyton's clothing, then undoubtedly we are getting somewhere—at last."

Later the house was locked up and the exhibit was handed over to the laboratory for an immediate report. While this work was in hand McLean and Brook paid a visit to Brayton Court Hotel. It was a comparatively new business, and having no licence the facia board described it as a 'Guest House'. Small as it was it was first class in quality, and the vestibule was gay with floral decorations and tasteful furnishings. McLean asked to see the manager, and on presenting his card was shown into an office behind the reception desk, where an immaculately dressed middle-aged man sat at a table.

"Good evening, Inspector," he said. "What can I do for you?"

"I have reason to believe that a man in whom we are interested rang you up recently. He may have wanted to speak to one of your guests, or merely to make an enquiry. His name is George Colby. Do you know anything of him?"

"No. I can't say that I do."

"Have your guests telephones in their bedrooms?"

"Yes. Any calls would be switched through to the bedrooms. If there is no reply we use the loudspeaker in the public rooms."

"How many guests have you at the moment?"

"Twenty-two. That is our maximum number."

"May I see the list?"

"Certainly."

He produced a room chart, and McLean glanced through the names, all of which were strange to him.

"Does the receptionist deal with incoming calls?" he asked.

"Yes. It is part of her duty to attend to the switchboard."

"Can she be spared for a moment?"

"Certainly. I'll have her sent in."

The smart receptionist arrived in a few moments, and McLean asked her if she remembered receiving any message over the telephone from a man named George Colby.

"Yes," she said. "It was yesterday. He asked for Mr. Trimble, and I put the call through to Mr. Trimble's room. Mr. Trimble was there and took the call."

"Is Mr. Trimble in the hotel at the moment?" asked McLean.

"No, sir. He went out about half an hour ago."

"How long has Mr. Trimble been here?"

"Only a couple of days. He and his sister arrived together."

"Where did they come from?"

"I can't remember at the moment. Would you like to see the register? His address is in it."

McLean nodded and the receptionist went out and soon returned with the register. She indicated Mr. Trimble's entry. It was a single entry for himself and sister, and the address given was Hull. But McLean was no longer interested in the address. He turned to Sergeant Brook, his eyes gleaming as they invariably did when something of importance was emerging.

"Brook, have you got that slip of paper with the pencilled message?" he asked.

Brook fished out his note-book, and drew the slip from under the rubber band. McLean took it and laid it under the entry which Mr. Trimble had made in the hotel register. The handwriting was identical.

"Thank you," he said to the receptionist. "We will wait for Mr. Trimble to return."

17

HALF an hour passed, and then the receptionist came to the small writing-room where McLean and Brook were beguiling the time with some magazines.

"Mr. Trimble has just come in, with his sister," she said. "They have gone to their rooms—numbers ten and eleven."

"You did not tell Trimble that we were here?"

"No, sir."

"Good. We will see him in his room. Is it number ten or eleven?"

"Number ten, sir."

As soon as she had gone they mounted the staircase, and found that number ten was at the end of the corridor on the first floor. McLean knocked on the door, and a voice invited him to come in. He opened the door, and stood gazing with surprise at the dark face of the occupant, who seemed to share his own astonishment, but with far less pleasure.

"So Mr. Trimble is really Mr. Knullah," said McLean. "That saves my department some valuable time, for they are busy looking for you."

Knullah quickly regained his self-possession.

"Why should you look for me?" he asked. "Have I no freedom of movement?"

"Not when you are an important witness in a murder case. I asked you not to change your address without informing me."

"There were reasons why I could not give you another address. When I left Raven's Court I had no place to go to. I had to find myself a room, and that was not easy."

"Had you also to change your name?"

"Yes. I think you know why. My relations with Mrs. Mannering were not what her husband believed them to be. He drew the wrong conclusions, and did her a grave injustice."

"Yet she is here with you—or so I presume?"

"Yes, until she can make up her mind what she will do. But all that is beside the point. Why do you wish to see me?"

"I have some questions to ask you—very important questions. Do you know a man named George Colby?"

"No."

"Your memory is very short. He telephoned you yesterday, and you spoke to him from this room."

"Oh, that man! I couldn't make out what he was talking about. He must have confused me with someone else——"

"It won't do," interrupted McLean. "Here is a note which was found in that man's possession. Do you deny that this is your handwriting?"

Knullah scanned the note.

"I do. It's rather like mine, but it was never written by me."

"These foolish denials won't help you. You knew Colby before you came here. You knew him at the time when a man who called himself Robert Peyton was murdered. That he should ask for you yesterday by the false name in which you registered proves that you must have seen him quite recently."

"I can only repeat that you are making a mistake. But even if I did know this man what would it signify?"

"It might signify that you aided and abetted him in one or more criminal acts, for this man Colby is at this moment in custody."

"Then surely the matter is simple," said Knullah. "Take me to this man and let me hear what he has to say about our alleged association."

McLean smiled and shook his head.

"It is a little too simple," he said. "You shall be confronted with Mr. Colby at the right moment, and not before."

"May I ask what is the right moment?"

"You may ask but it is not my intention to tell you. Now I should like to see Mrs. Mannering. Brook, will you go to the next room and ask Mrs. Mannering to come here?"

Brook went out and was absent for a few moments. Knullah sat down on the bed, shaking his head sorrowfully.

"She knows no more about this man Colby than I do," he said. "Why should you trouble her like this, when already she has so much unhappiness?"

"Who is responsible for that?"

"There is much you do not know, Inspector."

"It is because I am painfully aware of that that I wish to widen the scope of my knowledge."

Brook then returned with Mrs. Mannering. As usual she was perfectly controlled, but succeeded in making her resentment known through the medium of her dark eyes and her shapely but firm little mouth.

"I'm sorry if I am causing you any inconvenience, Mrs. Mannering," said McLean. "But it is necessary that I ask you some questions."

"What are the questions?" she asked. "If they concern my poor niece I have already told you all I know."

"They concern Mr. Colby, who is now in custody."

"But I do not know anyone of that name."

"Do you recognize this handwriting?"

McLean showed her the slip of paper, and she hesitated for a moment.

"It looks rather like Achmed's," she said.

"It is not my handwriting," cried Knullah.

"Please be quiet," snapped McLean. "Now, Mrs. Mannering, this slip of paper, bearing Knullah's writing, was found in Colby's possession, and yesterday Colby rang up Knullah and spoke to him. Do you still say that you do not know Mr. Colby?"

"I do."

"Very well. We will leave that matter for the moment. Why did you leave your husband and come here with Knullah, under an assumed name?"

"I refuse to answer that question. I think you have no right to ask it."

"Is it your intention to return to Raven's Court?"

"I have no plans for the future. I need time to think things over."

"Have you a passport of your own?"

"No. When I came to this country I travelled on my husband's passport."

"And you?" asked McLean of Knullah.

"I had a passport, but it fell out of date, and I destroyed it."

McLean cautioned them, with some emphasis, not to leave their present address without informing him, and then left the premises, but not before he had seen the manager and clarified the situation.

"It is absolutely essential that I keep in touch with Mr. Trimble and his sister," he said. "If they attempt to leave the hotel please telephone me at this number."

Back at Scotland Yard McLean waited for the report on the metal dust, but the evening was well advanced before this came to hand. Brook watched his face as he read the document, and soon knew that it was favourable.

"Everything perfect," said McLean. "It was blood of the same group as that of the murdered man—at least two months old. Three rather uncommon metals have been identified in that handful of dust, and these correspond with the dust adhering to the clothing, previously identified. I think we can rule out coincidence."

"Will you see Colby now?"

"Yes."

Again the prisoner was brought before McLean. He looked

wild-eyed and ill—quite different from when McLean had last seen him.

"Mr. Colby," said McLean, "I have a statement from Miss Coombes at Windsor. I propose to have it read to you. Brook, will you read that statement?"

Sergeant Brook opened his note-book, and commenced to read his shorthand notes. The prisoner's face grew almost purple as Brook proceeded, and his hand went to his stomach as if in pain. Finally Brook finished and closed the book.

"Have you anything to say to that?" asked McLean.

"It isn't true. I don't know why she should tell such lies."

"Here's a note found in one of your suits at your house. Take a look at it."

Colby gave a quick glance at the note which McLean held before his eyes.

"It's nothing," he said. "A fellow brought along a car which he wanted me to buy. I turned it down."

"What was his name?"

"Dobson. He knew I sometimes bought second-hand cars."

"The man who sent this note is a Syrian named Achmed Knullah."

"Well—he called himself Dobson."

McLean stared at Colby intently.

"I suggest to you that he brought the car to take away the body of a man which was lying on the floor of your workshop."

"No. I'm no murderer. You can't hang such a crime on me."

"Who was the man who was kept a prisoner in your workshop for days, and finally shot? He called himself Peyton, but that wasn't his real name. Who was he?"

"I don't know what you're talking about. I'm ill and want to see a doctor."

He staggered towards a chair, tried to get a grip of it and fell heavily. The waiting constable moved towards him, but McLean waved him back, and leaned over the groaning man. On his lips and lower jaw was a trickle of blood.

"Get a doctor," he said to Brook. "He really is ill."

A police surgeon was soon on the spot. He spoke to the stricken man, but Colby seemed incapable of doing anything

151

but groan and move convulsively. But the doctor was not long in diagnosing the trouble.

"He'll have to be taken to hospital at once," he said. "I think it is a duodenal ulcer which has burst. I shall have to use your telephone."

In less than five minutes two men arrived with a stretcher and the half-conscious man was taken away. McLean gave a little sigh.

"Is it serious?" he asked the doctor.

"Could be. It depends upon a lot of factors. They will operate at once, if my diagnosis is confirmed. You are not likely to hear the result until tomorrow morning. Well, I must get along to the hospital."

"And I thought he was shamming," said Brook, when the doctor had left.

"So did I until I saw the blood round his mouth. Brook, our luck is of the oscillating type. As soon as we take two paces forward we slip back one. I'm certain that Colby could tell us exactly what happened to Peyton so-called, and why."

"There's still Mr. Knullah."

"Yes, but what have I got against Knullah? Only the fact that he knew Colby, and wrote that note to him. At this moment it is Colby who is my star witness. If he didn't actually kill Peyton I believe that under pressure he will turn King's Evidence. If we solve the Peyton case we shall be a long way to solving the death of Miss Rostan. Ring up my wife and tell her that I cannot be home tonight."

Brook picked up the telephone, but McLean reached out and took it from him.

"I'd better face the music," he said. "She'll understand, bless her."

But there was no reply from Valerie, and McLean asked the operator to keep the call in hand.

"You'd better pack up, Brook," he said. "It's been a long day. I dare not miss a chance of getting a more forthright statement from Colby. I can snatch a bit of sleep in that chair later on."

Brook did not attempt to argue the point, for he was indeed both tired and hungry. When he had gone McLean did a little paper work, and then again tried to get through to Valerie, but with no better result.

"I've tried the number several times," said the operator. "Am I still to keep the call in hand?"

"Please."

It seemed a little strange that Valerie should be absent from the house for so long a period at that hour, but he concluded that she had taken the dog out for a run on a more than usual lengthy route. Curiously enough he was not at all tired, nor hungry. It seemed to him that he had reached an important juncture in his investigation, and that he was on the verge of solving one half of the problem. It all hung upon Colby. If the pending operation was successful Colby might be frightened into confessing the part he had played in the matter of Peyton's death, always provided that he had not actually encompassed it, and McLean believed he was merely the tool and not the murderer. If by some mischance he did not recover then there was still a good chance that he would tell the truth, guilty or not guilty, before he went the way of all flesh.

But as time passed and the telephone remained silent, he became worried about Valerie. Again he got in touch with the operator only to be told that there was still no response from the number he wanted. His anxiety increased. It was now past eleven o'clock, and he could not imagine Valerie being out at that time of night, or so sound asleep that she could not hear the telephone ringing.

It seemed absurd to imagine that anything could have happened to her, guarded as she was by a highly trained police dog, and yet there was that strange silence to be accounted for. In this case of his a number of irrational things had already happened. There was the forced entry of his house, followed very quickly by the shooting-up of his car. Neither of these events could have been the work of a normal balanced brain, for they could not have altered the investigation in the slightest degree. They suggested a near lunatic as the instigator.

At shortly after midnight he rang up the hospital to enquire after Colby. There was a somewhat significant delay, but finally the surgeon who had conducted the operation came to the telephone.

"Bad news," he said. "The patient never came out of the anaesthetic. There was always that possibility, for I found he had a bad heart. But the operation had to be performed, and

153

we did our best to get him through it. He died only a few minutes ago."

McLean hung up the receiver with a little sigh of disappointment. His star witness was no more. He had carried to eternity the secrets he was reluctant to divulge, just as Denise Rostan had done. He had thought this to be a lucky day, but relentlessly the scales were redressing the balance. But at least he was freed from an all-night vigil. There was the mystery of Valerie's silence to be settled—and that without a moment's delay. Within five minutes he was in his car, racing through the deserted streets towards his home.

When he reached the house it was in complete darkness, and his heart thumped painfully as he leapt out of the car and opened the front door with his key, calling for Valerie as he did so. Then Rex came trotting into the hall, wagging his tail with obvious pleasure, and half McLean's anxiety vanished. The lounge was empty and he ran upstairs. Valerie was lying on her bed, clad in a dressing-gown—dead asleep. It was a long time before he could wake her.

"Oh, lord!" she yawned. "It's you."

"Yes, but what have you been doing? I tried to get you on the 'phone half a dozen times."

"I had a headache so I took a couple of sleeping tablets and came here for a lie down."

"A couple! You must have taken the whole box."

"No—only a couple. I've had a nice sleep, and my headache has vanished."

"So has mine," laughed McLean.

18

HARRY MONTAGUE was finding his new life full of absorbing interests, but not yet had he recovered from the tragedy which had overtaken the woman he had loved so deeply, nor was he quite settled in his mind whether she had been a worthless adventuress or merely the victim of circumstance. That she had lied to him on some matters was undeniable, but that alone did not put her completely outside the pale. Many otherwise excellent persons were sometimes driven to untruths, to conceal matters that were painful to discuss. Whatever others might think or say to him, she would always remain a joyful memory.

Helen, well aware of his feelings, never mentioned Denise. She believed that time would effect a cure for his periodical fits of depression, and she did her best, with marked success, to be a blithe spirit about the place.

It was on the morning following McLean's stunning discovery that Helen came across to the Dutch barn where he was busy to inform him that a visitor had come to see him.

"An old acquaintance of yours. He says his name is Murphy, and I've an idea you once mentioned him to me."

"Not Joe Murphy?"

"Yes. He says you gave him this address when you last saw him—that he meant to write to you, but never did."

"He certainly never did. I'll come and see the old scoundrel."

He went back to the house with Helen, and found Joe in the sitting-room, as brown as a berry, and his blue eyes twinkling with merriment.

"Well, this is a surprise, Joe!" he said, as he wrung Joe's hand. "In case you haven't guessed, I'm a farmer now."

"Darned if you don't look like one too," laughed Joe. "What wouldn't I give to be on the land instead of rushing round the world selling insurance. Since I last saw you I've travelled about twenty thousand miles."

"This is my sister Helen who has taken me into partnership. Actually she's the real farmer, and I'm learning the business. It's a good business too."

"He's far too modest," said Helen. "He's taught me more about machinery than I ever dreamed of. When our neighbours' tractors refuse to go they send for Harry. But can I get you a drink?"

"It's an idea," said Joe. "I still haven't signed the pledge."

"Whisky or beer?" asked Harry.

"Beer in the morning. Whisky at all other times."

"I confess I had written you off," said Harry, when Helen had gone for the beer. "But did you have a good holiday?"

"Holiday! I had only a fortnight, and then the Company packed me off on a terrific jaunt. I finished up in Bombay again where I picked up a wonderful slice of business, and something else too which will interest you. Remember old Peyton?"

"Do I remember? I've every reason to remember him. Don't you know what happened to him?"

Murphy stared at Harry curiously.

"Go on," he said. "I'll have your news first."

"He was murdered. His dead body was found on a Surrey heath, and the police got busy and hunted up pretty well all the passengers who were on the *Rantala*. Didn't they trace you?"

"My wife wrote to me and told me she had had a call from the police asking for me. But she told them I was abroad and likely to be away for a considerable time. They didn't tell her what their business was. Did they get the murderer?"

"No. But they established that Peyton's name wasn't Peyton, and the case is still open."

Joe was now very excited.

"Did you tell them about that queer remark which Peyton made the night when he got drunk?" he asked.

"Yes. I think they take the view that Peyton was hoist with his own petard, and that his enemy got in the first and final blow."

"Curiouser and curiouser," said Joe. "Now you hear what happened to me."

At that moment Helen came in with the refreshment—beer for the two men and a sherry for herself. Harry poured out the drinks, and Joe swallowed half a glass of beer before resuming.

"While I was in Bombay I ran out to Poona to see a business associate," he said. "We had occasion to look up an old case of incendiarism, and I went with him to the office of an English newspaper, to look through the files. The one I was interested in was five years old. I found the case and read the evidence. It ran over the page and as I turned it over I saw the photograph of a man on the opposite page. I nipped it out while no one was looking. Here it is."

He produced his wallet and extracted a folded piece of old newspaper, holding it up for Harry to see. Instantly Harry drew his breath hard.

"Peyton!" he gasped.

"Yes. Unmistakable, isn't it? It says here his name is Ambrose Watling, and that he was charged with robbery and violence in the private house of a rich merchant. A servant in

156

the house was seriously injured, and the booty was considerable. It was known that he had associates, but they got clean away with the jewellery. Watling was sentenced to five years' penal servitude. What do you think of that?"

"Amazing! It explains a lot. Evidently he served his sentence, and changed his name. By some means he must have heard that his associates were in England, and he came here to settle accounts."

"Sure! But what had he to settle?"

"Perhaps they squealed on him—gave him away to the police."

"But if he knew that to be the case he could have put the police on their track. No, it must have been something else— something which put the idea of murder into his mind. But to think that you and I sat and played Bridge with him night after night, believing him to be a respectable old man. It goes to prove you can't go on appearances. But your friend Denise Rostan wasn't taken in as we were. I remember that she mistrusted him from the start and——"

He stopped as he saw Harry wince, and Helen spilt some of the sherry from the glass in her hand.

"What's wrong?" he asked. "Have I dropped a brick?"

"Just a tiny one," replied Helen. "You see, Denise Rostan met with an unfortunate end quite recently."

"Sorry," said Joe. "But what do you mean by 'unfortunate end'? Not what happened to Peyton—I mean Watling?"

Harry nodded, and then proceeded to tell Joe the details, while Joe stared incredulously, hanging upon every word until Harry had finished.

"What a bag of trouble!" he said. "And what tough luck on you. But I don't quite get it. Do the police believe that she was involved in Watling's murder?"

"That is my impression, but Inspector McLean, who has the case in hand, is pretty tight about it all."

"But—you don't believe it, do you, Harry?"

"I try not to, but there is the established fact that she visited Watling in his cabin at night, while pretending that she disliked him. Have some more beer, Joe. Your glass is empty."

Helen filled the empty glass, and then looked at the clock on the mantelpiece.

"I've got some chores to do," she said. "I'll leave you two

boys to dig up the past, but don't dig too deep. See you before you leave, Mr. Murphy."

"Surely!"

"Did your sister ever meet Denise?" asked Joe, when he and Harry were alone.

"No. It was all arranged that she should when—when the blow fell. What a fool I was not to have proposed to Denise when I had the chance. But I didn't know how much she meant to me until she had left the ship. I might have saved her life."

"I don't see how you work that out," said Joe. "From what you've told me it looks as if the trouble was already brewing. Your sister doesn't believe in her, does she?"

"What makes you think that?"

"It was in her eyes while we were talking about Denise—a kind of silent resentment. It's rather a pity she did not meet Denise because then she would have got a better idea of her. Hell! I can't believe that she could have got herself mixed up with murder. I won't believe it."

"Thanks, Joe. I'm hoping that one day perhaps the whole truth will come out. Until then I'm going to keep my faith in her. There's one thing you must do, Joe—take this picture of Watling to Inspector McLean, and tell him how you came by it. Up to now he's been investigating the murder of a completely unknown man. This may help to put him on the right trail."

"I'll do that, but how do I get at him?"

"You can telephone him from here. I've got his number. It would save time to make an appointment."

"Okay. You find me the number."

The call was put through, and after a little delay Joe was speaking to McLean, explaining whom he was and where he was. Finally he hung up the receiver and came to Harry.

"That fellow doesn't let the grass grow under his feet," he said. "Offered to come down here, and at once. Is that all right with you, Harry?"

"Quite all right. Like to have a look round the farm while you're waiting?"

"Surely. I need to stretch my legs a bit. Far too much sitting in 'planes and cars. Makes a fellow all fat and flabby. Wish I had your figure."

"You look very well as you are. That little bit of rotundity adds dignity."

"Dignity, my foot! It's in the wrong place, and you know it. Well, let's go."

Despite his overweight Joe proved to be a good walker, and he praised everything he saw, from the new cowsheds and tidy yards to the beautiful herd of Guernsey cows, placidly grazing in the lush meadows.

"One of these days I'll buy me a farm," he said. "And spend the remainder of my days sitting on a fence sucking straws."

"God help the farm," laughed Harry. "I'm beginning to learn that you don't really own a farm. It owns you, and if you don't do as it tells you you go broke."

They had scarcely completed the whole round of the fields when Harry saw a long car coming up the drive towards the house.

"Inspector McLean, breaking records," he said. "I didn't know one could get from London as quickly as that. He'll probably kiss you when he sees what you've got to show him. Did you tell him what it was?"

"No. All I said was that I had some information to give him about the man known as Robert Peyton."

McLean and Sergeant Brook had left the car, and were waiting for the two approaching men. Harry introduced Joe to them and McLean took in Joe at a glance.

"I tried to get in touch with you some time ago, Mr. Murphy," he said, "but was told you were not available."

"I very seldom am," replied Joe. "I'm just a poor fool who gets projected all over the globe in the cause of big and prosperous business.

"You said you had something to tell me about the man known as Robert Peyton?"

"Yes. You will appreciate that until I arrived here today I had no idea that Peyton had been murdered. I first met him on board the *Rantala*, and knew no more about his past than Harry did. Well, I had occasion to visit India again recently, and there, whilst looking through an old newspaper, I saw this."

Joe handed the cut-out picture to McLean, who scanned it very closely, and read the caption underneath.

"Do you recognize him?" asked Joe.

"No. Do you mean this is Peyton?"

"But can't you see it is?"

"The body which we found had scarcely any face left," said McLean.

Joe winced.

"I wouldn't have your job for something," he said. "But anyway that is the man we all knew as Peyton. Harry will bear me out there."

"No doubt whatsoever," said Harry. "It was not the sort of face one is likely to forget."

McLean's eyes gleamed at this piece of good fortune.

"You've done me a great service, Mr. Murphy," he said. "What was the name of the newspaper from which you took this cutting?"

"The *Sunday Echo*. It's a small newspaper published in Poona. I've pencilled the date on the back. It's June the tenth, 1947."

"Were there no details of the trial of this man—Watling?"

"No. I looked for that in the earlier issues, but they didn't report it. I dared not ask the editor, because having mutilated his file I felt a bit guilty."

"Naturally. Well, that can all be checked up. Now, is there anything you can tell me about Denise Rostan, who was also a passenger on that ship?"

"In what connection?"

"Was she friendly with Watling during the voyage?"

"Neither friendly nor unfriendly. To the best of my knowledge she never spoke to him. But I know she had a very poor opinion of him."

"What makes you think that?"

"Her attitude when she was near him. She looked at him contemptuously, and once she said she couldn't think what Harry and I were doing playing Bridge with such a dissipated old crook."

"You think she really meant that?"

"I'm sure she did."

"Well, we'll leave it at that. May I keep this cutting?"

"Of course."

"Then I won't detain you any longer."

Murphy and Harry stood and watched the car disappear down the drive.

"He's certainly no time-waster," said Murphy. "I'm glad I haven't done a murder."

160

19

McLEAN was immensely pleased with his new information. At last he appeared to be making real progress. In the car he looked again at the photograph, and gave a short little laugh.

"Humiliating to reflect that we have been trying in vain to identify that dead man, and Mr. Murphy has it served up to him on a plate," he said.

"You think it's going to help?" asked Brook.

"It will be surprising if it doesn't. Something is bound to be known about Watling's associates. I want a verbatim report of that trial, and I want it without too much delay. If there's any hitch I shall fly out to India, but I hope that won't be necessary. We will see what we can do over the air."

On reaching his office McLean met with a surprise. He was informed that Mrs. Mannering was waiting to see him.

"Most certainly we'll see her," he said. "I wonder what she has on her mind. Run down to the waiting-room and bring her up."

Brook went out and returned very shortly with Mrs. Mannering. She was wearing yet another costume, and McLean reflected that every time he had seen her she had been differently dressed.

In her gloved hand she was carrying a newspaper.

"You wished to see me, Mrs. Mannering?" asked McLean.

"Yes. You told me not to leave my present address without letting you know."

"Do you wish to leave it?"

"I—I think so. This morning I saw an advertisement in the newspaper. Perhaps you will read it. It is marked with a pencil."

McLean took the newspaper from her. It was folded to bring the 'Personal' column to view, and a small advertisement was marked with a cross. The advertiser requested Mrs. Zolta Mannering to get in touch with him without delay, and it was signed 'Cedric'.

"Your husband?" said McLean.

"Yes. I telephoned him, and he begged me to return to him. I said I could not return while he believed me to be guilty of infidelity, which wasn't true. He said he didn't believe it any longer, and that he had spoken in anger, and would never refer to the incident again if I would come home."

"Did you agree to do that?"

"Yes."

"And Knullah—does he get his job back?"

"No."

"Have you told him what you propose to do?"

"Not yet. I shall do so before I leave."

"When do you propose to leave?"

"This evening. Will that be all right?"

"Certainly. But it is understood that neither you nor your husband will leave Raven's Court while this investigation is taking place?"

"I understand that now, and I'm sure my husband does. But, Inspector, you don't really think that I—or my husband —had anything to do with my niece's death?"

"I have never suggested that," replied McLean. "But I cannot have important witnesses moving from place to place without my knowledge. It involves the police in enormous work keeping in touch with them. The witnesses must be immediately available."

"Yes—of course. I will not offend again."

"Good. Well, that's all, Mrs. Mannering."

"Thank you, Inspector."

Brook opened the door for her, and in a moment she was gone.

"Large-hearted man, Mr. Mannering," said Brook, as he came back to his desk. "Believes in platonic friendship, no doubt."

"But not in Achmed Knullah. I don't trust any of them, and my distrust grows. It's time I stopped some bolt-holes. We'll start with the air services and continue with seaports. No passages abroad for the Mannerings nor for Mr. Knullah. Take down these descriptions and we'll get the information circulated without delay."

When this was done and the machinery set in motion, McLean turned his attention to the photograph which Murphy had given him. For some hours priority cables passed between Scotland Yard and the Indian police, and at last his efforts were rewarded.

"Full report of the trial of Watling, with all relevant information, is coming by Comet 'plane tomorrow," he told Brook. "That should be splendid grist for our mill. Now we'll see if Mrs. Mannering has gone back to her devoted husband. Ring up that hotel and ask for the manager."

McLean was soon speaking to the hotel manager. He was told that Miss Trimble had left an hour previously, giving her new address as Raven's Court, near Maidenhead.

"You should have told me, as you promised to do."

"I'm sorry, Inspector, but I have been out of the premises and have only just returned. I was just about to ring you."

"Is Mr. Trimble still with you?"

"Yes. I saw him just now."

"Good. But don't slip up on him, please."

"I won't. But it's not easy, you know. I've never had such a thing happen before."

"It can happen in the best regulated hotels."

"Clumsy fool!" ejaculated Brook, as McLean hung up the receiver.

"He has my sympathy," said McLean. "We've made his position difficult. He can't very well tell all his staff that certain of his guests are suspect by the police. His natural retort to us is, 'Why don't you do your own dirty work?'"

"Did he say that?" asked Brook.

"Not in so many words, but he did suggest that it might ease matters if I arrested Knullah."

"Would it?"

"It would help him, but not us. I can arrest Knullah on some minor charge, and then he would probably close up like an oyster. I am hoping that ultimately we shall frighten him into telling us quite a lot."

"If he doesn't die on us as Colby did."

"I can't see Knullah dying that way. He looks a particularly virile person."

McLean arrived home late that evening, to find his patient and industrious wife finishing a crayon sketch of Rex, who was reposing on the hearthrug, looking the picture of innocence and contentment. Valerie took her husband's kiss on the nape of her admirable neck.

"Oh, it's you!" she said, turning her head.

"Who else might it have been?" he asked.

"That's telling," she replied. "A neglected wife must have some form of diversion. I've a very admiring milkman."

"Then he ought to be good for a pound of farm butter."

"You brute! Now, what's wrong with his mouth? I simply can't get it right."

"Whose mouth?"

"Rex, you idiot. He's a wonderful model—quiet as a statue, except for his mouth. He will keep moving it."

"Looks all right to me," said McLean, quizzing the sketch. "Well, let's have some food—if you've got any."

"I've got some bread and cheese," said Valerie demurely.

"You've got something better than that unless I misjudge that glint in your eye. What happened to the cold mutton?"

"Rex had it."

"You mean he stole it?"

"Oh no—he wouldn't do that. I gave it to him as a reward."

"Reward for what?"

"He killed a chicken when I took him for a walk this morning."

"But he's trained not to do that. You should have called him off."

"I wasn't near enough."

"Whose chicken was it?"

"I haven't a notion. It was in the lane, miles from anywhere, and there was I with my shopping basket on my arm, and a dead chicken lying on the road. What could I do but— but——"

"Bring it home and cook it?"

"Exactly! There was nothing wrong with it. He just bit it through the neck. I expect it was rude to him. One shouldn't waste good food in times like this. Of course you needn't eat it if you have a conscience in the matter."

McLean shook his head at the dog, who lowered his handsome head on his forelegs as if in shame.

"Roast chicken or bread and cheese?" asked Valerie.

"Now you're demoralizing me as well as the dog. All right— roast chicken it is."

McLean's moral sense seemed not to be unduly violated during the ensuing meal, and Valerie was quick to notice a brightness in his eyes that had been absent for many days.

"What's happened?" she asked. "Did that dead man—Colby—leave a confession behind, after all?"

"Nothing so simple. But this morning I saw another passenger from the *Rantala* who had hitherto not been available."

"Good gracious! Are you back on that old case?"

"I've never been away from it. Solve that and I am near to solving the death of Denise Rostan."

"What did the new witness have to say?"

"Not much, but he gave me something of the greatest importance. This is it."

McLean delved into his pocket and handed her the newspaper cutting which Murphy had given him. Valerie glanced at the reproduced photograph, and made a wry face.

"Nasty looking specimen!" she said. "Convicted of robbery with violence. Well, that doesn't surprise me. Where does he figure in the Peyton case?"

"He is the case. That is Robert Peyton so-called."

"How interesting! But does it really help, now that he's dead and buried?"

"It helps enormously. While I was investigating an unknown man I didn't know where to turn for information concerning his past and his associates. Already certain facts have been given me, and within thirty-six hours I hope to learn more. I won't go beyond that, but I promise you that when this case is all nicely tied up, you and I will slip away to some quiet spot in Devon or Cornwall, and spend a week or two really enjoying ourselves."

"Jam tomorrow," said Valerie with a smile.

"The best pleasures are those which we have to wait for."

"Oh, I'm not complaining. In fact I'm getting quite a kick out of this case—so far as I understand it. How far have you really got? Recapitulate for me."

"I can do that now, with more certainty than I might have done yesterday. It all started five years ago, when this man—Ambrose Watling—and some associates broke into the home of a very rich Hindu, and stole a great quantity of jewels. A servant who opposed them was seriously injured, but afterwards he was able to identify Watling, who was suspected of being the ringleader. The jewels were not found and Watling was given a sentence of five years. He was released from jail about six months ago. At this period Denise Rostan was in India. Presumably she had married a young Hindu in Algiers. They separated after a short time, and the husband, in ill health, went back to his family, who had never approved of the marriage. The sick man grew worse, and when he knew death was near he expressed the desire to see the woman he had married. The family consented and Denise hurried to India, arriving there in time to be with her husband at his death. Dates are speculative here, but the facts are not. Some time after this we find her on a ship bound for England—the ship which brought young Montague here, and also Watling, who had by some means possessed himself of a passport belonging to the real Robert Peyton, which he must have faked to suit the circumstances. Despite Montague's assertion that Denise did not know Watling, and never spoke to him, it is in evidence that she visited Watling's cabin on more than one occasion. She herself finally admitted this, but pleaded that he had invited her there to have a drink."

"You didn't believe that?"

"No. I am convinced that she went there while Watling was absent, for the purpose of finding out where he was going. In short, she was acting on instructions from some other person, who wanted Watling kept under observation."

"One of Watling's old associates?"

"Obviously. There must have been some double-crossing, for there is reason to believe that Watling was on his way to England to settle some account. He boasted of it one evening, when he had had too much to drink. He and Denise Rostan disembarked at the same port—Naples, the girl ostensibly to stay with some friends in Rome. But her real reason was to keep in touch with Watling."

"Go on."

"There is a gap in our records until we find the dead body of Watling on that lovely heath not far from Guildford—a body so disfigured that identification by normal means was impossible. Then, after a lapse of time, Denise Rostan is traced to the home of her uncle, Cedric Mannering, at Raven's Court. You know what happened there. Montague, who was in love with her, begged me to tell him where he could find her, and I stretched a point in that matter and put him in touch with her. He saw her and was surprised at the change in her appearance. He invited her to spend a few days with him and his sister on the farm which they ran jointly. She agreed to do so, but put off her visit for a long time. One evening she telephoned to say she would like to come the next day. As you know, she was not able to keep that promise, for she was murdered the next morning."

McLean was silent for a few moments, while he let his mind range over the subsequent evidence and events. Then he resumed.

"When I examined her effects I found part of a letter intended for Montague, which convinced me that she intended to tell him the truth about her relationship with Watling. I believe that she had trailed Watling in the belief that she was helping someone to escape his wrath, only to discover finally that she had encompassed his death. It was then that she turned to Montague, the one man she could trust, but her intention became known, or at least suspected. She was murdered cleverly and deliberately. And who would have better cause to murder her or cause her to be murdered than the person who killed Watling?"

"Do you think you know who that person is?"

"Not yet. But we are getting nearer and nearer to the truth. He is a person whom she had no cause to mistrust, or she would not have eaten sweets which he provided, and which brought about her death."

"What about the man you arrested—Colby?"

McLean shook his head.

"I believe he was merely the cat's-paw in the matter of Watling, and I had a case against him strong enough to have forced him to speak, had he lived a little longer. Knullah was mixed up in that affair, but to what extent I can only guess."

"That still leaves Mannering and his wife. Are they not also under suspicion?"

"Very much so. But I must confess that I have absolutely nothing tangible against them, and there is evidence to support the view that at the time their niece was murdered they were both at Raven's Court."

"Oh, dear!" sighed Valerie. "It's all very complicated.

Would it be correct to say that you really haven't a single clue to the identity of the person who actually killed that poor girl?"

"No. I have a very good clue. The only one in this very strange case. The murderer of Denise Rostan left something behind him which may yet hang him, if only I can find the gap into which it fits. So far I have failed."

"Oh, Robert! This is the first time you have mentioned such a thing."

"I've been reluctant to make too much of it. It was just a page torn from the end of a loose-leaf diary, on which was drawn an acrostic. An ingenious thing well known to people interested in such things. It was found between the leaves of a book which the girl was reading just before her death. It was a volume containing examples of acrostics and other puzzles, but the volume failed to give that example. I can imagine the circumstances in which that sheet of paper got into the book. I can almost see the drama enacted."

"Tell me, Robert. I was once bitten by the same bug."

"The girl was in the punt, moored at the end of a charming backwater, reading the book of puzzles, when someone she knew intimately approached her either by water or by the footpath on the bank. He got into the punt and chatted, offering the girl some wrapped sweets, which she accepted. I should mention that she was extremely partial to sweets, and quite clearly the visitor was well aware of the fact. The poison in the sweets was slow in acting, so he kept the conversation going by taking an interest in the book which she had been reading. I think he may have said 'I know an acrostic better than any of these' and then drew the thing on a page of a pocket diary. All the time the girl was munching the sweets, and coming under the influence of the poison. Before going into a coma she slipped the paper bearing the acrostic between the pages of the book. When she was past all help, he disposed of the box which had held the sweets and stole away. That is my imaginary picture."

"You make it sound very real, Robert. But have you got the acrostic?"

"Not here. It is in the dossier of the case. But I can draw it for you—exactly as it is."

He produced a sheet of paper and with a pencil swiftly

168

drew the acrostic, and passed it across to Valerie, who examined it with marked interest:

"My word, it's clever," she said. "I've never seen it before. My Latin is just good enough to translate it, except the word 'Sator'. Is it 'Farmer'?"

"Ploughman."

"Oh yes. But why have you put in these little ticks?"

"Those are present in the original, and they fog me completely. It looks as if, after completing the acrostic, the writer checked it against something else, but what? I've asked myself that a hundred times, and the answer doesn't come. I've shown it to a few experts, or alleged experts, without divulging my real interest in it, but got no help from them."

"But, Robert, isn't it possible that Denise had this acrostic before she went out in the punt that morning?"

"It is possible but unlikely, for the book had only arrived that same morning by post. Had the acrostic been in her handbag, which was very small, I should expect it to show signs of folding, or creasing. But it was perfectly clean and flat."

"But she could have slipped it into the book just before she left home," argued Valerie.

"That's a reasonable suggestion, but I prefer my own interpretation. It's simpler, and is in keeping with other evidence of another person in the punt. Of course I may be wrong, but even so it doesn't dispose of the friend who stayed with her in the punt long enough to leave certain traces behind him. Who was that unsuspected friend?"

20

CEDRIC MANNERING sat in the big lounge at Raven's Court with a bottle of whisky and a syphon of soda-water on the low table beside his chair, while he smoked one of his enormous cigars, in the reflective mood of a man who has much to occupy his mind. It was by no means cold, but he loved heat, and the big electric fire was full on. A soft knock on the door brought Emily to the scene. She had discarded her apron and cap, and was now dressed less soberly.

"Yes, Emily," he said.

"I have laid the table for two, sir. You told me I might go out with Cook when that was done."

"That's right, Emily. I am expecting the mistress at any moment. There is no need for you to wait any longer."

"Thank you, sir."

The door closed, and Mannering turned again to his discarded morning newspaper. For some minutes he interested himself in the stock market quotations, and then laid the paper down as he heard the sound of an approaching car. He guessed it was his wife, and went out through the hall to the front door. The taxi had just stopped, and Mrs. Mannering was searching her handbag for money to pay the driver, who nodded at Mannering, and then dumped several suitcases just inside the open door. In a few moments he was away and Zolta was in the lounge, flinging off her coat and hat.

"Thank God!" she said. "Cedric, get me a drink. I'm gasping."

Mannering produced another glass, and helped her copiously, topping up his own glass afterwards.

"Cheers!" she said, and sat down on the arm of his chair.

"So it didn't work?" he asked.

"No. That inspector found us. It was through Colby. He is in custody."

Mannering stared at her incredulously.

"In custody? Are you sure?"

"Quite sure. Achmed was questioned about him. Of course he denied all knowledge of him."

"But Ned wouldn't give away anything. I don't understand it. Why was Colby arrested?"

"I don't know. But couldn't it be in connection with Ambrose?"

"Too long ago. I must get to the bottom of this. Colby can be trusted up to a point, but McLean is an astute devil, and wouldn't make an arrest unless he had good reason. You saw him?"

"The inspector? Yes. He came to the hotel, and questioned Achmed, and then me."

"What did he ask you?"

"He asked me if I knew George Colby, and I said I didn't. Then he showed me a written message, and asked me if I knew the handwriting. I said it looked like Achmed's."

"Why the hell did you say that?"

"Because I realized that Achmed had signed the hotel register, and that it would be silly of me to deny something which was obvious."

"But what was this message?"

"It had no date or signature, and said that the writer would call with a car, and that Colby presumably must be ready at midnight. It must have been that night——"

Mannering stopped her with a fierce gesture, rose from his chair and paced to and fro, his big face agitated, and his forehead bespangled with small beads of perspiration.

"Colby must have been mad to keep that message by him," he said. "Anyone but a born idiot would have destroyed it. But it's no use wailing. Something has to be done. Pressure may be brought to bear on Colby, and if he talks——"

He stopped as the telephone-bell rang, and after a pause picked up the receiver. An angry conversation ensued, and finally he laid down the receiver, and turned to his wife.

"That was Achmed, speaking from the railway station. He left soon after you, and caught the next train."

"Why? I told him he must stay at the hotel until he had further instructions."

"He wouldn't say. He's coming here in a taxi."

"Curious. He must have something important to tell us."

171

"I've got something important to tell him. Have another drink?"

Zolta was quite willing, and for a moment or two she sat sipping the strong mixture.

"Why did you want me to come back, Cedric?" she asked.

"It served no good purpose your staying there, once McLean knew where to find you, and this place was damned lonely without you. If I brought Achmed back too it would look very suspicious to Inspector McLean, who suffers under the delusion that my wife was unfaithful. I wanted you both out of the way while this investigation continues, and I was foolish to agree to your going to London. I suppose he knew you were coming back here?"

"Yes. I showed him the advertisement in the newspaper, as you suggested, and he had no objection."

"He couldn't object—the swine!"

"Oh, he's not so bad. He's always very polite and considerate."

He looked at her from under beetling brows.

"Make no mistake, my dear, he's as clever as they make 'em, and damned pugnacious. I've got to get you and Achmed to some place where he can't reach you——"

"Can't you trust us to be discreet?"

"Not with McLean. He'll go on asking you questions, all cunningly phrased in order to trip you up. Be sure that he has already taken steps to prevent your getting out of the country. I wish I knew just how far he has got—how much he has unearthed—if anything."

Zolta's dark eyes surveyed him intently as he produced a handkerchief from his pocket and wiped his moist forehead.

"Not losing your nerve, Cedric?" she asked. "Maybe it is you who should go far away from McLean's cunningly devised questions."

"Rubbish! I know best," he retorted with some heat.

"All the same, I wish Duke were here. Where has he gone?"

"I've no idea. He never tells me anything."

"Your fault, Cedric. It was silly of you to quarrel with him. If there should arise a state of emergency Duke is the man to deal with it. I suppose he hasn't gone for good?"

"Keep your mind off Duke. It was you who caused all the trouble."

"It was your stupid jealousy. Duke and I——"

"I don't want to revive all that. Ah, that sounds like Achmed."

"No. It's only an aeroplane. Achmed can't be here for a few minutes. I think I'll go and powder my nose."

Mannering nodded rather sullenly, and Zolta left the room. Some minutes passed, during which time Mannering had two more whiskies, and started another cigar. Finally there came the unmistakable sound of a car, and Mannering went to the front door and opened it. Achmed was already outside, with a newspaper clutched in his thin brown hand, and the electric door lamp illuminating his very serious face.

"Why the hell did you want to come here?" demanded Mannering, as they passed through the hall. "You could have said what you had to say on the telephone?"

"This is no time for lectures," lisped Achmed. "There is something in the evening paper that you should see. That is why I left the hotel soon after Zolta, and caught the next train. Here—read it!"

Mannering took the newspaper, and read the short paragraph which Achmed indicated.

A man named George Colby, who was arrested in connection with a serious crime, died early this morning in hospital after an unsuccessful operation.

"You see?" asked Achmed. "I should have been a fool to have stayed on at the hotel, where McLean could pick me up at any moment."

"Why should Colby's death make any difference?"

"Dying men make statements which they would not otherwise make. McLean must have known there was a risk of death, and have been standing by. He knew I was associated with Colby. How do I know what Colby may have told him?"

"You've no brains at all. If Colby died early this morning and made a statement, McLean has had hours and hours to act, and has done nothing. The obvious deduction is that Colby died without uttering a word and——"

He was interrupted by the entrance of Zolta, who, in her brief absence, had done marvels with her face and hair.

"What's the trouble?" she asked.

173

"Colby is dead," said Achmed.

"Isn't that somewhat convenient?" she asked. "There is a proverb about dead men telling no tales."

"There should be another about dying men who like to put themselves right with Allah," retorted Achmed. "Cedric thinks that because I'm still free Colby must have died without making any statement to the police. I'm not so happy about it."

"But why not? That's a reasonable conclusion."

"Not at all. Maybe he likes a cat-and-mouse business, waiting to see which way the mouse will jump."

"And how has he jumped?" snarled Mannering. "Right back here—to involve me in that business. I hope you had sense enough to leave your baggage behind you?"

"Of course I did."

"Then you can get back to it, and wait until I have completed certain arrangements."

"Not I. I've got a passport, and it's just in date. I can be in Paris tomorrow morning by getting a seat on the night 'plane. I don't like the way things are developing. All I need is some cash."

Mannering looked at him witheringly.

"You ignoramus," he said. "The moment you produced your passport anywhere in this country you would find yourself under arrest. Don't underrate the police, especially Inspector McLean. At least have the sense to play the part of an innocent man. Running away is madness, unless you can be sure of success, and the odds are a hundred to one against that."

"Well, what's the alternative?"

"I've told you. Go back to the hotel, and by tomorrow night I hope to be able to get you out of the country for good. Later on Zolta and I will join you. Of two risks choose the lesser, and what I am advising is the lesser by a long chalk."

Achmed dithered and looked at Zolta for her opinion.

"Cedric is right," she said. "Despite your fears and argument I'm certain that McLean would have snatched you immediately if Colby had made any confession."

Achmed looked again at Mannering.

"Are you sure that this precious plan of yours will work?" he asked.

"I'm sure of nothing, except that your own plan isn't worth

a moment's consideration. Do you imagine that I want to see you arrested?"

"I should think not, but you are still capable of making mistakes. You made one when you fell for Zolta. That was the start of all——"

Mannering's eyes blazed with resentment, and he made a quick movement towards Achmed, as if to assault him. But Zolta caught him by the arm and restrained him.

"You're just like two quarrelsome boys," she said. "We can't afford to quarrel just now. Cedric, where are the servants?"

"I let them go out together. But Emily laid the table before she left."

"Then let us have some food. I'm hungry."

"Me too," said Achmed.

"You can join us on condition that you return to the hotel in an hour."

Achmed gave a reluctant nod and the trio then walked to the dining-room, and sat down to a cold but excellent meal.

21

M c L E A N and Brook spent most of the following day at Colby's house, searching for any possible evidence of the existence and location of Colby's alleged sister, or of any other living relatives. But his search was vain and ultimately he came to the conclusion that the sister was a figment of Colby's imagination.

"Just an excuse to explain his presence on that stretch of road," said McLean. "By the way, how is the arm behaving?"

"As good as new," replied Brook. "But when I think I might have got that little packet in my back it makes me see red. And then him dying on us! There's no justice in this world."

"That remark may prove to be a bit premature."

"You think the Comet may put us back on the trail?"

"I've got my fingers crossed. At this moment it is killing space at five hundred miles an hour, with my little package aboard."

"Let's hope it don't catch fire."

"Brook!"

"Well, everything happens to us, and this morning my shaving mirror fell and broke. You don't believe in omens?"

"No more than I believe in fairies. What's that you've got?"

Brook handed him an over-coloured pictorial postcard, which had fallen from a pile of paper-bound, dusty novels which he was putting back on a shelf. It depicted the Taj Mahal, and was addressed to George Colby. The stamp was an Indian one, but the franking was smudged and undecipherable. It was addressed to Colby at an address in Bombay. The message was brief and to the point.

Expect to be back Monday—Duke.

"So Mr. Colby was also in India at some time," mused McLean. "It's a point worth remembering. A pity about the bad franking, but it's obviously years old."

Having locked up the house they went back to the office, where some paper work engaged them until eight o'clock. Then McLean rang through to the airport, and was informed that the Comet was on time and was expected to touch down in half an hour.

"We'd better leave now," he said.

They drove to the airport, arriving there in good time to see the Comet make a splendid landing. Within a few minutes the small sealed package was in McLean's hands, and he and Brook went back to their car, switched on the ceiling light and broke the seals.

"It's all here," said McLean. "The verbatim report of the trial of Ambrose Watling, with three good photographs of him, for what they are now worth, and a number of depositions taken by the police prior to the trial. I think we'll get back to the office and digest the material in better light and greater comfort."

The subsequent close perusal of the new information had the effect of raising McLean's hopes to the highest pitch, and cancelling out the disappointments and set-backs of the past weeks and months. When he had finished he looked up at Brook who had been watching him closely.

"Now I know why Ambrose Watling came to England with

murder in his mind," he said. "That was a point which always intrigued me. He had a wife—a beautiful young woman believed to be a Syrian subject. The Indian police tried to locate her after Watling's arrest, but failed."

"That's curious," said Brook. "Achmed gave his nationality as Syrian."

"He did indeed. You and I have fallen down rather badly in one respect. We overlooked a certain facial resemblance between Mrs. Mannering and Achmed, chiefly because the circumstances suggested that Achmed appeared to be in love with his beautiful young mistress. But suppose she happened to be Achmed's sister, wouldn't that explain certain queer happenings in this case?"

"By Jove, it would! Mannering wanted us to believe that fiction. It smelt a bit when he was willing to have her back again."

"But that's not all," said McLean. "The Indian police give a very detailed description of Mrs. Watling. It fits Mrs. Mannering like a glove. And that I think is the reason why Watling came to England soon after his release from prison."

"You mean that Mannering ran off with Watling's wife?"

"I think so. What better motive for murder in a man of Watling's character? His confederates got away with the booty, plus his wife, and he went to jail for five long years."

"That's it!" said Brook, excitedly. "You've got it all tied up beautifully. Watling came after Mannering, and got what he hoped to hand out, because Mannering's niece had cunningly trailed him all the way from India. Then Mannering, fearing she might betray him, brings off a double event."

McLean shook his head.

"I wish it were just as simple as that, but we are dealing not with a single miscreant but a well-organized gang. This gang is suspected of having carried out big and bold robberies in Cairo and Cannes before transferring their activities to India. Their leader is known as the 'Duke', and his real identity is a mystery."

"The Duke!" exclaimed Brook. "That postcard of the Taj Mahal was signed 'Duke'."

"I'm not overlooking that fact."

"It could still be Mannering."

"It could, but we have to prove it, and I mean to attempt

that without delay. We go to Raven's Court immediately, but before we leave here's something to enforce the law, if that should be necessary."

McLean opened a drawer and extracted two shining automatics. He slipped out the magazines to make sure they were fully loaded, and then replaced them, and handed one of the weapons to Brook, who grinned his approval.

An hour later the big fast car was gliding up the drive at Raven's Court in the brilliant moonlight. It was a lovely nocturnal picture, with the river turned to silver, and the taller trees in the grounds throwing deep shadows. The clock on the dashboard gave the time as 10.45.

"Hope they haven't gone to bed," said McLean. "If so, we'll rout them out."

The car was driven into the shadow of the house, and after the ignition was locked McLean and Brook went to the portico and rang the bell. It was Mannering himself who answered the summons, and he looked not a little surprised to recognize his two callers.

"Sorry to disturb you," said McLean. "But there are one or two matters I wish to clear up."

"You certainly choose most inconvenient times to ask questions," said Mannering. "But come in."

"I presume Mrs. Mannering is here?"

"Yes, but she is on the point of retiring. I also."

He was about to conduct McLean to the library, but the door of the lounge was half open, and McLean could see Zolta sitting by the electric fire, smoking a cigarette, and clad in a tweed suit.

"I should prefer Mrs. Mannering to be present," he said, and moved towards the door.

"As you wish," grunted Mannering.

Mrs. Mannering rose as they entered, and stubbed the end of her cigarette into an ash-tray. She smiled quite pleasantly at the visitors, and McLean smiled back equally pleasantly.

"Do sit down, my dear," said Mannering. "The inspector apparently has some news."

Zolta resumed her seat, but the others remained standing.

"Well, Inspector?" said Mannering. "Be good enough to make it as brief as possible."

"I will. Mr. Mannering, how long have you been married?"

"Nearly six years. I think you asked me that before."

"I did, but I do not appear to have any details about that marriage. Where did it take place?"

"At the English Protestant Church in Beirut."

"I presume you have the marriage certificate?"

"Not I, but my wife probably has."

"It is somewhere," said Zolta, "but at the moment I do not know where."

"Do you think you could find it?"

"Oh yes. Tomorrow——"

"I should prefer to see it now."

"My dear Inspector," said Mannering, "you surely don't expect my wife to start a search at this time of night?"

"I'm afraid I must insist. Mrs. Mannering, will you try to find the certificate?"

"Of course. There are only a few places where it can possibly be. Excuse me."

She rose and walked with her usual grace out of the room. Mannering shrugged his shoulders.

"I must say, Inspector, I can't see what useful purpose this demand serves, nor why it should be so desperately urgent."

"I assure you it is necessary—and I regard it as urgent."

"But what can it have to do with my poor niece's death?"

"I may be in a better position to answer that question when I have seen the certificate."

"Well, you know your business."

He took up a newspaper, and generally expressed his resentment of McLean's attitude. McLean countered by taking out his note-book, and turning over the pages very slowly, but his glance never entirely lost sight of Mannering's face. It was quite a long time before Mrs. Mannering returned to apologize for her inability to find the certificate.

"It's a long time ago," she said. "And I've never needed it for any purpose."

"I suggest there never was a marriage," said McLean.

"That's rather an insulting suggestion," retorted Zolta.

"It is not intended to be insulting, but merely as a matter of fact. Had there been such a marriage, you, Madam, might be open to a serious charge."

"What charge?" blurted Mannering, angrily.

"I think Mrs. Mannering knows," said McLean. "I was referring to the crime of bigamy. I have information which causes me to believe that Madam was already married, and her husband living, at the time when you state this other marriage took place. If she denies this there are means of proving it. What do you say, Mrs. Mannering?"

Zolta's bosom heaved a little, and Mannering's piercing eyes became focused on her. It looked as if this was a situation utterly unforeseen by both of them. But Zolta was by no means slow-witted.

"The truth appears to be out, Cedric," she said. "Yes, Inspector, I was untruthful just now. I think most women in my position would have tried to cover up certain things in her life. There was no marriage at Beirut. I left my husband, who treated me most brutally, and came here to snatch what happiness I could. It is, I suppose, a relationship which is commonly known as 'living in sin' unless my husband has since died, which I think is quite likely, since he was a chronic alcohol addict."

Mannering took up his cue with alacrity.

"I apologize, Inspector," he said. "I couldn't do other than support my wife in this matter. Our relationship during these six years has been a happy one, but not one which any sensitive woman would wish to publicize. We have always hoped that the time would come when we should be able——"

He was interrupted by a long ring at the door-bell.

"The servants have retired," he said. "Will you excuse me——?"

"Sergeant Brook will save you the trouble," said McLean, with a swift glance at Zolta's concerned face.

In the pause which followed it looked as if Mannering's raised hopes had suddenly received a set-back, and when Brook returned the cause was apparent, for Brook brought with him the lithe figure of Achmed Knullah.

"Just caught him before he started to run, sir," said Brook.

"That is untrue," gasped Achmed. "I came to ask Mr. Mannering if he would give me back my job."

"At this time of night?" asked McLean. "And how did you propose to get back to London, in the event of Mr. Mannering refusing? The last train would have gone. Oh no, Mr. Knullah. You were on the run."

"I swear——"

"Save your breath. Sit down there, and I will deal with you in a moment, when I have finished with Mr. Mannering."

"God! Is there more to come?" snarled Mannering. "I've explained to you the exact position here. Can't you leave us in peace?"

"What were you saying when your late lackey arrived?" asked McLean.

"Does it matter?"

"Yes. I think you were about to say that you hoped the time would come when you and your mistress could be married, meaning when you could prove that her husband was dead?"

"Yes."

"What was his name?"

"I forget."

"Well, Madam at least will not forget."

"His name was Watling—Ambrose Watling," said Zolta.

"And you do not know what happened to him?"

"No. Nor do I greatly care."

"Then I will tell you. He was sent to jail, in India, for a brutal robbery. After five years he was released, and he came to England vowing vengeance on the man who had run off with his wife—a fact which must have been made known to him while he was serving his sentence. But he was outwitted, and taken to a workshop where he was finally done to death. That workshop belonged to a man named George Colby, a man of whom you denied all knowledge. Watling went under the name of Robert Peyton. Do you still say you did not know Colby?"

"Yes."

"Very well. We will see what your brother has to say."

"My brother!"

"I suggest that Achmed is your brother, and that you and he and Watling were members of a gang of international crooks at the head of which was a man known as the 'Duke'. You are all involved in the murder of Watling. Now, Mr. Knullah, I have proof of your association with Colby. About three months ago you went to Colby's house, round about midnight, with a car. You used that car to transport the dead body of Watling to a remote heath in Surrey where you hid it under some bushes. Under whose instructions were you acting?"

Knullah was now thoroughly scared. He opened his mouth

to say something, and then stopped. Again McLean asked the question, taking note of Mannering's reaction.

"I warn you that you may be charged with that crime," added McLean.

"No," blurted Knullah. "I had nothing to do with it. The 'Duke' had a pull on me. He told me he wanted to remove something late at night, and needed a closed car. I stole a car from a park near a night club, and drove it to his place. I—I didn't know what the cargo was to be until I saw it. I tried to back out but he threatened me with a pistol. When he came back I left the car where I had found it. I knew Colby in the past as the 'Duke'."

"So Colby killed your brother-in-law?"

"I suppose so. But I didn't know whose body it was, because he wrapped it up in a blanket."

"Do you expect me to believe that?" asked McLean scathingly.

"It's the truth."

"And are you suggesting that Colby also poisoned Denise Rostan?"

"I know nothing about that."

"I think you know a great deal. I propose to arrest you in connection with the first murder."

"But I swear——!"

"Sit over there, and be quiet."

Knullah moved to the seat indicated, and McLean turned his attention to Mannering.

"You knew this man Colby—called Duke?"

"No. But I had heard his name mentioned."

"By whom?"

"Watling."

"Did you suspect that Watling was working for him?"

"My wife—I mean Zolta—told me that she believed her husband was engaged in a life of crime."

McLean turned to Zolta, who was by far the calmest of the three.

"Did you not know for certain that your husband was a criminal?" he asked.

"No—not until he was arrested."

"Were you living with him at that time?"

"No."

"Did you know the 'Duke'?"

"No."

"Did you not know that your brother was associated with him?"

"No."

"I find it difficult to believe."

"But it's true," said Achmed. "I told her nothing."

"You speak when you're spoken to," growled Brook.

McLean then took a page from his note-book, and handed Mannering a fountain pen.

"I want you to write on that—to my dictation," he said.

"Why should I be treated like a naughty schoolboy?" retorted Mannering.

"Why should you decline to write a simple sentence if you are the innocent man you claim to be?"

"Well, make it brief."

"Write these words, *'Expect to be back Monday'*."

Mannering wrote the sentence at a speed which convinced McLean that it was his normal writing, and McLean, on examining it, was disappointed to find it was utterly unlike that on the postcard which had been signed by 'Duke'.

"Satisfied?" asked Mannering.

"Far from satisfied. This man who was known as the 'Duke' is wanted on a charge of murder in another country. Knullah asks me to believe that he was George Colby. Quite an astute move when he knows that Colby is dead. I am convinced that the 'Duke' is very much alive, and that you all know where he can be found. In the circumstances I am going to take all of you into custody."

"You can't do that, Inspector," said Mannering. "You may have grounds for arresting Achmed, but for me and my wife you need a warrant."

"I need no warrant when I have grounds for believing that you three have planned to leave this house tonight."

"That is nonsense. What grounds can you possibly have?"

"Knullah's visit here, and your wife's clothes. Does she usually dress like that in the evening?"

"She has been walking all day."

"All the more reason why she should take the first opportunity to change into more appropriate garb. You, too, appear to be warmly clad as if for a long journey. I think I will take a look round before we leave. Brook, take charge here for a few minutes. Oh, you had better make sure that the two men are not carrying anything lethal."

McLean waited while Brook 'frisked' Mannering and Achmed in most businesslike fashion, greatly to Mannering's resentment.

"All right, sir," he said finally.

McLean went rapidly through the main downstairs rooms, and then continued his search upstairs. Failing in his quest he came downstairs, and left the house by a side door. In the garage were two cars, but neither of them contained any baggage.

He came out and looked across the moonlit lawns. The top of the pagoda could just be seen above the trees, but the boat-house was in full view. He hurried across to it, expecting to find the door locked. But it was open, and piled up inside were half a dozen large suitcases. They were all weighty, and locked.

Did it mean that the party planned to escape by means of the river? What other conclusion could be drawn from the piled baggage? It seemed a peculiar method to adopt when fast cars were available. But as he stood and pondered there came to him the unmistakable sound of an airplane approaching from the south. He went outside, hoping to see its lights, but he saw nothing. Suddenly the engine cut out, and there came dead silence. Quite clearly the machine was landing somewhere, or had already landed.

Then suddenly he saw the whole thing. Mannering was cunning enough to guess that he, McLean, would have taken the obvious precautions, and had countered the move most ingeniously. Farther up the river there were long straight reaches, on which a small seaplane could 'land' easily in such bright moonlight as now prevailed. He looked at his watch. It was dead midnight. This was the appointed time.

He hurried back to the house, and found Brook guarding the three disconsolate prisoners. They all stared at him mutely, but he said nothing. He picked up the telephone receiver, and then changed his mind, and went into the library where there was an extension. In a few seconds he was talking intently to local police headquarters.

"This is Inspector McLean speaking from Raven's Court.

I am about to make several arrests, but in the meantime there is a job I want done. Somewhere on the river a mile or two above this place there is, I think, a seaplane waiting to pick up my unlucky prisoners. I want that 'plane taken into custody, along with the pilot. It requires swift action, for he may not wait very long. I will wait here until I hear further from you. Is that clear?"

He was assured that action would be taken without a moment's delay, and then he returned to the lounge, feeling that he had drawn his net very tightly.

"Do we leave now, sir?" asked Brook.

"Not yet. I am expecting a telephone message shortly. Gentlemen, you may smoke."

"Kind of you, Inspector," said Mannering, and took his cigar case from his pocket.

Knullah did not look as if he wanted to smoke, and his beautiful sister sat quietly as if she were posing for her portrait. Mannering lit his cigar and began to fill the room with pungent smoke.

"You seem pleased with yourself, Inspector," he said.

"I wasn't aware that I displayed any such emotion."

"It's in your eyes."

"Perhaps I felt a sense of relief at frustrating your plans for escape. Have you the keys of the suitcases?"

"What suitcases?"

"The suitcases in the boat-house."

"Oh, those! I removed them from the launch this afternoon. We always keep some clothing on the launch in summer, but now I propose to lay the boat up. Do you want the keys?"

"Not immediately."

Achmed's oily eyes were moving uneasily in their sockets, and he looked from time to time at the marble clock on the mantelpiece.

"Yes, it's well past midnight," said McLean, "and your friend must be wondering what has happened. Very soon, I hope, he will get an answer."

McLean was sitting with his back towards the door, and Brook came across to him, apparently to ask him something, when suddenly the most unexpected thing happened. The door was quietly opened, and McLean, through the medium of the mirror opposite him, saw an immensely tall man, clad in a long coat, and wearing a hideous Guy Fawkes mask over all his features. In his hands was a tommy-gun, held as steady as a rock.

"Don't move," he growled, "or I'll shoot you to pieces. Put up your hands!"

Brook was about to reach for his pistol when McLean stopped him, with a quick gesture. Heroics were plain suicide in the face of that murderous weapon, and the eyes that glinted through the holes in the mask.

"Achmed, they may be armed. Search them. Quick!"

Achmed, trembling like a leaf, seemed not to like that task, but the harsh impelling voice hustled him on, and he quickly found the weapons, one of which he handed to Mannering, while he retained the second.

"Now, where shall we put them?" asked the masked man.

"The smaller cellar," replied Mannering. "Past the servants' hall, and down the steps. There's an iron door at the bottom. I'll show you. There's no time to be lost."

He opened the door into the hall, and led the way. McLean and Brook followed, and the masked man and Achmed brought up the rear. They were drawing near the cellar steps when Brook, incensed by loss of dignity, and heedless of McLean's warning glance, turned swiftly, apparently with a view to taking Achmed by surprise. There was a burst of fire from the tommy-gun, and five or six bullets missed Brook by inches, ricocheted along the wall and smashed into the blank wall at the end.

"One more move like that, and it will be your last," said the tommy-gunner, in curious grating tones. "Get on!"

Brook gave a grunt of pain as the end of the tommy-gun was pushed into his back, and from somewhere above there came a scream of alarm.

"The servants!" said Mannering. "Achmed, you're not needed. Go up and lock them in their rooms. Hurry!"

Achmed turned and went, and in a few seconds Mannering opened a door on the left, and switched on a light, which revealed steps going downwards. The situation was hopeless and McLean knew it. He had no doubt at all that the man behind the tommy-gun was in deadly earnest. Finally Mannering opened a very solid iron door at the bottom of the steps, and stood by while the prisoners passed through it. Then the door slammed on them, and there came the sound of a key being turned in a noisy lock, followed by retreating footsteps.

"What a flop!" groaned Brook. "No sooner we are in luck than we are out of it. Why didn't we bargain for that?"

"How could we? I saw a switch on the wall as we came in. It's here somewhere. Ah!"

There was a click and an electric light came on, just above the iron door. It revealed a large cellar, half full of boiler fuel, and above the pile a circular hole down which the fuel was shot. But this opening was far too small for any full-sized male to squeeze through it, and the ventilation it afforded was very inadequate for a long stay.

"Any ideas, sir?" asked Brook.

"None which promises to ease this situation immediately. There is an old crate over there. Bring it and we'll rest our limbs and have a smoke."

Brook brought the crate, and McLean produced a cigarette-case and a lighter.

"It may not be quite as bad as it looks," he said. "They planned to get away by the river in a boat."

"That's a barmy idea, isn't it?"

"Not when the boat can connect with a seaplane, not very far up the river. I heard it when I was outside."

"I heard it too," said Brook. "Gosh, that was smart of them. But why did you use the telephone?"

"To inform our local colleagues about the 'plane. They promised quick action, but whether it will be quick enough is quite speculative."

"Then there's still a chance they can be put in the bag?"

"Just a chance. But the gang have the advantage of knowing just where the 'plane is. It's very much touch and go, and you and I are incapable of doing anything about it."

"And all through that murderous swine with his tommy-gun. Who is he? Can it be possible that at last we have seen the 'Duke'?"

"I think it's quite possible."

"I've got it! He's the fellow who piloted the 'plane. He had time to get here, didn't he?"

"Scarcely time, I should have thought. And I see no reason why he should have come, armed with that weapon, even if he could get ashore without swimming."

"He could have carried a rubber dinghy."

"But they had obviously arranged to go to him, so there was no need for him to come rushing here."

"If they get away I think I'll go and hang myself quietly."

"Not you, Brook. We've had other disappointments. Better have a sleep."

"Sleep!" said Brook, disgustedly. "Look here, sir. Can I have a go at that door? There's a big hammer over there by the coal."

"You won't make any impression on that door, Brook."

"Well, I can try, and it will do me good to have a bash at something and let off steam."

"All right."

Brook got his sledge-hammer which had obviously been used in the past to break up large coal. He poised himself before the door, and then commenced to deliver heavy blows near the lock. The noise was tremendous, and from time to time he would examine the door, only to find it as immovable as ever.

"No good!" he grunted at last. "I'm through."

"Thank goodness!" sighed McLean. "Now come and rest. If you can't sleep you can at least engage in contemplation."

"About what?"

"I'm sure you can think of something."

It was about half an hour later that the dead silence was broken by the distant double ringing of a bell.

"The telephone!" ejaculated Brook.

"Yes. I asked our colleagues to telephone me here when they had something to report. It may be good news or bad. Your guess is as good as mine."

"When they get no answer are they likely to come here?"

"They may—but if they do they will find the place locked up, and will assume that we have gone off with the prisoners."

"And then?"

"Sooner or later they will find that you and I are missing, and a search will ensue. All we can do is to exercise that blessed virtue—patience."

The telephone-bell ceased to ring, and McLean lighted another cigarette. Calm as he was outwardly, his mind was a turmoil. If the seaplane had got away, he had not heard a sound of it, but he doubted if he would have heard it from his present position. No, it was not safe to draw any favourable conclusions from the long silence. By this time the gang might be in another country and all the precious weeks of intense investigation largely wasted.

22

IT WAS about an hour later that the silence was broken. A door was heard to slam, and Brook, who was almost asleep, made an ejaculation, and stared at McLean.

"Yes, I heard it," said McLean. "Where's that hammer? We must do something."

Brook found his discarded hammer and hurried to the door, on which he beat an ear-splitting tattoo, until McLean told him to desist for a moment. When he did so there came the sound of feet on the stone stairs outside.

"Golly!" cried Brook. "Someone's really coming."

"Yes, I think so."

McLean went to the door, and called out loudly. A high-pitched voice replied, and the next moment the key grated in the lock and the heavy door was swung open. On the threshold stood the tenant of the Pavilion—Mr. Cartland. He was wearing a thick dressing-gown over pyjamas, and leaning heavily on his stick.

"Inspector McLean!" he gasped. "This is amazing! Whatever has happened? The maid—Emily—came and woke me up. She told me an extraordinary story about shooting, and later some fearful banging, which she thought came from down here. She said she had been terrified, because she had been locked in her room."

"That's perfectly true. How did she get out?"

"She finally climbed out of her window to the lower roof, and from there jumped. Unfortunately she sustained an injury to her ankle, and had almost to crawl to my place. She stated that she called out to the cook, who occupies the next room, and was able to make herself heard. The cook also is locked in her room, according to Emily. But I came here first. Had a little trouble getting in. Had to break a window in the front of the house. Emily had told me that the family had left. She saw them leave from her bedroom window."

"I'm much obliged to you, Mr. Cartland," said McLean. "Brook, run upstairs and release the cook. Let her come down if she prefers to."

Brook hurried off and Cartland made his way up the steep steps, gasping a little as he did so. By the time he and McLean reached the hall Brook was there with the cook, who was fully dressed and seemed scared out of her wits.

"There was a dreadful noise of shooting," she gabbled. "I woke up and screamed. I got out of bed and went to my door, but it was locked. Then Emily knocked on the wall, and told me that she too had been locked in. Then, much later, there were terrible bangings, and Emily called to me and told me she couldn't stand it no longer, and was going to try to get out. I think she must have gone———"

"Emily is all right, except for a sprained ankle. She's over at the Pavilion," said McLean. "You'd better stay here, while I help her to get back."

"Oh, I don't want to stay here alone!"

"Then Sergeant Brook will stay with you. But first I want to use the telephone. Excuse me, Mr. Cartland."

"Certainly."

But when McLean went to the telephone he found that the line had been cut in such a manner as to make an immediate repair impossible.

"No good," he said to Brook. "They put the instrument out of order before they left. You'd better stay here with Cook while I go with Mr. Cartland and see what damage that girl has sustained. Perhaps I could use your telephone, Mr. Cartland?"

"Of course. The garden path is the quickest way. I hope I shan't hold you up. I'm not very mobile."

They left the house by the main door, but McLean stopped at his car, and took a two-inch bandage from the first-aid outfit. Cartland limped on to save time, and McLean quickly overtook him.

"Strange goings-on, apparently," said Cartland. "According to Emily the Mannerings left in a terrific hurry. Did they lock you up———? But, I oughtn't to ask you that."

"I may as well admit the fact."

Cartland shook his head.

"A strange household," he ruminated. "I've been away for

a few days, and only came back this morning. I wanted to talk to Mannering about a leak in my roof. He snapped my head off and told me if I wasn't satisfied with the place I could find myself another home, and he rang off before I could make a suitable retort."

"He has a good deal on his mind."

"Did you know he has sacked his valet?"

"Yes."

"That's astonishing too, considering how he cracked the fellow up. Personally, I never trusted him. I don't like people who can't look you straight in the face. Well, here we are."

They entered the Pavilion, where McLean found Emily nursing her right ankle. Unlike the cook, she was not fully dressed, and was clutching a coat around her to cover up the fact.

"I'll attend to you in a moment, Emily," said McLean. "I have to make a telephone call. Where is the instrument, Mr. Cartland?"

"In my bedroom. First to the left along the passage. I find it more convenient there."

McLean went to the bedroom, where the bed was disturbed, and found the telephone on the bedside table. He hesitated for a moment, and then picked up the receiver and dialled the number of the local police headquarters, bracing himself for the worst possible news. He asked for Inspector Anthony, and was asked to wait a few moments. Hanging above the instrument was a telephone chart, with the comparatively few numbers neatly typed, but a recent addition had been added in pencil. It was A.K. Temple Bar 21756. Before McLean could grasp the full significance of that his colleague Inspector Anthony was on the line.

"McLean!" he said. "I rang you at the house, but got no reply."

"I wasn't in a position to reply. Tell me the worst—what happened?"

"The worst is that the 'plane and the pilot got away. We missed them by a short head. The pilot saw us in the bright moonlight and did a proper moonlight flit. Oh, but wait, there's better news to come. We got Mannering and his wife, and also the Arab chap. They're here awaiting your pleasure."

McLean drew a deep breath of intense relief.

"Good work, Anthony!" he said. "That's the most welcome bit of news I've had for a long time. See you shortly. I've got a few things to tidy up here."

"Okay. Good-bye till later."

McLean hung up the receiver, and then looked again at the telephone chart. He knew the number. It was the Brayton Court Hotel where Mrs. Mannering, so-called, had stayed temporarily. And the initials A.K. stood for Achmed Knullah. Again the tide had turned and was flowing fast in his favour. Going to the door he quietly turned the key in the lock, and then swiftly opened drawers and delved into the pockets of several garments. It was in the drawer of the bedside table that he found something of enormous interest. It was a pocket-diary, the pages of which were identical with the torn-out sheet containing the acrostic found between the leaves of the book which Denise Rostan had been reading just before her death, but all the pages up to the present date had been torn out. At the end were some blank sheets, and on one of these was inscribed a curious design:

$$
\begin{array}{c}
A \\
P \\
A \\
T \\
E \\
R \\
A\ P\ A\ T\ E\ R\ N\ O\ S\ T\ E\ R\ O \\
O \\
S \\
T \\
E \\
R \\
O
\end{array}
$$

It was not the design itself which riveted his attention, but the ticks placed against all the letters. Wasn't it significant that similar ticks also appeared in the letters of the acrostic? Were these two things really related, or was it merely one of those rare coincidences that crop up on occasion? Finally he slipped the diary into his pocket, unlocked the door and went back to the sitting-room.

"Sorry to be so long," he said. "I had trouble in getting through."

"That's all right," said Cartland. "I've been giving Emily some refreshment."

"It's very strong," said Emily, sipping the drink. "I'm sure it's intoxicating."

"Not at its present strength," laughed Cartland. "Anyway, it will do you good."

"Now let me have a look at that ankle," said McLean.

The girl put up her leg somewhat reluctantly, and McLean, after manipulating the foot very carefully, was convinced there was no fracture.

"Nothing worse than a slight sprain," he said. "This bandage will give you some relief, and tomorrow you can see a doctor."

The bandage was fixed and Emily found she was still able to get her shoe on.

"Do you live near here?" asked McLean.

"Oh no. My home is in Wiltshire."

"Then you had better go back to the house, and stay with Cook. Can you walk or shall I bring the car round?"

Emily stood up, and tried her game ankle.

"I can walk," she said.

"Good! We won't keep Mr. Cartland up any longer. He has already been sufficiently disturbed."

"Not at all," said Cartland. "Glad to be of service. All the same, I shall welcome my bed."

He saw them off the premises, and wished them good night. Emily made the journey with commendable speed, and seemed rather to enjoy the unusual experience of a walk in the moonlight with a police inspector. They reached the house to find Brook entertaining the cook in the large kitchen. The older woman was still very nervous.

"Aren't the master and mistress coming back?" she asked.

"Not tonight, anyway," replied McLean.

"Oh, but I don't like staying here——"

"You'll be perfectly all right. You and Emily had better turn in together, and tomorrow you can both go to your homes.

There's nothing to be afraid of. Sergeant Brook will be down here."

This information caused Brook to stare, but it satisfied the two women, and a little later they went upstairs together.

"I'm sorry, Brook," said McLean. "But it's the best way to solve this problem. There are other reasons why I should like you to stay."

"That's all right," said Brook. "But what about Mannering? Did he get away?"

"He did not. He and Mrs. Mannering and Knullah were taken into custody. But the pilot of the 'plane made off."

"That's fine—except for the loss of the pilot. Do you think he was the tall fellow who barged in here?"

"No."

"Then what became of him?"

"I think I know, but don't ask me to commit myself at this moment. I want to go to local headquarters in connection with the prisoners, and also to dispatch two men to watch a certain place. I think you'll have a quiet night here, and Cook will doubtless provide you with an excellent breakfast. If you find anything to drink that's none of my business."

"And when shall I see you again?"

"Tomorrow morning, I think. Now I must go."

McLean's heart was light as he entered the car and set it in motion. At police headquarters he lost no time in getting two good detectives sent to the vicinity of the Pavilion with instructions not to permit its lone occupant to leave, and then he heard from Inspector Anthony the details of the capture. No resistance had been offered although Mannering and Knullah were found to be in possession of automatics.

"Mine and Brook's," said McLean. "Did you see any sign of a fourth man?"

"That's curious," said Anthony, "because when we first caught sight of the rowboat making towards the 'plane I could have sworn there were four persons in it. But a cloud obscured the moon for a few moments, and then I saw only three. We argued a good deal about that, but Mannering, when questioned, swore there had never been more than three of them."

"I think there were four," said McLean.

194

"Then he must have slipped overboard, and got away. Do you want to see the prisoners?"

"No. They'll simply continue to lie. I expect you want to snatch some sleep, and so do I."

He was on the road again a few minutes later, making for London along completely deserted roads. At his office he turned out the fat dossier of the Peyton-Rostan case, and extracted the original acrostic and the postcard of the Taj Mahal which had been sent to the dead Colby, and signed by the 'Duke'. That had yet to be compared with the single handwritten word on Cartland's telephone chart. He believed it was the same handwriting.

23

VALERIE MCLEAN sat in her riverside home awaiting the arrival of her wandering husband. Over the telephone had come the message that he was on his way home, with no explanation of his lateness. But in his voice there was a ring of unmistakable elation, which was evidence that the day had not gone too badly for him. It was the dog who gave her warning of his master's approach. He detected and recognized the sound of McLean's car some seconds in advance of Valerie, and wagged his tail to make known the fact.

"You're a clever lad," said Valerie, reaching out and rumpling his neck.

Within a minute McLean was inside the house, hugging his wife warmly.

"Steady!" said Valerie. "Leave me some breath to tell you what I think of you. What a time for a respectable married man to arrive home. Aren't you ashamed of yourself?"

"My darling—I hate myself."

"Not you. You're oozing self-approval. Don't tell me you've solved your case."

"It's as near solved as can be. Three of my suspects are in jail, and the fourth is at this moment sitting on a powder keg, which before very long will blow him sky-high."

"You mean Mannering?"

"Mannering is in jail. I was referring to the big chief who

controls Mannering and his cronies, and who poses as an ex-missionary. He lives in a converted building on Mannering's estate, and plays the part admirably. But tonight I found the diary which I have searched for all these weeks. But get me a drink, and I'll tell you the whole story."

Valerie sat and listened to McLean's exciting narration, and when he had finished he handed her the diary. Valerie turned over the pages, and then stared at him.

"But what use is this?" she asked. "There's nothing in it."

"Yes there is. A few pages from the end. I've turned down the corner."

Valerie found the turned-down page and glanced at the diagram. She shook her head and then looked up at him.

"What does it signify?" she asked.

"Don't you notice anything particular about it?"

"No. Except that all the letters are ticked."

"That's the whole point. Here's the acrostic which I found in the punt. That also is ticked. Can't you see an association?"

"I'm blessed if I can."

"Well, I can't blame you, for I missed the real connection at first. You see, there was never much doubt in my mind that the murderer of Denise Rostan left that torn-out sheet behind him—probably at the girl's request. This diary in itself is no proof that the man who owns it was her murderer, for there must be tens of thousands of identical diaries in existence. But my case is strengthened by the fact that the acrostic and the double 'paternoster' are associated in the most ingenious way. I discovered that in the car while I was racking my brains for the connection. Can you see it now?"

Valerie stared from the acrostic to the other design, and then suddenly light came.

"Why—the letters go to make up the other design," she said. "It's a kind of anagram, and every letter is used up—by adding the alphas and omegas to the design."

"Exactly!"

"Robert, this is wonderful! I can understand the girl wanting to keep the acrostic. How clever of you!"

"Clever of me! You mean clever of the man who worked that out in the first place. He has probably been in his grave for the best part of two thousand years, and would be amused now if he could see to what use his genius was put. What

196

is remarkable is that a cold-blooded murderer should be in possession of this piece of rather obscure knowledge."

"Is he the man you know as the 'Duke'?"

"I think so."

"And a double murderer?"

"That is my conviction now. I think he killed Denise Rostan because by some means she discovered that he had murdered Peyton so-called."

"But Mannering was her uncle. You would have thought that he would have spoken——"

"Would a man who had closed two mouths effectively stop at closing others in an emergency? When the 'Duke' is safely behind iron bars I have an idea that Mannering will be willing to tell us all he knows. In any case he is an accessory, as are his wife and Knullah. Early tomorrow morning I shall arrest the 'Duke'."

"But will he wait for that? Surely he must realize that he is suspect?"

"He cannot do anything but wait, for I have two armed men keeping him under close observation. Moreover, like many homicides he suffers from an inflated ego. He has played his part very cunningly, but can have no idea of the extent of my knowledge concerning him."

"But he may miss his diary which you now possess."

"He may, but he had already removed the pages containing his memoranda. He certainly overlooked the page bearing the design, but even if he remembered it he is the sort of man to doubt my ability to make anything of it. No, I expect to find him bland and charming, and hypocritical as before. I am looking forward to the operation which, I hope, will put an end to his criminal career."

"And then a holiday?"

"Yes—definitely. But I must prepare my case first."

"Ah, I thought there might be a snag in it."

McLean enfolded her in his arms.

"There's no snag. I know I'm a dreadful husband. This case has taken up so much of the time which really belonged to you. But all real happiness has to be bought. It doesn't settle on one like manna from heaven. But we'll make up for all the lost hours, and perhaps then I'll think seriously of retiring from a profession which demands so much——"

"Robert, you idiot! If you did, I'd divorce you. You're the right man in the right place, and I'm the right woman. Never mention such an insane thing again. Oh, dear, I'm so tired. Come on to bed."

The alarm clock by the side of McLean's bed aroused him from what had seemed but a few minutes of slumber, and he put out his hand, switched on the light and silenced the clock. Valerie, but two yards from him, stirred and then blinked her eyes.

"Anything wrong?" she yawned.

"Time for me to get up."

She raised herself a little and looked at the window.

"But it's still dark!"

"All the same—it's half past five. Stay still, and I'll bring you a cup of tea."

"You won't. You get into the bathroom and I'll get things moving. But what a time to start work! I didn't know you had set the alarm for this ungodly hour, or I would have put it on a bit."

"You'd better stay where you are."

"No. I'll see you off, and then come back and finish my dream."

The dawn was breaking when McLean kissed his wife and got into his car.

"Oh, one thing more," said Valerie. "Give me a ring when you've really got that terrible man where he belongs."

"I will."

"And, Robert, dear—take care of yourself."

"That's one thing I'm particularly good at. Now you go and get some more shut-eye. Cheerio!"

Driving in the amber morning sunlight was quite a pleasant occupation, and he thought the country had never looked more beautiful, and not for a long time had his mind been less encumbered with teasing problems. But when he drew near to Raven's Court there arose a small element of doubt. There were no reasonable grounds for doubting the outcome of his journey, and yet that tiny cloud would insist upon intruding itself. So many times disappointment had come at the moment when success looked certain.

Finally his car passed up the drive at Raven's Court, and

198

when he rang the door-bell Brook himself appeared, with rather sleepy eyes.

"Didn't expect you so soon, sir," he said.

"Did you get any sleep?"

"Yes—quite a lot. If it hadn't been for a couple of owls making love I'd have got more. Can't think why they want to make such a song about it. Any fresh news, sir?"

"We are going to arrest the 'Duke'."

"Now?"

"As soon as possible. Have you had any breakfast?"

"Cook is just getting me some—in the kitchen. But that can wait."

"No. You get on with your breakfast. I'm going to find the two men I sent to watch Mr. Cartland's movements."

"That crippled gentleman? Is he involved?"

"Very much involved. Unless I am making the greatest mistake of my life he is none other than the 'Duke'."

"But——!"

"You get your breakfast. I'll explain everything when I have seen the two detectives. I'll be back shortly."

McLean went off on foot, taking the road route to the Pavilion rather than risk being seen across the garden. He found his assistants nicely placed to observe any movement at the Pavilion without being seen themselves.

"Anything happened, Stevens?" he asked of the senior detective.

"Absolutely nothing, sir. When we arrived last night there was a light burning in one of the rooms. Then it was doused and there has been no movement since dawn."

"Good. I am going to make an arrest almost immediately. I'll post you when I come back in the car with Sergeant Brook. In the meantime, take care you are not seen."

"Very good, sir. And if he should attempt to break out before you get back?"

"Then you must take him. But I warn you he is a dangerous fellow. Still, I'm hoping, and believe, he won't try that."

By the time he got back to the house Brook had made quick work of his breakfast, and was ready for anything. In the car McLean handed him an automatic.

"The one you lost last night," he said. "Now there are one

or two things I want to prove before I take Cartland. I propose to use his telephone again, or pretend to, so that I can check some handwriting on the chart which hangs above the instrument. If you are left alone with him for a few seconds, watch him like a lynx, and don't let him leave the room, for somewhere in that place I believe there is a tommy-gun."

Brook gasped at this.

"You mean that it was he who held us up? It's hard to believe, sir. That swine was much taller, and had a different voice. He showed no sign of a limp——"

"You underrate the 'Duke', Brook. Just you watch him, and take no chances."

"I will," said Brook, grimly.

"Then we'll get on our way."

McLean was soon within a very short distance of the Pavilion. He parked the car in a sheltered place, and then found the two watchers, who reported that they had seen no sign of Cartland.

"We are going to call on him," said McLean. "I don't want either of you to come closer to the house until we are inside. Then, and only then, get in as close as possible. These are merely precautions. There may be no trouble at all. But be on your toes all the same."

The two men signified their clear understanding of the instructions, and then McLean and Brook strolled out into the open and made their way to the short drive which led to Cartland's front door. On ringing the bell there was no immediate response, but after a few moments the door was opened, and Cartland, in a dressing-gown over pyjamas, and leaning on his stick, appeared. A smile broke over his face as he stared at his early visitors.

"You don't get much sleep, Inspector," he said.

"As much as my case will allow me. Last night we arrested your landlord—Mannering. He is singularly dumb on some points, and I should like your help."

"Certainly—if I can be of any help, which I rather doubt. Please come in."

They accompanied him into the sitting-room, where he switched on the electric fire, and then settled himself into a comfortable chair.

"I'm still very sensitive to cold, after spending half my

life in hot climates," he said. "I'm sorry to hear about Mannering. I suppose it's in connection with that poor girl?"

"Yes. Can you possibly remember the date when she came to Raven's Court?"

"No. I think she was there some time before I first made her acquaintance. That would be only a few weeks before—before her death. Three weeks at most."

"Did you ever see her in the grounds with any person other than Mannering or his wife?"

"No. When I saw her she was always alone. I got the impression she wasn't very happy."

"Did she ever mention having been in India?"

"No. I can't remember that she did."

"I want to show you a photograph. It is of a man whom I believe was a friend of Miss Rostan. It is possible that he might have been hanging round the house, and that you may have seen him."

McLean produced the photograph of Watling, and Cartland gazed at it, and then shook his head.

"I don't think I've ever seen him," he said.

"That's a pity," sighed McLean, and returned the photograph to his pocket. "Can you tell me anything about Mannering's personal servant—Knullah?"

"I saw him once or twice, when I had occasion to go to the house to see Mannering. He seemed to me to be very devoted to his employer, and Mannering once told me that he was a most admirable servant."

"You did not know that in fact he was Mrs. Mannering's own brother?"

"Her brother! But that's incredible."

"True, notwithstanding. He has admitted the fact."

"But why should Mannering employ him in that menial position?"

"He had his reasons. Oh, while I remember—may I use your telephone again? The one at the house is still out of order."

"Certainly."

McLean rose, and Brook, who was sitting near the door, remembered McLean's warning, and put his right hand down close to his hip.

In the bedroom McLean hastened to the telephone, taking

from his pocket the Taj Mahal postcard, with a view to comparing the writing with that on the telephone chart, but one glance at the chart caused him to utter a quick ejaculation. That last telephone number, inscribed by hand, had been heavily scored out. He came back at once to the lounge.

"Line engaged?" asked Cartland.

The preliminary fencing was over, and McLean got down to hard facts.

"Mr. Cartland," he said, "why did you obliterate a telephone number on the chart—since I was here last night?"

"I invariably do that when a number is no longer in use."

"Whom did you require at that number?"

"An old friend—who has since left."

"A friend whose initials are A.K.?"

"Yes. A Mr. Alfred Knowles."

"Not Achmed Knullah, who had the same telephone number for a short time?"

"My dear Inspector," laughed Cartland, "that is indeed an astonishing suggestion."

"It is not a suggestion but an accusation. For what purpose did you telephone Knullah, when you have just stated that you knew him only by sight?"

"You are labouring under a misapprehension. I think this questioning has gone too far."

"Not far enough, Mr. Cartland. Why do you pose as a cripple?"

"I beg your pardon!"

"Why do you pose as a cripple?"

"Really, this is more than I can tolerate! I will answer no more questions."

"Your failure to answer questions in a case of murder can be interpreted in only one way. Show me that assegai wound in your leg and I will readily beg your pardon."

"I'll show you nothing," retorted Cartland, with a fine display of hurt pride.

"Then I'll show you something. Do you recognize this diary?"

McLean pushed the diary under Cartland's big nose.

"I recognize nothing."

"It's yours. I took it from the drawer in your bedside table last night. Do you deny it is yours?"

"It could be. I used one like it to make shopping lists, which I tore out daily."

"Yes—quite a lot of the pages have been removed from this diary. But there is one at the end which you overlooked. Do you remember it?"

"No—I do not."

"Then take a look. It may revive your memory."

McLean opened the page that was turned down, and showed Cartland the diagram, who gave a little grunt of feigned amusement.

"One of my doodles," he said. "I often scribble such things. Do you see anything sinister in that?"

"I see murder, because I happen to have the counterpart. A page from this diary which was found in the punt in which Denise Rostan met her death. You should have taken more care about that, Cartland."

"You must forgive me if I fail to follow your strange reasoning. Are you accusing me of murdering Mr. Mannering's niece?"

"You will be formally charged at police headquarters. I propose to take you there immediately."

Cartland shrugged his broad shoulders.

"Very well," he said. "I was merely trying to prevent you from making a grave error. Will you give me time to make myself more presentable? A man feels rather less of a man without a coat and trousers."

"Sergeant Brook will bring you some clothing. Brook, you'll find what is necessary in the bedroom."

Brook at once vanished through the doorway, and Cartland made an attempt to rise to his feet from the rather low chair in which he was sitting, only to fall back with a wince of pain on his face.

"Give me a hand," he begged.

"You will do very well as you are until Brook is back with your clothing."

"Presumably you don't trust me?"

"No more than I trusted you last night, when you held a tommy-gun in your hands."

"Your obstinacy and imagination know no bounds. Last night I rendered you a service, and this is how you repay it. You will never get me on that charge, Inspector."

"If I do not, you will be held on an extradition order from the French Government, in connection with the murder of a man at Cannes, years ago, for I know you to be none other than the celebrated international criminal known as the 'Duke'. It is merely a question whether you hang in England or are beheaded in France."

For the first time the smug conceit left Cartland's face, and it was clear that this bolt out of the blue had struck him hard. He stared almost crazily at McLean and then turned his baleful glance to Brook, who entered with some clothing over his arm. Suddenly his right hand went to his mouth. He swallowed hard and then closed his eyes, and gave a groan of agony, rolling from side to side in his chair.

"He's done it!" cried Brook, and ran to the chair, dropping the garments on the way.

McLean shouted a warning, but Brook had already placed himself in jeopardy. With lightning speed two immensely strong hands went to Brook's throat and fastened on it like a vice. McLean produced his automatic, but between him and Cartland was Brook's big body, rendered powerless by the complete stoppage of his breath. Cartland, now upright, backed to the casement window on the garden side, and as McLean ran forward Cartland launched Brook at him with all his strength, and then, while McLean took all the force of Brook's body, smashed through the casement window and went running across the garden towards the grounds of the big house. McLean fired two shots into the blue to bring the two detectives on the scene and then went after the escaping man.

As Cartland passed the two beehives he overturned them and almost instantly the air was black with infuriated bees. McLean covered his face with his hands and charged through the noisy throng, wincing as a dozen stings were plunged into his neck. He saw Cartland pass through the boundary gate, and break to the left. Still pursued by bees, McLean put the last atom of his strength into his long strides, and began to gain a little on the fugitive, whose unexpected action seemed futile on the face of it. But McLean feared there was a certain method in his madness, and he recalled the murderous weapon of the previous night. Somewhere Cartland had that tommy-gun concealed, and might see in it his last chance to beat the odds against him.

McLean came out of a shrubbery to see Cartland still running at great speed away to the left, and almost parallel with the river bank, and then he realized that his objective was not the river, but the pagoda. There could be only one reason for that, and McLean had no doubt what it was. It was in the pagoda that Cartland kept his lethal weapon, and once in possession of it his capture would be a matter of extreme difficulty, not to say danger. Whipping out his automatic he fired two low shots. They went close to Cartland's legs, but did not stop him. Sixty yards divided them, and Cartland had but a hundred yards to go. McLean gave one glance behind him, and saw Brook and the two detectives coming up. But they might as well have been a mile away so far as the immediate issue was concerned.

Cartland was now clearly flagging, but so was McLean, for the pace had been terrific. Notwithstanding, he drew closer and closer, until but fifty yards divided them. But now Cartland was at the door of the pagoda, with the key in his hand. In a second or two the door was open, and Cartland passed through it. McLean reached it just as the key was turned on the inside. He fired four shots into the lock and then pushed the door open. Cartland was out of sight, but McLean could hear him running heavily up the stairs above. It looked as though the race was over, and in a sense it was, for suddenly there was a loud creak and the staircase and upper floors crashed down. McLean crouched against the wall, but was hit by a baulk of timber which brought blood from his head and injured his shoulder. When the dust had subsided he looked into the debris and saw Cartland, pinned down by a rafter. His eyes were open and he was struggling in vain to free himself. Not two yards from him, mixed up with a number of items, was a sack, from the open end of which protruded a tommy-gun. Brook and the two detectives appeared just outside the door, all gasping for breath.

"Are you hurt, sir?" gasped Brook.

"No—not seriously. There's your man—with the weapon he was after. He must have been within reach of it when everything came down. You may need an ambulance for him. Get him outside as quickly as you can."

While McLean mopped the blood from his head injury, which was only superficial, the party worked their way into the debris, and finally reached Cartland. Brook had the great pleasure of handcuffing him before the heavy timber was removed from his chest.

"Strangle me, would you—you son of a ——!" growled Brook.

"That will do, Brook," remonstrated McLean. "Let him get up—if he can."

"My right leg's broken," said Cartland.

McLean came forward and quickly found this to be true. Moreover, it was the leg in which Cartland had received his imaginary assegai wound, which caused Brook to remark caustically that Cartland had wished that on himself.

The injured man was carried outside, where McLean was compassionate enough to have the handcuffs taken off, since they now served no useful purpose. One of the detectives went across to the Pavilion to telephone for an ambulance, and McLean and Brook searched the debris. In a partly smashed wooden box was a considerable supply of ammunition, a pair of boots, with soles two inches thick, and a cheap Guy Fawkes mask!

"I think this clears up last night's incident," said McLean.

24

At five o'clock that evening McLean came home to his anxious wife, who welcomed him literally with open arms. Then, carefully, she removed his hat and stared at a shaven patch and a strip of medical plaster.

"You poor dear!" she crooned.

"It's only the slightest cut. But it's ruined my hat."

"But what's wrong with your neck? Why are you wearing that scarf?"

"I ran into half a million angry bees, and twenty-three of them had a go at me. That was the 'Duke's' last gesture. I'm sure he injected some of his own venom into his pets. Well—let's have some tea—with plenty of jam."

Over the meal Valerie heard all the details up to the time of Cartland's removal to hospital, and she gave a little sigh to realize that at last the case was ended.

"I suppose there's no doubt he will be convicted?" she asked.

"None at all. Mannering made a clean breast of everything when he was confronted with Cartland. He and the others feared him like the devil—and with good cause. It was a thoroughly organized gang, engaged exclusively on large-scale robberies. Even now we do not know Cartland's real name. To his associates he was always known as the 'Duke'. Colby was the expert safe-cracker, and after the big Indian robbery he came to England and started that small engineering business. I think it was simply a cloak to cover other activities in England. But the 'Duke' knew where to find him when he needed him."

"And the girl—Denise?"

"She was never a member of the gang. Mannering used her to trail Watling, because he knew that she happened to be in India when Watling was released from jail. Mannering swears that she did not know that he was involved in criminal pursuits, and that she trailed Watling to an address in London only because she believed that Mannering and his so-called wife were in great danger from Watling. This was undoubtedly true, and it was Colby who was given the task of inducing Watling to visit him, pretending that he had broken with the 'Duke' and Mannering, and was on Watling's side. We know what happened in that place. Watling was held a prisoner for some days, while Mannering and the 'Duke' made up their minds what to do with him. Mannering was for buying him off with money, but the 'Duke' had other ideas. One night he went to Colby's house and shot Watling. That is Mannering's version and I am inclined to believe it. Denise knew nothing of this until we began our investigation. Then her eyes were opened to the truth. She believed that Mannering had murdered Watling—not the wily ingratiating 'Duke', who made it a point of being charming to her. Torn with remorse and fear she finally made up her mind to confide in the man she secretly loved."

"Montague."

"Yes. But the 'Duke' was not so easily tricked. Mannering swears that he knew absolutely nothing about the 'Duke's' intention, and was horrified when the news of Denise's death reached him. Of course the 'Duke' denied having had anything to do with the murder, and made a counter-accusation. Well, you know the rest. They still had associates abroad who could be called in an emergency. The result was the arrival of the 'plane which was to take them all to safety. I now know the name of the man who brought that 'plane, and have taken steps to have him apprehended. That, my dear, is the end of the story."

"Not quite. Was it the 'Duke' who sent Colby to shoot you up in the car?"

"I shall never know, for that business was never mentioned to Mannering. But I think we may assume it was."

"Quite a nice satisfactory ending," mused Valerie. "I'm glad for Harry Montague's sake that Denise Rostan wasn't the cheap adventuress she appeared to be. I hope you'll tell him so one day."

"I shall."

"And Mrs. Watling—the main cause of all this tragedy—what will they do to her?"

"Curiously enough, she's the one person who comes out of it rather well. I doubt if she will be called upon to face any charge. When her lord and master comes out of prison I think he will find himself in the exact position of her late spouse, and we may find history repeating itself."

It was later that evening that McLean put on a dress-suit, and stretched a collar round his still swollen neck, while Valerie, looking her burning best, surveyed herself in her long mirror and smiled to reflect that she would see a little more of her husband in the near future.

THE END